DEATH OF
MR. DODSLEY

DEATH OF MR. DODSLEY

A LONDON BIBLIOMYSTERY

JOHN FERGUSON

With an Introduction by
Martin Edwards

Poisoned Pen
PRESS

Introduction © 2024 by Martin Edwards
Cover and internal design © 2024 by Sourcebooks
Cover image © London Picture Archive

Published by Poisoned Pen Press, an imprint of Sourcebooks, in association with the
British Library
P.O. Box 4410, Naperville, Illinois 60567-4410
(630) 961-3900
sourcebooks.com

Death of Mr. Dodsley was first published in 1937 by Collins, London.

Cataloging-in-Publication Data is on file with the Library of Congress.

Printed and bound in the United States of America.
VP 10 9 8 7 6 5 4 3 2 1

CONTENTS

INTRODUCTION

Death of Mr. Dodsley, first published in 1937, is a "biblio-mystery" from a Scot who combined ministry in the Episcopalian church with a varied and successful literary career. John Ferguson was in his heyday described as "one of the most delightful stylists in the genre," yet he has largely been forgotten during the seventy years since his death.

This story centres round the murder of a bookseller in London's Charing Cross Road, long regarded as a home-from-home for bibliophiles. Richard Dodsley's corpse is found lying on a carpet in his shop by Constable Roberts in the early hours of the morning. For clues, the Scotland Yard detectives Inspector Mallet and Sergeant Crabb do not have much to work on, although they find three cigarette ends and a woman's broken hair-slide at the scene of the crime and notice that several books are out of position on the shelves. Further, they discover a note indicating that, a couple of months before his death, Dodsley consulted a private detective, Francis MacNab.

During "the Golden Age of Murder" between the two

world wars, both Father Ronald Knox and Canon Victor Whitechurch achieved a considerable reputation in the field of literary detection. John Alexander Ferguson (1871–1952) is rather less well-known, perhaps partly because his series detective was, for all his amiability, a relatively low-key character who is not quite as memorable as many of his peers in vintage crime fiction. Not much has been written about Ferguson over the years, so I shall take this opportunity to sketch an outline of his life and work.

Ferguson was born in Callander in Perthshire and worked as a clerk on the local railway before becoming ordained as an Episcopalian minister. His ministry took him to places such as Dundee, Guernsey, and Glasgow, and it was not until he was in his forties that he began to carve a literary reputation. Shortly before the First World War, he achieved success as a playwright, thanks to his widely admired one-act play *Campbell of Kilmohr*, set in the aftermath of the Jacobite rebellion of 1745. Professor Alan Riach has said that the play concerns "the predicament of a Highlander confronted with the sly duplicity of a Lowlander's military interests. It would have some resonance after the First World War in its treatment of loyalty and betrayal. In the 21st century, in the context of the international popularity of the TV series *Outlander*, it warrants reappraisal."

In 1915 Ferguson became school chaplain at Eversley, an exclusive girls' school then based at Sandgate, a coastal village near Folkestone in Kent. The following year, he wrote a paper for the Folkestone War Refugees' Committee on how the town could best help Belgian refugees. 1918 saw the publication of his first thriller, *Stealthy Terror*, and on the Kent Maps Online website, Professor Carolyn Oulton points out that: "In a memorable scene in Folkestone, the narrator watches human 'butterflies' on the Leas, as they gather round a military band. The bandstand had been erected in 1893, when Folkestone ranked as one of the more fashionable Victorian resorts. But as Ferguson's readers would have been well aware, the Leas promenade gives on to what would later be designated The Road of Remembrance, along which thousands of soldiers had passed on their way to the trenches." The novel, which recounts how John Abercrombie, a medical student who is staying in Berlin shortly before the war, is drawn into taking charge of a secret document, enjoyed success on initial publication and also, decades later, as a green Penguin paperback.

Two more thrillers, *The Dark Geraldine* (1921) and *The Secret Road* (1925), followed; the respective settings were Perthshire and India. *The Man in the Dark* (1928) was subtitled *An Ealing Mystery*; although the story is as much a thriller as a conventional whodunit, Francis MacNab, Ferguson's Scottish sleuth, plays a part. In 1976, the book was dramatised for radio broadcast on Radio 4. *Murder on the Marsh* (1930) is a detective novel principally narrated by the journalist Godfrey Chance, who acts in effect as MacNab's "Watson". MacNab is asked by Ann Cardew to solve the puzzle of her father's strange behaviour. Shortly after this, James Cardew dies. There is no obvious sign of foul play, but MacNab wonders if an ingenious crime has been committed.

Ferguson then changed publishers, and *Death Comes to Perigord* (1931), perhaps his best-known detective novel, appeared under the legendary Collins Crime Club imprint. The greatest strength of this mystery is the unusual setting, on the island of Guernsey. It was followed by two more Scottish novels, *Night in Glengyle* (1933), an adventure story, and *The Grouse Moor Mystery* (1934), which has an "impossible crime" ingredient, before Ferguson turned to writing about London in this book. By the time *Death of Mr. Dodsley* was published, Eversley School had relocated to Lymington, on the Hampshire coast. Although Ferguson remained school chaplain for a while, the dedication to the novel indicates that at the time of publication he was living at Cerne Abbas in Dorset. Thereafter he moved to Culross before retiring in 1946. His final mystery, *Terror on the Island* (1942), again benefited from his knowledge of Guernsey. His non-criminous work includes *Dalgarney Goes North* (1938), a novel in which he returned to Scottish history and chronicling the aftermath of the '45.

Dorothy L. Sayers was among Ferguson's admirers. She heaped praise on *Night in Glengyle*, saying in the *Sunday Times* that "your reviewer quite forgot to be cunning and was properly taken in by the surprise-packet at the end," although, like her successor as crime critic for the *Sunday Times* Milward Kennedy, she was less convinced by Ferguson's adherence to the tenets of "fair play" detection. In the first major full-length study of the genre, *Masters of Mystery* (1931), H. D. Thomson described Ferguson as "one of the most delightful stylists in the genre." Ferguson's determination to vary the backgrounds of his books as well as the type of stories he wrote strikes me as interesting and rather impressive, and it is good to see a novel of his back in print in Britain after a very long absence from the shelves.

Martin Edwards
www.martinedwardsbooks.com

A NOTE FROM THE PUBLISHER

The original novels and short stories reprinted in the British Library Crime Classics series were written and published in a period ranging, for the most part, from the 1890s to the 1960s. There are many elements of these stories which continue to entertain modern readers; however, in some cases there are also uses of language, instances of stereotyping and some attitudes expressed by narrators or characters which may not be endorsed by the publishing standards of today. We acknowledge therefore that some elements in the works selected for reprinting may continue to make uncomfortable reading for some of our audience. With this series British Library Publishing and Poisoned Pen Press aim to offer a new readership a chance to read some of the rare books of the British Library's collections in an affordable paperback format, to enjoy their merits and to look back into the world of the twentieth century as portrayed by its writers. It is not possible to separate these stories from the history of their writing and as such the following stories are presented as they were originally published with the inclusion of minor edits made for consistency of style and sense, and with pejorative terms of an extremely offensive nature partly obscured. We welcome feedback from our readers.

To Charles Winterbourne.

Dear Charles,
You may recall the night on which you talked to us on detective fiction. Among other things you said you had no taste for a problem set in artificial conditions such as never could arise in real life. What you wanted was a problem and its solution, without any fancy frills and cheap thrills.

It is because this is an attempt to fulfil the conditions then laid down that I place your name in this book.

Yours,
J. A. Ferguson.

Cerne Abbas,
Dorset.

BOOK I

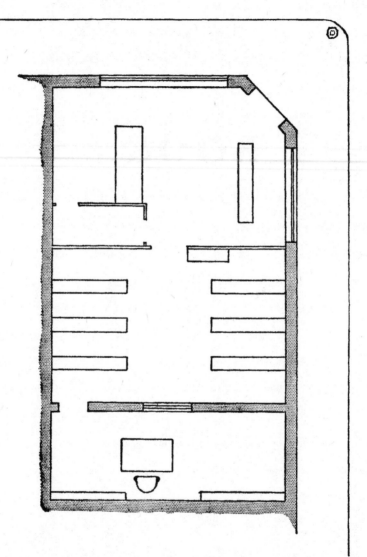

CHAPTER I
An All-Night Sitting

COMMANDER MALE, AFTER RECORDING HIS VOTE ON clause five, loitered about for a moment or two in the Lobby. The House of Commons was in for an all-night sitting, and Male had it in his mind to take a breath of the fresh night air on the terrace. Still new to politics, the wordy struggle and bickering over this measure was the sort of fighting for which his previous life in the navy had not prepared him. He was, too, left a little bewildered by the almost endless variety in type and character he met among the members. Accustomed so long to the ordered routine of a great battleship, where no one ever wasted a single word, where a single glance told one to whom one spoke and dictated the manner in which he should be addressed, Male needed some time to adjust himself to his new environment.

But he was immensely interested in his fellow members. There was this man Grafton, for instance, the fellow who now stood in the centre of an eagerly jabbering group in the Lobby. Male eyed the group curiously. He had heard Grafton described as a coming man. The phrase had caught his attention. For Grafton was at least in the late forties; at any rate somewhere about the age when, had he been in the navy, all his future would have lain behind him.

Male watched the group with interest. It did him good to look at Grafton. It restored his buoyancy. Unlike his friend, Charles Kendrew, the Kentish squire who had taken to politics as a refuge from the boredom of country life, Male had, after the old-age limit retired him from the service, entered Parliament as a dignified means of still remaining useful to his country. And to hear Grafton referred to as a coming young statesman somehow seemed to give him back his own lost youth.

He had heard much about Grafton from Kendrew, and overheard more from others. Unlike Kendrew and himself, Grafton, it appeared, had not taken to politics as a refuge from anything, but as a career. Having climbed out of very humble beginnings on the ladder afforded by one political party, he had changed over to another as soon as he achieved sufficient distinction to make himself a welcome recruit. The press, too, had begun to give him space, since his speeches were often of that rare type which induces a chuckle from readers, even when the readers disagreed with the views Grafton expressed. And no doubt it was this capacity for ironic humour, this gift for saying the unexpected thing, which made him in opposition such a destructive critic, that had brought David Grafton his great chance that night. For it was he who was down to put that critical amendment to the ninth clause on which, it was agreed, the fate of the Government hung that night.

Male, on the point of passing towards the terrace, had his arm taken by Kendrew who, with Henry Everard, had been making for the reading-room. Everard eyed the group around Grafton with extreme disfavour.

"Infernal upstart," he muttered half to himself. Everard was young, but being a member of an old family with a political history which extended back to the Revolution, had entered Parliament as naturally as a son enters an old-established family business; and, in fact, more than any other member he moved about the House with the proprietary air.

But Male was hardly prepared for what followed. As the three were about to pass the group around Grafton, Everard pulled up on its fringe and stood listening to the comments some one was making on some recent speech of Grafton's. Male observed that when Everard's presence was noticed an awkward little pause ensued, a pause in which eyes were turned upon the intruder. Everard did not allow the silence to last long.

"Wonderful, Grafton, wonderful!" he said, with a wave of the hand as if joining in the general chorus of congratulation. Then, in the next breath, while every one was dumb at the tribute from a quarter so unexpected, he added in a tone of careless insolence: "And is it really true that your father was a gas collector in Leeds?"

Male could have sworn that the only thing in the group that moved was Grafton's suddenly tightened jaw. In the hush the two men eyed each other. Everard had ceased to be among the number Grafton now needed to consider.

"Yes," he nodded, "it is really true that my father was a gas collector in Leeds. And if your father had been a gas collector in Leeds, you would have been a gas collector in Leeds."

Abashed by the snigger which the unexpected retort evoked, Everard somehow failed to get out his intended gibe about the son's ability to distribute what the father had collected. Then, while the others melted away to the different rooms, to smoke, read, refresh themselves, or sleep in the big easy-chairs, leaving the more conscientious to save the House from being counted out, Male made for the terrace. An all-night sitting did not trouble him. His life in the navy had accustomed him to keep awake and alert all night; but he had not yet overcome his distaste for a fetid and stuffy atmosphere.

On emerging his first glance went to the sky. Overhead the night was a clear, cold, uniform blue; but in the south-west his keen eye discerned a low bank of blackness which, with the wind in that quarter, might mean heavy rain later on. While cutting a cigar he watched the dark cloud, idly speculating as to how soon it might be overhead. After regarding the sky for a little he took out his watch and putting the glowing end of his cigar to the glass, saw it wanted but three minutes to one. His calculation was that the rain would be coming down in half an hour. He had come out just in time.

Commander Male began his promenade in his old quarter-deck manner, hands held negligently behind his back. Below him the reach of the river loomed black and silent, the long chain of street lamps on the Surrey side reflected as bright yellow spots on the river's inky surface. He liked to feel he had the terrace to himself. In the dark and with the glint of the river below him, he could imagine himself back at sea again and still young. He was tired of listening to speakers on beetroot and Milk Boards and pigs. He was tired of all the figures of speech about exploring every avenue, and leaving no stone upturned, and ploughing the sands and so on. Why the representatives of a sea-power like Britain should invariably confine themselves to agricultural figures of speech he could not imagine. But he admitted to himself that David Grafton never employed such hackneyed phrases.

As he paced to and fro his mind turned on Grafton. In Grafton he recognised something akin to himself. Grafton had "drive." He did not waste words. He knew what he wanted, and went straight for it. And that was why every one spoke of him as a coming man. But Male suspected that even those who recognised Grafton's power did not perceive that the secret of it resided in the fact that, clever as he was at saying the right thing at the right moment, he had still more the promise of *doing* the right thing at the right moment. And as a sailor Male could appreciate that capacity. As for those blighters who gave no promise to do more than talk—

In his impatience Commander Male wheeled round abruptly, and then discovered he was not so much alone as he had supposed. Just as he turned he caught sight of a shadowy figure moving towards him. His first thought was that it must be Kendrew, who, well knew his liking for the fresh air, had come to look for him. Male quickened his pace. But when the figure stopped short and then turned quickly aside out of his path to make for the terrace wall, Male judged it must be some one who wished to avoid him.

Now Male's eyesight remained still as good as it had been on that far-off day when he was tested for his cadetship. In fact he was rather proud of his sight as being one quality, at least, which had not led to his retirement from the navy. So he did not think that this abrupt turning aside at sight of him had anything personal in it. The man, whoever he was, had simply caught sight of the glowing end of his cigar as he wheeled round, and had stepped out of his path. He did not wish to meet any one just then, probably because he was thinking out some speech he would make later on in the debate.

More with a view to testing his eyesight than from any idle curiosity as to the identity of that shadowy figure, Male watched the man. He was certainly moving more quickly than one does who is lost in thought, unless indeed, Male smiled to himself, he was a more than usually rapid thinker. Then suddenly—some swing of the arm, or the outline of the square shoulder, or the poise of the body—suggested to Male that the man was Grafton. But he could not be sure that the suggestion had not come from the fact that he had just been thinking of Grafton.

So it came about that Male curtailed the length of his promenade, keeping well within the radius of the lighted entrance. He wanted to identify the man on his return, merely to see whether he owed the suggestion to his eyesight or his imagination. But the man did not return. Then the rain he had foreseen took Male unaware, and he made for the entrance. Once inside, the remembrance of his calculation as to the coming of the rain came back to him and he took a look at his watch. It gratified him to see that his estimate as to the set and velocity of the wind had not been out by more than four minutes, for the time was 1.31.

In the reading room Male found most of the chairs already occupied, though few of the occupants were reading. Ben Wallesely, the bulky red-faced representative of a Lancashire mining constituency, lay back in his chair breathing stertorously, his huge hands clasped over his stomach. Not now was Ben on the sort of night shift which kept him awake. But Ben, in common with the whole House, would be alert enough when the storm broke over that fateful ninth clause. Meanwhile the guillotine had only fallen on the sixth clause. Male, the man of few words, highly approved of the guillotine. So did Kendrew, for by the regularity of its fall one could reckon just how long one's nap would last. Kendrew, however, when Male caught sight of him over in the corner behind Ben Wallesely's chair, seemed to be deep in some newspaper. An empty chair with its back to the wall stood close to Kendrew. Male made for it as Kendrew, looking up, caught his eye. Something was amusing Kendrew. He thought it must be something in the newspaper which Kendrew used to beckon him over. He was about to take the vacant chair when his friend stopped him.

"Not that one, Male. That's Grafton's," Kendrew murmured.

Then Male perceived a book lying in the seat of the chair obviously placed there to retain possession during the temporary absence of its occupant. So tiptoeing across, Male procured another chair, wheeling it carefully up alongside Kendrew's. As soon as he was seated Kendrew touched his knee and drew his attention to the book on the neighbouring chair. It lay face downward with its covers exposed. The jacket bore the title *Death at the Desk,* and carried the picture of an elderly man, half lying on a writing table, with a bullet wound in the temple from which the red blood ran down his chalk-white face. But if Male was surprised to find Grafton, with the fate of a government in his hands, condescending to detective fiction at such a moment, he was startled when he read the author's name. For at the foot of the body appeared the name, M. G. Grafton.

"Any relation?" he asked.

Kendrew comprehended.

"His daughter," he said.

Male's eyes went back to the book. He marvelled at the capacity for detachment it revealed in Grafton. That a man who might within the next hour or so bring down a government could become absorbed in a murder story, even if his daughter were the author, struck him as super-human. Or should it be subhuman? he asked himself. All the same, he wanted to see Grafton return to that chair and take up the book. To judge by the look of it, if the book had been put down where the reader left off, he had not got very far into the story. Male wanted to judge for himself whether Grafton was as cool and self-possessed as that book suggested, whether the man would not betray some symp-tom of nervousness, some sign of a quickening pulse as the moment for his attack on the ministry approached.

Yielding to a sudden impulse, Male rose and picked up the volume. Yes, the book had been put down at the place where the reader left off, for the corner of the page itself had been turned down. And at the point where the corner ceased to cover the text, Male's eyes lighted on these words underlined by a pencil:

> The prophet who was slain by a lion had a nobler end
> than Bishop Hatto who was eaten by rats.

Replacing the book, Male turned to find Kendrew look-ing at him.

"As curious as all that?" Kendrew inquired after a prodi-gious yawn.

"Only seeing how far he'd gone," Male remarked as he reseated himself.

"Well, it's a good hour since his secretary handed him the book," Kendrew explained.

"Ah," Male smiled, "then he's not quite so cool as all that."

Kendrew did not understand.

"As all what?"

"He's only on page twenty-seven. That looks as if he must have been thinking of something else."

Kendrew laughed in a way that made Ben Wallesely stir in his chair protestingly. Male was about to ask his friend what his laugh meant, but at that moment the bell went for the division of clause six, and all the room struggled up to file out for the lobbies.

On their return, however, they had a chance to talk more freely, since Ben Wallesely had apparently gone elsewhere in search of a quieter corner. But when asked why he had laughed, Kendrew did not understand till Male explained. Then Kendrew laughed again.

"Oh," he said, "I just saw that what you said confirmed what I'd just been reading in that paper. It was a notice of the book and I read it simply out of curiosity from seeing the book in Grafton's hands."

"But why laugh?" Male insisted.

"Well, the chap said he'd found the book heavy going. At any rate words to that effect. And it was funny to have that verdict confirmed by the author's own father, when you found he'd only reached the twenty-seventh page after an hour's struggle with it."

"That may have been because his mind was on something else," Male suggested. "Or it may have been that he was making sure of the clues; they're usually given early on in the story, you know."

But Kendrew waved this aside.

"That's a bad shot anyhow," he asserted. "Don't you see he hasn't come back to go on with it? He leaves the book lying there. And," he added, stooping to pick up the *Daily Record* which had slipped off his knees, "if you read that, you will know why."

Male took the paper and at the place Kendrew had tapped with a rather irritated forefinger, found the notice of Miss Grafton's novel. Male read the notice with interest. But he would have read it with an interest far more intensive had he known that it was destined to attract the interest of the police at a later date. It read as follows:

Death at the Desk by M. G. Grafton. Of Miss Grafton's book it may be said with truth that it contains many points in detection which are both new and good. But, unfortunately, we must add that what in it is good is not new, and what in it is new is not good. We do not cavil at the inherent improbability of her plot: the plot of a detective story may even verge on the impossible, and yet if the author be sufficiently skilful to make it sound plausible while we read on, it will pass muster, provided the book has other merits. But what have we here? The story of a prosperous bookmaker who is a secret blackmailer, who having sent his victim a letter calling him to his office in the middle of the night, when he is there alone, gets himself promptly "done in" by his prospective victim.

Now blackmail as a motive for murder is good enough, blackmail being itself a form of murder; but it is not new. What, however, is new in Miss Grafton's use of this motive is her notion that any blackmailer could be so stupid as not only to get into touch with his prey by such a letter but fix such a rendezvous at such a time simply because he and the pigeon he proposed to pluck would be there alone. That, indeed, was asking for it. And our trustful blackmailer got it sure enough! For the pigeon, seizing his chance, promptly turned into a hawk and slew him on the spot. So far so bad. But worse is to follow. For the pigeon, having turned himself into a hawk, next turns himself into a goose. That is to say, instead of walking out of the office unseen and unsuspected, he places the corpse in a trunk, ropes it up and then, turning up the collar of his coat and pulling his hat well down over his eyes—always an impenetrable disguise on these occasions—he goes into the street, and having boldly asked a policeman where he can obtain a taxi, returns in it to pick up and deposit the trunk in the cloakroom at Charing Cross!

No, no, Miss Grafton. You must mend your psychology. A blackmailer never mistakes a hawk for a pigeon. Neither is it permissible to turn your hawk into a goose merely, as here, that it may lay golden eggs for the lynx-eyed detective. Indeed, the detective would need to be as blind as a bat and as brainless as the goose he is after to take more than a day for such a job.

Male laid the paper on his knees.

"Well," he said, "let's hope Grafton hasn't seen that. If she were my daughter I'd—"

As he paused Kendrew bent towards him.

"Forbid her to write any more," he suggested.

Male tapped the paper viciously.

"Maybe, but only after I'd given the fellow who wrote this a damn good hiding."

For a second Kendrew wondered why they should bother to talk about the Graftons at all.

"Oh," he said in a tone of dismissal, "it's only your own paternal pride that makes you say that. I don't believe Grafton has any."

Male protested.

"Now, now, Charles! I like a good party man myself but, hang it all, you needn't go so far as to deny a political opponent can have fatherly feelings."

Kendrew hesitated and then glanced around the room before replying. Satisfied with the symptoms of weariness and inattention he saw displayed on the faces and attitudes of those in their neighbourhood, he bent forward.

"Well," he said slowly, "I happen to know that he turned his daughter out of the house. She'd got mixed up with some young man in a bookseller's shop in Charing Cross Road. At least that's what I've heard." He glanced at the *Record* on the other's knees. "As for that notice, when I saw him reading it I certainly did see his face flush with anger, but that, you may be sure, was because it hurt his personal not his paternal pride."

"Oh, you know he's read this then?" Male asked.

Kendrew slewed himself round impatiently in his chair.

"Certainly. His secretary handed him the paper as well as the book. It was when I saw his sallow face darken as he read that I turned curious. When he left I got hold of the paper, and when I lighted on that notice I knew why he was reading yesterday's *Record*."

Male glanced down at the paper he was smoothing out on his knees. Kendrew was right: the paper was that of the day before. Male glanced at his friend, about to make some comment, but seeing Kendrew had laid himself back in his chair, with muscles relaxed and closed eyes, he let him get on with his doze. Kendrew was not in the least interested in Grafton. So not himself feeling somnolent, he started off idly probing for the cause of his own mild interest in the man. The secret when at last he seemed to come on it brought a smile. Yes, it must be that, he thought. Grafton was a man of at least his own age, and Grafton was being referred to as a coming man, while he himself had been retired from the navy on account of his age. Kendrew, he knew, was three months older than himself; but then Kendrew had never—what was the jargon they now used?—developed an inferiority complex, since there was no age limit for country squires.

"Wonder where he is now," Male said involuntarily.

Kendrew lifted his head, starting out of sleep.

"What was that?" he asked, blinking.

"I was just wondering why Grafton hadn't returned," he explained.

Kendrew sat up.

"I'll tell you. He's probably gone to the Chamber to get the nap he couldn't get here."

"Sorry," Male said as his friend lay back again.

But when he glanced at the clock and saw the hands nearing the two-thirty, he knew that the bell for the division would sound at any moment. After that the fun would begin. Then there would be no sleep for Kendrew or any of them—least of all for Grafton.

CHAPTER II
The Open Door

CONSTABLE ROBERTS OF E. DIVISION CAME SLOWLY
out of the dark alley back again into Charing Cross Road.
The rain had stopped. Just enough had fallen to freshen
things up, and make the long empty street shine in the lamp-
light. The air came cool and sweet, gradually regaining its
clean, early morning flavour. As he stood for a moment on
the edge of the pavement savouring the freshness, Roberts
heard the distant St. Martin's clock strike three. He had the
street to himself. Only a very occasional taxi went sailing
past. In all the length of the houses opposite there were but a
couple of little lighted windows, and only the lights from the
street lamps glinted back from the closely shuttered shops.

Roberts, removing his thumb from his belt, resumed his
slow patrol. He moved quietly along, throwing a look here
and a glance there at the shuttered fronts of the shops, his
hand sometimes going out to examine a padlocked door.
The vague, vast hum of London's traffic had for a few hours
ceased to vibrate in the air, and at that hour even slight
sounds struck on the ear with an unfamiliar distinctness.

Constable Roberts, however, had not covered more than another hundred yards of his beat before his ear became alert to a sound which did not come within the category of those night sounds which could be safely ignored by an intelligent officer. It was some one running. Running a few steps and then walking, hurriedly, like a person urged to run who is yet incapable through exhaustion of keeping it up. His ear at once told him the steps were coming towards him. Roberts took up his position under a lamp and waited, becoming alert when he heard other rapid footsteps some way behind the approaching man. For a moment or two the first man did not see Roberts under the lamp. As subsequently described by Roberts he was a short man, of slim build, somewhere in his late twenties, dark-eyed and clean-shaven. But his face was not clean, for he had apparently slipped and fallen on the wet road, so that some of the grit and grime of the pavement had been transferred to his features, though he appeared to have dined too well to be conscious of the fact. Roberts could not restrain a smile. He had obviously been making a night of it, and was far from steady in his progress, though his balance seemed better when he ran than when he walked. The dark cloak he wore was unbuttoned, revealing an expanse of white shirt front, which seemed all the more extensive because of the sharp contrast it made against the dark street and the murky countenance. His silk hat was far back on his head, his little black tie under his right ear, and his fingers clutched an unlit cigarette.

The man had almost passed when Robert's outstretched arm stopped him. He pulled up with an abruptness that very nearly sent him headlong.

"Ah, there you are at last. Mustn't pass the traffic signals," he nodded. His enunciation was thick, and laborious for want of breath. "Jus' the ver' man I'sh lookin' for," he added, sidling over. Laying a hand on the lamp-post for support, he stared up at the officer who stood like a tower above him.

Police Constable Roberts was a young officer not unfriendly in his natural disposition, but just a little nervous about losing his dignity if he unbent at all. He had not yet achieved that poise which more experience would bring. Yet stiff as he held his upper lip when on day duty, he could offset this by a certain attitude of tolerant condescension on such an occasion as this.

"D'you know, such a strange thing happened to me jus' now," the young man said confidentially. As he blinked up his tone changed. "Why do policemen wear a strap under their lower lip? Don't it—hurt—you—at all?"

Roberts's left hand tipped the silk hat forward to a safer position on the other's head.

"You look as if you'd need a strap to your own hat," he said. "Better be off home now or your breakfast will be cold," he added, beginning to move forward to meet the man who had followed. The glint of bright buttons on the tunic told him the newcomer was his sergeant. Sergeant Barrett surveyed the young man with a smile.

"Ah," he remarked, "I wondered why he ran. Drunk, is he?"

"But not incapable and not disorderly," Roberts commented.

The young man, swaying a little, replaced the watch he had just produced and stared back at them with vacant eyes.

"Better be off home," the sergeant waved a peremptory hand at him.

The other waved a less steady hand back at the sergeant.

"But what about that door up there?"

"What door?" Sergeant Barrett demanded.

"The door I was telling him about."

Roberts cut in.

"You didn't mention any door. What door is it?"

The man blinked in surprise.

"Didn't I? Funny. I meant to, you know. Came looking for you jus' to tell you. Thought you might be—inter—interested."

"Well, what about it?" the sergeant inquired, half tolerantly, half interested.

"Funny a cat should open it like that, and then shut it again, don't you think so?"

"A cat? Did you say a cat opened and then shut the door?" the sergeant asked.

The young man nodded solemnly.

"Right in my face as soon as it saw me," he declared.

The officers exchanged a glance.

"Sure it wasn't a rat?" Roberts suggested.

"A rat—why should it be a rat?" the other asked with indignation.

"Why should it be a cat?" Barrett asked. "Rats is what whisky makes you see when you've had too much, not cats."

"I tell you it was a cat I saw, and it shut the door in my face as soon as it saw me."

The sergeant's interest deepened, and his tolerance decreased. He took hold of the bewildered roysterer and gave him a shake or two.

"Pull yourself together and out with it straight," he said. "What door opened and then shut?"

The shaking was not without its sobering effect, even though it had not been vigorous enough to make the cigarette drop from the young man's hand. He held it up now.

"I wanted to light this, y'know. Saw a light up in a window. That's what put it into my head. See the idea?" He waved the cigarette. "Light up there. Fire down below. Result: a smoke for me on my homeward way. I take out my cigarettes. Funny how things get into a fellow's head—ideas, I mean."

"It is," Barrett sarcastically agreed, "very funny how things get into the head. But what about that door?"

The sergeant became impatient.

"Another idea he had," he remarked.

"Not a bit of it. I was just telling you. As I say, I got the idea of having a smoke and fished out my cigarette case. Like this." His hand went fumbling to the outside pocket of his cloak. "Hallo, it's gone! That's funny again."

Barrett turned to his officer.

"He's just silly drunk; but you'd better have a look at the door," he said in an undertone before moving off on his own round.

Robert's patience also gave way. But he waited till the sergeant was out of earshot and then came close up to the man.

"A lot seems funny to you tonight," he said. "But if you don't get off home at once you'll find yourself in a place that won't seem a bit funny when you wake up in the morning."

The other, who was now fumbling through all his pockets, seemed not to have heard.

"Must have left it with Jerry," he muttered to himself. Then he looked up startled. "That's funny too. Couldn't have left it with Jerry or how'd I have got this fag? Let me see." His hand went up to his forehead. The diamond stud on his shirt front, catching light from the street lamp, sparkled in the constable's eyes. "Let me see," its owner repeated slowly.

Roberts, trying to be patient, sighed with repressed exasperation.

"After it was over," the other continued, "Jerry and I took a taxi. We had an argument who was to see the other home. Was Jerry to drop me at my place or was I to drop Jerry and then go on?" He shook his head. "I forget how we settled it, I really do, officer. What happened to Jerry, you ask? I don' know. What happened to the taxi then? Don' know that either. But what I ask you is: if I dropped Jerry at Jerry's place where is the taxi? And if Jerry dropped me at my place why am I not there now?"

"Ask me another—when you're fit to take in the answer," Roberts brusquely replied. "Now then, move along."

Roberts, without giving him time to obey, took him under the arm and removing him from the support of the shutter, led him along with him up the street. It is true that the constable, not knowing in which direction his "place" lay, did not know whether he was leading him towards or farther away from his home. He had no intention of arresting him, for the man, though a little fresh as he had put it, was not disorderly nor actually incapable, and Roberts was really a kindly fellow and not of the type who would be ready to trump up this encounter into a charge of obstructing the police in the execution of their duty. So it was that partly to test his capability and partly under the belief that a little exercise would assist his recovery, he led the young gentleman along with him on his beat. In about fifty yards they were walking side by side.

"This is about the place, I think," the young man said, pausing to look around.

"Where you left the taxi?"

"No, no! Don't remember that. Where I saw the door

open itself and then shut in my face. It's at this corner, I think. Must be, for I remember being hit and knocked down by that lamp-post," he added, pointing ahead, not quite so unsteadily, at the lamp-standard on the corner. But as a lamp-standard stood at every corner, the identification did not seem quite so conclusive to the constable.

His gaze ascended to the signboard above the window.

"Yes, that's right; it was a bookseller's shop," he cried.

Roberts knew the shop; he knew all the shops. The one indicated was that of H. Allom at the corner. But as there are about as many booksellers' shops in Charing Cross Road as there are lamp-posts, even this counted for little. Roberts, however, went over and tried the door. Stooping, he peered in at the keyhole. All was dark inside the shop.

"Oh, it's shut now," the young man nodded. "I knew that. In fact, I saw it being closed."

Roberts left the door and came across to where he stood on the edge of the pavement. The street was as silent as the grave.

"Look here," he said. "Just tell me exactly what happened at this door."

"Nothing, That was the funny thing. Not a word was spoken, by him or me."

"Begin at the beginning," Roberts suggested.

The young man's face took on an aggrieved expression.

"Haven't I been doing that ever since I found you?" he cried; "and don't you stop me every time with—with unintelligent remarks?" He shook his head sorrowfully. "Mus' say I'm very disappointed with you."

The patient Roberts tried to keep him quiet; but his emotional ducts once opened, now overflowed. He seemed about to weep.

"Expected something better from the police," he said, "now they're going to Eton and Harrow for their men."

Roberts's jaw stiffened.

"'Ere, that's enough. You be off home, or I'll have you up for insulting behaviour," the exasperated constable growled, beginning to push his man along the street, with that successive series of sharp little shoves in the small of the back which invites retaliation. Roberts felt he had been let down; that he was being played with.

"You're incapable too," he snapped, "as well as guilty of insulting behaviour."

But when his man had been propelled across the street towards the district in which he supposed this West End gentleman probably lived, his flurry of anger evaporated. The foolish young man, however, still nursed his grievance. No sooner had the patient constable left off pushing him towards another constable's beat than he turned round with his protest.

"Incapable!" he cried, recovering his breath. "Doesn't that prove what I said? If I'm incapable, how could I be capable of any kind of behaviour?" He came forward to tap the officer's chest. "If you'd been at a good school you'd have known better than that," he said, wagging his head.

Roberts, thumbs in his belt, surveyed the man thoughtfully, half doubtful whether it was not his duty to make an arrest. A chance remark let fall by a superior about the over-zealous type of young officer who made too many arrests on trivial charges, tipped the balance in this man's favour. Roberts turned and moved away, lest the silly young man might create a disturbance which would compel an arrest. At first it looked as if an arrest could not be avoided. The young man followed him, clinging to his grievance with that persistency characteristic of one in his condition.

"Incapable—indeed!" he scoffed.

"Well," Roberts said, "just let me see you stand on one leg."

The other put up his hand in protest.

"No, no! You don't try the leg theory on me. Been barred by the M.C.C. Every one knows it isn't cricket. Incapable, indeed! It's your behaviour that is insulting. You don't know who I am—I—"

"Look here," Constable Roberts broke in with intense decision. "Make your choice. Go home now, or I bundle you off to Bow Street."

The reply was prompt.

"Take me to the station then. You'll see, my fine fellow. If there's—there's anything fishy happened in that shop, and I tell how you wouldn't listen to me—well, that's how for you, my lad."

Roberts could not restrain a smile at the air of portentous gravity with which this threat was delivered by the unsteady little figure looking up into his face. It was not often the lonely hours of his night duty brought him any such comic relief. The fellow was actually looking at his watch as if to report the time. Roberts laughed.

"What did you think you saw?" he inquired.

"Shan't tell you now."

"What! You refuse information that may be vital to the police. That's very serious," Roberts said with mocking gravity.

"I didn't. You refused to take it. That's the point." Roberts shook his head.

"Oh, I heard all about the lighted window, and Jerry and the taxi and the cigarette case if that's what you mean," he said. "The only thing you kept mum about was what happened to that door, which is all that interests me."

The other caught at his arm and pointed back at the door.

"Look here, that door, when I thought I'd have a cigarette I went up to it, to shelter the match from the wind, you know."

"Why, man, there's not been a breath of wind all night," Roberts interjected.

"Wrong there, officer. I felt it blowing on my cheek. Otherwise why should I go to shelter my match in the door?"

The big policeman, thumbs in belt, considered the question as if it were a problem set him in the art of detection.

"I know," he nodded suddenly. "There wasn't any wind, but from the way you were swaying about when you came along the street, you must have thought you were fighting your way through a gale. How's that?"

"Out!" snapped the other, turning on his heel with a dexterity that was ample evidence of his recovered balance. Roberts watched his progress along the street. Beyond a missed step and stutter now and then the going was good. Roberts went back into Charing Cross Road in a benignant mood, and with the pleasurable feeling that he had, with the best results, played the paternal part towards a very foolish young gentleman.

Constable Roberts was, as has already been remarked on, a young officer, and the vision of the ideal officer as drawn by the departmental instructor whose classes he had attended, yet remained fresh in his mind. It was no part of his duty to make as many arrests as he could, rather was it the duty of a good officer to avoid making arrests when possible, always keeping in mind that his function was the prevention rather than the punishment of crime. Of course, Roberts told himself, there was no question of crime in the case of this young man. But what the superintendent instructor had said about crime applied equally to the ideal officer functioning as Guardian of the Peace. There too, his duty was to prevent rather than to punish. And Roberts resumed his patrol, satisfied that he had handled the present case in a manner which would have won him the approval of the police lecturer.

All the same he crossed the street to have another look at H. Allom's door. The young man's story about the door having opened and shut itself before his eyes was a fantastic notion, due either to the flickering of the match he had struck or to the condition of his head, which made him suppose the whole city of London was reeling and rocking about him while he himself alone stood firm on his feet. Silly young ass. Yet it was just as well to have a second look at the door. Unlike most of the shops in the street, H. Allom's was entered by the door round the corner in Crown Court. At both sides of the door stood high show-cases filled with books in the daytime, and these formed a good enough screen for any one trying to force an entry.

Roberts stole up quietly and, after shoving firmly at the door, put his eye and then his ear to the keyhole. Not the slightest sign of life came from within. After remaining for quite a time in his attentive attitude, Roberts straightened himself, pushed his lamp back along his belt, and leaving the door, prepared to resume his patrol up the street. It was a fine night now, the air fresh and crisp to the lungs and clear to the eye, just as if all the dust of the long day's rioting traffic had settled down and gone to sleep. It would be a long time yet before his eight hours were up, and he could expect no more diversion such as he had extracted from the interlude just ended.

Something made him throw a glance back down the empty street towards the spot at which he had first met the young gentleman. He could not see so far, but some distance off something attracted his attention. Close to a shop door a little shadowy object appeared to be dancing about, now this way, now that, circling round some object lying on the pavement. He stood quite still to watch. At first he took it for a little dog. Then, going back to make sure, he decided from the quickness of its movements that it must be a cat. Nothing unusual in seeing a cat on his nightly rounds. He moved on, trying to see just what the animal was playing with. When the cat backed away and put its chin on its two paws, crouching for a spring, the small object caught a glint of light, but before Roberts remembered the young man's missing cigarette case, the cat had made its spring, propelling the thing with a metallic scraping towards the shop front. Roberts, fearing the case would be pushed down the iron grating beside the window, made a dash for it. The cat, which had been too much engrossed with its own antics, pulled up at the last moment, and, after one wild stare at the running figure, bolted wildly away. But not before Roberts had time to understand why he had at first taken it for a little dog: the cat was a Siamese. Then he picked up the small gold cigarette case. So the young fellow hadn't after all left it either in the taxi or with his friend Jerry. He had probably lost it in some fall. He certainly must have fallen, and now the case was stained by the same dirt and slime of the pavement which Roberts had seen on its owner's face. And the way in which that cat had shoved it about had not improved its condition. But it was, though small, a very good case. Roberts could see that, as soon as he began to wipe it clean with his handkerchief.

But as he was about to pocket the case and resume his promenade, a thought pulled him up. If the case had been dropped here where had the young man got the cigarette he had tried to light down the Crown Court corner? Roberts glanced up. Regent Court, at least, just there, was not unlike Crown Corner—not unlike it in more than having the usual lamp at the corner facing the usual bookshop. The young man had mistaken the one for the other and led him too far up the street, that was all. To be sure Regent Court formed a *cul de sac*, while Crown Court was only the top of the narrow street at its far end; but many people not handicapped as that young man had been, missed seeing that difference even in broad daylight. So if he had mistaken the one for the other—!

Roberts suddenly pocketing the cigarette case, stepped over quickly and gently put his hand to the door. It yielded to his touch, moving back an inch or two in a way that abruptly sent every muscle in his body tense and straining. He stood rigid for a little, listening at the aperture. It might well be that the door had been left unfastened at closing time by some assistant. He knew the shop. The name above the door was Richard Dodsley, a very old business, not like H. Allom, who having only a girl assistant would be sure to do the locking up himself. Much the same, however, as they looked to the eye, he knew Dodsley's to be an important shop. His sergeant had given him a nudge one afternoon, and whispering the name of a statesman with a world-wide reputation, had drawn his attention to a gentleman in the act of leaving Dodsley's with a book under his arm. So, little as it looked like it, there must be money in a business which numbered such celebrated men among its customers. Roberts brought his Wooton lamp round to the front of his belt, pushed the door open, and stepping inside, switched on his light.

At first he could see nothing of the symptoms usually very evident after a burglarious entry. Nothing lay scattered about. He flashed his lamp over the floor and all along the serried ranks of books in their variegated bindings. Passing behind the counter he found the till, so far as violence went, bore no trace of having been forced. He wondered if there was a safe anywhere. He felt there was sure to be something more than a till in a business which was patronised by members of His Majesty's Government. But his flashing lamp nowhere showed up the familiar green front and brass knob of the typical steel safe, unless it was hidden by the heavy dark curtain in the right corner at the far end of the shop.

He went towards the corner, feeling that the open door must be an oversight, since even that curtain would have been torn away in the hasty reckless search characteristic of a burglar's methods. But a surprise awaited him when he pulled the curtain aside. The curtain covered an opening which gave access to an inner room. Roberts hesitated at the entrance. It was pitch dark inside, except for the one ray of light from his own lamp, which threw into brilliant relief the coloured binding on the wall facing him. He had an odd sensation that this inner room was not unoccupied, and began to sweep his lamp about, wishing it covered a wider area than that spot of light at its extremity.

The searching light passed along the row of books, up and down the floor, till it picked out the leg of a table and then ascending, threw into brilliant prominence the telephone standing on the writing table with the white pages of a book lying open alongside. Suddenly Roberts, seeing something on the pages of the book, deflected his light on the position which the chair would normally have occupied. He got the chair at once. It was one of those swivel chairs with tripod legs, and it had been swung round so that it now faced the door. Any one sitting in it would have been looking straight at Roberts himself.

Then Roberts, impelled by what he had seen on the white pages of the book, directed his light on to the carpet. It was a fine Turkish patterned carpet with a lot of red in its design. In a moment, however, he saw a red which was not there by the weaver's design, and beyond the stain lay the body of the chair's last occupant. Roberts remembered the man who was lying on his side. He was the elderly man he had seen bowing and smiling on the doorstep on that afternoon when Sergeant Barrett had nudged him to draw his attention to the two people then leaving this very shop. He had then thought the sergeant's nudge was intended to draw his attention to the lady, for Barrett was known to be a connoisseur in female charms. Only later did he learn that Barrett wanted him to observe her companion, the celebrated diplomatist, then regularly pictured in the daily press as he arrived at or left Croydon aerodrome on his many air trips to the various European capitals. But the shot man at his feet was certainly the elderly man he had seen bowing and smiling to the lady and gentleman that day.

It was the young constable's first experience of what looked like a murder case, and it rather overwhelmed him. He stood staring for a few flashing seconds while he took it in. He remembered that neatly trimmed short grey beard, the abundant grizzled and curly hair about the high white forehead as the man stood bareheaded, smiling and bowing to his distinguished client. But the forehead was not quite so white now. There was a dark hole over the right eyebrow with a yellow stain above it, and over its lower edge something red slowly welling up through the ugly orifice and down the white cheek.

Then Roberts jumped for the telephone.

CHAPTER III
Mr. Grafton
Takes His Chance

THE DEATH OF MR. DODSLEY DID NOT ATTRACT IMME-diate notice in the daily press. The defeat of the Government on the ninth clause of their bill quite overshadowed much more important news than the tragic event in a small book-shop in Charing Cross Road. And the news of that defeat, coming as it did just after three a.m., monopolised all the available stop-press space in the provincial editions of the great dailies. The House had adjourned after Grafton's amendment had been carried by a majority of eleven, and the great subject of discussion in the suburban railway car-riages that morning was whether or not the Government would resign. Later, when the London editions printed the names of those members who had gone over to the oppo-sition, it was argued that since those weak-kneed recalcitrants could easily be brought to heel, resignation was not called for. But papers of all shades of thought were unanimous in regarding the adverse vote as a personal triumph for Mr. Grafton. He had, it appeared, on this great occasion sur-prised even his friends.

The Chamber had rapidly filled as soon as the Government carried the eighth clause with an increased majority. When he rose to speak to the amendment on clause nine, Grafton faced a House stilled with expectation; the party opposite less apprehensive by reason, as the Lobby Correspondent of the *Daily Record* put it, of their enhanced majority in the previous division; and with Grafton's party less confident for the same reason. Not any longer it was thought was that ninth clause the heaven-sent opportunity on which Mr. Grafton could rise to greatness. But friends and foes alike sat up as he began, aware somehow that the moment was one in which Grafton might either make or mar his own future. And, again to follow the *Record*'s special reporter, that attentiveness certainly did not relax when the House began to see it was not listening to the Grafton it had come to know and expected to hear.

This was a Grafton they did not know. He began so very quietly, even stammering a little, feeling for his words. His party began to fear the occasion was going to be too much for him. In real apprehension they waited for an exhibition of confidence and grip of his subject, for the voice to rise in pitch, his face to quicken. Above all they wanted to hear those apt and telling phrases, the ironical humour, the incisive burlesque quotation from his opponent's speech and the rhetorical final question which reduced a previous speaker's argument to a flagrant absurdity. They got none of these. Nor was there any promise of their coming to be drawn from the restrained, almost solemn tone in which his arguments were developed.

Ben Wallesely nudged a back-bench neighbour who chanced to be one of Grafton's former friends in the party he had left.

"Lad, didst ever hear him speak like a parson before?" he inquired. "Reached end o' his tether, I reckon."

The other shook his head in disagreement.

"Grafty knows all the tricks, Ben, from ranting like a Methodist to sighing like a sucking dove. Which is when he's most dangerous," Norton added between his teeth.

Yet if Grafton's present style was familiar to Norton, the House found it new. Of course the momentousness of the occasion made the atmosphere of the House electric, and this may have accounted for some, though not all of the intense, almost breathless attention given to him. And it was this intent stillness which made possible this unwonted low-toned voice, appealing not to passion but merely to quiet reasonableness. No need at that moment for declamation or the short snappy phrase, reinforced by the clenched fist. Only near the end did Grafton allow a trace of his curbed passion to appear in his voice.

"The honourable member opposite seeks to buttress his case for the peace of Europe by going to the Bible for support," he cried. "I have no desire to follow the example he has set, for I have no wish to hear any words from the sacred volume bandied across the floor of the House. Yet it seems desirable to make it clear that that Book is not what his attitude seems to imply—a divine manifesto issued in support of the party to which he belongs. It may be that the hon. member has not recently given that Book much serious study. He has at least forgotten much of what at this juncture it is certainly convenient for him to forget. May I recall the experiences recorded in it of one whose case was exactly that of all of us. 'I laboured for peace,' he writes, 'but when I spoke to them thereof they made them ready for war.' Could any more words accurately represent the conditions of affairs in Europe today? Could any words more truly express our country's efforts on behalf of peace? But, like the prophet, we have laboured in vain and spent our strength for naught and in vain. No, the attitude we are now forced to adopt is that expressed in a later age but in the same Book, if we are to secure peace and unity."

Grafton paused for a moment and then, bending forward, like a man about to impart a great secret, almost whispered the next words: "When the strong man armed keepeth his house his goods are at peace; but when a stronger than he shall come—"

Commander Male leaned forward, exultant, pulses quickening, nerves tingling as he saw the long restraint the speaker had put upon himself about to snap. And snap it did. Grafton straightened himself and clenched his fists, as he flamed out the question as to whether that House was content to leave the country's existence dependent on the magnanimity of some other power better armed than itself. In this matter, he declared, the experiences of nations would not differ from that of the individual, and there was only one kind of defenceless man who escaped when he came face to face with a bandit, and that was the man who had nothing worth the taking. The hon. member would not be ashamed to see this country naked of defences. Well, in the history of mankind it had not always been a disgrace to be naked and yet unashamed. But to leave one's country naked, and extol the nakedness while he conceals the shame, would be an eternal disgrace.

"He assures us that today the Angel of Peace is abroad in the world," Grafton cried, "that only deaf ears can fail to hear the beating of her wings. Let him clear his mind of such cant and sentimentalism. Let him remember that there is another angel with at least as much substantive existence. Let him remember the Angel of Death, the beating of whose wings I seemed to hear while we talk of peace and others prepare for war."

Some members here stirred uneasily: this was too like the old-time oratory which the House had long ago learned to distrust. But Grafton, sensitive to that slight stir of discomfort, responded to it promptly, and somehow even deepened the impression he had made when he ended his speech in a tone almost conversationally colloquial.

"It's like this," he said quietly. "We're all for peace. Our only difference is about the way in which it can be secured. My friend opposite considers defencelessness our best defence. We, on the other hand, do not like to see our country in a position in which we would not care to see ourselves when we are in danger of attack from some personal enemy. When I am attacked I like to know that I have the means by which to defend myself, and the courage to use those means, when other methods fail. I would not like to see myself with my hands tied behind my back in such an emergency. And I doubt whether the hon. member would prefer his own hands tied behind his back at such a moment. But that, obviously, is how he would like to see this country. On this occasion, it seems what is sauce for the gander is not sauce for the goose."

Grafton sat down amidst a burst of affectionate laughter.

"The sting in the tail as usual," Norton remarked to his friend Wallesely.

"Where else wouldst tha' have it?" Ben laughed, tickled like many others, in spite of himself, by the deft way in which Grafton had manoeuvred to get the sting into his very last word.

Up in the press gallery Surtees of the *Daily Post* met the eyes of Murray of the *Morning Mail.*

"Excelled himself," Murray nodded tersely.

"Excelled?" Surtees thoughtfully repeated. "Oh, I don't know about that."

"Meaning?" Murray snapped. Little Murray of course adapted himself to the limits of the *Mail*, which being much smaller than the bulky *Daily Post*, used shorter sentences and fewer adjectives.

"Well," Surtees said, "to be in a position to say he's *excelled* himself you've got to know just precisely how much he's capable of. In strict logic, Murray, you might as well say—"

But Murray had already gathered up his notes and fled.

CHAPTER IV
The Morning After

SMALL AS IS THE SPACE RESERVED IN ANY NEWSPAPER for stop-press items, it cannot be said that the news there given is robbed of prominence. Ill-printed, with lines all askew and without caption the item may be; but readers vaguely feel that what is there printed must be import-ant, since the multitudinous wheels in the printing office stopped rotating at the last moment in order that this little item might appear. There are, indeed, some readers who each morning look for the stop-press news in their paper even before they look at what there is for breakfast.

Owen Brewster, Grafton's secretary, was not of this class. He liked his breakfast too well for that. Indeed, he got more than enough of newspapers in the course of his day's work to have any appetite for them quite so early. The morning following the Government's defeat, however, was an excep-tion. He had gone home with a headache long before the fateful ninth clause came up for discussion. And now he felt he owed it to Grafton to make himself familiar with all that had followed his own departure from the House, so that he could tell the others when they came down. Besides, that morning he found himself without his usual healthy anticipative appetite for breakfast. These late hours at the House played the very devil with a fellow. A sharp flurry of irritation came to him. Who was that ass who had babbled down there over the devastating effect of London's night-club life, and the drinking and dancing on the youth of the country? Not half so devastating as dancing attendance on any one of those long-winded legislators, anyhow. In a night club one didn't yawn one's head off, sitting on till one never wanted to sit down again, with nothing to do but wait and nothing to drink but words. There was exhilaration in the night club: it didn't get on your nerves. Brewster's impatient roughness with the paper indicated that his own nerves were not at their best condition that morning. Then he found the stop-press. Two items of news occupied the small square space:

STOP-PRESS

Government defeat. Opposition amendment on clause nine carried by a majority of eleven. House adjourned 3.15 a.m.

At 3.16 this morning Richard Dodsley, the well-known Charing Cross bookseller, was found shot dead in his shop. Death had occurred only a few minutes before the discovery by the police.

Brewster's eyes remained on those two items long enough to have read them over, word for word, thrice at least. Then he put down the paper with an odd gentleness and walked over to the window to stare outside. Grafton's house was a snug little Georgian house in Charles Street, with a view on the park. It belonged to his second wife's first husband, though it had been acquired at her instigation when she brought him up to London in pursuit of the social ambitions his large fortune had awakened in her. Mr. Clough, the proprietor of the world-renowned specific for all throat and lung troubles, Clough's Cough Cure, did not take kindly to the new life, and pining for his former pushful life in Lancashire, wilted away and finally died of a throat affection in less than twelve months from his retirement. And in another twelve months Mr. Grafton, having married the young widow, moved in from Finchley to the house in Charles Street, which opened up a vista both for him and his wife of much more than the trees in the park. Both were climbers, and both had hitherto been handicapped, she by her husband, who was uncouth in speech and appearance, and too set in his habits to change: Grafton by his first wife, who had been a vain, silly but pretty typist whom he had married, when still very young, in what must have been the one weak moment in his upward career.

Brewster must have been staring with unseeing eyes at the trees in the park for quite ten minutes before the door burst open, and young George Grafton entered, as usual in a hurry, making straight for the sideboard.

"'Morning, Brewster," he greeted the secretary. "Finished already?"

Brewster approached and stood uncertainly regarding the young man helping himself so liberally to the eggs and bacon.

"Not started yet," he explained.

George cast an appraising eye on him while hooking round a chair with his left foot.

"Yes, you do look rather peevish. Got that morning after the night before feeling, I suppose."

Brewster replaced the cover George had clapped down so noisily on the wrong dish, and helped himself to a small piece of steamed fish. Having deposited his plate on the table, he sat down and stared across at George.

"As a matter of fact, I was upstairs in bed hours before any of you," he said, flicking out his napkin.

George laughed as he tore up a large chunk of bread.

"Took the Bentley for a trial run on the Great North," he nodded confidentially. "Knew I'd nothing to fear from them last night—not with the all-night sitting. Got into trouble though, near Baldock, and I had the hell of a time underneath the engine. Must have been on my back an hour."

"Got wet, I suppose?"

"Not at all. Not a spot. But I did get pretty squiffy at the *Gryphon* after I'd got her back here in the garage."

"And just when did you get home?"

George waved his knife jocularly.

"Ah, just in the nick. My luck was in there, though only by the skin of its teeth, as you might say." He bent forward to explain. "I was just creeping upstairs when I heard his latch-key. Had only time to step inside my room. Well, he can do the soft toe business himself. I didn't hear him pass my door anyhow—just heard a door close gently. Had some practice at it in his own youthful prime," George nodded.

Brewster began to toy thoughtfully with his fish while George's towsy head bent over a second helping. Brewster could easily understand what a disappointment the young fellow was to his father. He noted that George, though well aware that his father had a big part to play in the House of Commons the previous night, showed not the least curiosity as to the result. In point of fact, all the father's concerns and interests were to the son no more than shadowy unrealities, George's own interests being fixed on motors, sports models for choice. And it was when Grafton realised that his son saw life only as a background to the motor industry that he consented to allow George to take up his present work in the garage off the Bayswater Road.

But hard as Grafton was on his son, Brewster considered the lad might have been a much greater parental tragedy. If he kept late hours it was through his all-absorbing devotion to his work, and not through any passion for night clubs and drink or dancing halls. And if he sometimes took out a girl in the Bentley Brewster divined that he did so merely from the feeling that a pretty girl gave the right last touch with which to set off a radiant sports car—she being to him a gadget more than a girl.

Some indeterminate sound took Brewster's quick ear, and he knew Mrs. Grafton was at the door.

"'Morning," she greeted them both.

"Hallo! Didn't think you'd be down yet," George returned.

"Great news, isn't it?" She beamed on Brewster as she came forward.

Brewster set the grape fruit down before her.

"Not unexpected, though," he commented.

"What news?" George inquired.

But when she explained he merely said, "Oh, that," and went on with his breakfast. Brewster expected her to flash out some rebuke; but probably elated by the reflected glory of her husband's triumph, she only smiled. For a time the talk confined itself to the vote of last night and its possible consequences.

Brewster, covertly watching Eve Grafton, felt sure she

was now seeing herself as one of the big political hostesses of the future, at Downing Street, perhaps, giving receptions at which distinguished statesmen, ambassadors, attachés, and foreign diplomats in brilliant uniforms would bow low over her hand or murmur how pleased they were to meet her. Yes, Brewster told himself, that was the sort of triumph she must be picturing. For she looked as if she had been at it all night. To judge by her eyes and the pallor of her face, she had not slept at all, and yet she was in an unusually good humour. More evidence of this came when George, having at length finished eating, pushed away his cup in which the spoon still stood, and leaning his elbows on the table, began to fill his pipe. Mrs. Grafton, a stickler for table manners so far as she knew them, did not approve of pipes. She considered them most plebeian, and when in similar absent-mindedness George had done the same thing, he had been pulled up sharply and told to refrain till he got outside. Yet this time she ignored the pipe.

"George, you have dropped your serviette," she said.

George came back from his meditations on what he could get a three and a half-litre Invicta to do. She repeated her admonition, and George, dropping a hand to the floor, looked over twinkling at Brewster:

> *"Nobody mentioned in Debrett*
> *Ever speaks of a serviette."*

he chanted in a sing-song voice. Mrs. Grafton arrested her cup in mid-air.

"Why ever not?" she inquired, staring.

George shook his head as he pulled the *Daily Post* towards him and began to read.

"Don't know, I'm sure. I can only tell you that's what my form master at school told me in my first term."

Eve Grafton, a little bewildered, glanced to see what Brewster made of this. But Brewster's face was like wood.

"Well," she said, "if that doesn't go to prove all they say about the uselessness of what they teach you in those public schools is correct." She turned to Brewster. "Fancy saying a thing like that to a boy! Why shouldn't he refer to his serviette? If what I've heard is true, they often speak of worse things. At least there's nothing immoral in a serviette."

Brewster, aware he was being challenged, stirred in his chair uncomfortably. A sudden whistle from George, however, relieved him from the need for comment. He looked up to see George staring wide-eyed at the newspaper.

"By jove!" he cried. "By heavens, that was quick, though."

"What is it?" Mrs. Grafton laughed. "Some new speed record, I suppose."

Without a word George handed her the *Post*. Brewster knew what she was going to read. He was half prepared for what followed if the simple-minded George was not. He noted the sudden change in her face. She had apparently to read it aloud to take it in. *At 3.16 this morning Richard Dodsley—the well-known Charing Cross bookseller—found shot dead in his shop.*

"Yes," George cried, "but look what follows. The police were on it a few moments after. Mighty quick that, you know. Just shows what they can do when they stick to their job and leave us motorists alone."

Neither of them listened to him. Brewster watched the woman. After a moment she threw down the paper and got to her feet.

"Oh, it's too dreadful," she cried, "too, too dreadful."

George, astonished, paused with the lighted match at his pipe.

"Why?" he said. "What's the matter? I don't see——"

She cut him short, almost stamping her foot.

"Don't you see who the man is?" she demanded stridently. "Dodsley. Don't you know who Dodsley is?"

George, completely nonplussed, looked across at Brewster as if to see what the secretary made of this outburst.

"Why, of course I know who he is. I've been in his shop more than once." He hesitated for a moment. "As a matter of fact I passed it last night myself on my way home, but what has——"

"But don't you see how this hits your father?" she cut in impatiently.

"Father?" George stared.

"Yes. Hadn't Margery to leave home because of her connection with this man's nephew?"

George's face darkened.

"Very unfair that was, too. Father never even saw him, you know."

"It was enough to know he was employed in a second-hand bookshop," she snapped. Mrs. Grafton bought few books, but she would as soon have bought a second-hand hat as a second-hand book.

"Well, he's been to Oxford, which is more than I can say," George said defensively.

This self-depreciation seemed only to move his step-mother to a renewed outburst.

"If he had never been to Oxford he never would have got to know Margery. That's what you forget."

Brewster had not overlooked this fact. It had indeed been in his mind for quite a time. For it was through his acquaintance with young Dodsley at Oxford that Dick got to know Margery. In the ordinary way the two men might have passed through Oxford without ever striking up even a casual acquaintance, for Brewster was in his third year while young Dodsley was only in his second term, besides being members of different colleges. Shaw's *Man of Destiny*, an O.U.D.S. production, chanced to bring them together, however, for Brewster played Napoleon to whom he had a certain facial resemblance, while Dick Dodsley was shoved in to take the part of the young lieutenant as substitute for Tommy Lawson who got sent down five days before the play's production. Young Dodsley's only qualification for the part, however, seemed to be that he was familiar with the words through having spent many hours with the book in his hands listening to and prompting Lawson.

All this flashed through Brewster's mind in the few moments while Mrs. Grafton walked up and down, while George sat with his unlit pipe, bewildered as to the cause of her anger. Queer, Brewster thought, that if Tommy Lawson had not got drunk and assaulted a policeman after a club supper, George Grafton would now be smoking his pipe in peace. Still more queer it was to remember that if Lawson had not struck the policeman, Dick Dodsley would never have met Margery Grafton. There was more of destiny in that play than the man who was its author could have dreamed, Brewster thought again, remembering that day in Oxford Street when he met Dodsley while out shopping with Margery and introduced them to each other.

Brewster remained fully conscious all this time that Mrs. Grafton was getting at him and not at George in all she said. But the innocent George had no such thought. He stared almost helplessly at his stepmother's back as she now stood gazing moodily through the window.

"But look here," he said at length, "hang me if I can see what all this fuss is about." Then as Mrs. Grafton still kept her back to the room, he added in a persuasive, reasoning tone: "After all, things are just the same as they were yesterday."

That brought her face round swiftly.

"Are they?" she demanded. "Is that all you can see? You think it makes no difference to us that this man has been murdered?"

"I don't see how it does. After all, I don't suppose he was murdered by his nephew. In fact, if it comes to that, is it certain he was murdered? The paper doesn't say he was."

This time she did stamp her foot, the acquired veneer of speech and manner peeling off.

"What a fool you are," she cried. "Don't you see it makes no difference to us whether the man was murdered or not. There's bound to be an inquest. Then Margery's connection with those people will come out, and there's more than one dirty rag of a newspaper will make the most of that—to throw mud on your father, at this moment, just when he was about to make his position secure. Why, the papers on the other side will simply wallow in this sordid affair; it's a gift to them if there's going to be a general election."

At this Brewster felt compelled to intervene.

"Oh, come, Mrs. Grafton," he expostulated mildly. "That is exaggeration. I grant you Mr. Grafton has plenty of enemies—every distinguished man has—who would be glad to damage him; but I don't see how they can make capital out of this man's death." He laughed lightly. "Surely you aren't suggesting they will hint Mr. Grafton shot the uncle because of the nephew's association with Margery."

"No," she asserted, "I don't suggest anything so nonsensical. That could not damage him, since nobody would believe it. But they don't need to hint at that, even if they dared. They've got something quite as damaging to a political career, and that is ridicule. They can suggest that the uncle shot himself because of the nephew's association with the daughter of David Grafton."

Brewster pondered this, a little staggered. It was not so absurd as it seemed to George. There were always ways in which it could be safely suggested, and there were those who could suggest it. In his mind's eye he saw the headlines:

BOOKSELLER SHOOTS HIMSELF.

Nephew recently engaged to daughter of Mr. Grafton.

Nothing libellous there, though none the less the suggestion would be that this was a case not of *post* but of *propter hoc.*

Unexpectedly, Mrs. Grafton broke down. But as she made for the door, dabbing her handkerchief to her eyes, she turned.

"I—I can't bear it," she cried. "I can't bear to think of it. Just when everything was going so well. Just when Lady Jesson had invited us to Datchlands; on the very morning when I received a note of congratulation and a card for her next reception from the Duchess of Lymington—that— that we should be mixed up in such a—such a squalid affair."

As the door closed, George gave vent to a prolonged whistle of such variation in pitch that it sounded like his own motor horn.

"So that's the fly in her ointment," he nodded. He bent forward over the table and spoke more eagerly, "I say,

Brewster, you don't think this will really damage Father, do you? I mean that Dodsley's uncle shot himself—if he did shoot himself."

"Of course not," Brewster replied, getting a reassuring tone into his words. "How could Mr. Grafton be blamed for what this man did to himself?"

In his relief at hearing this, George at last got his pipe going.

"Just what I think," he nodded.

"Mrs. Grafton is probably unduly nervous," Brewster remarked. "The chance that Margery's name will come out at the inquest is very remote."

George sighed out a cloud of smoke.

"She's always had her knife into Margery—that's about the size of it," he remarked. "She puts out this new idea to make more trouble between her and Father. Hanged if I can see why. She's always been nice enough to me."

Brewster thought he might as well explain the position. Poor George, he knew so much about his motor-cars and so little about women.

"Nice to you, yes. But you're a nice boy, George," he said.

George stared and then asked sharply:

"Do you mean Margery isn't a nice girl?"

"No, only that she is a girl."

"I don't follow you."

Brewster smiled indulgently.

"It's simple, George, very simple. Margery and Mrs. Grafton are not so far apart in age, and it's not unusual for two women to develop a certain jealousy of each other when a young wife finds a grown-up daughter as head of the house into which she marries. And after all," he added, "the—the antagonism isn't all on one side, you know."

George's brow puckered in laborious thought for a few moments. "I know Margery didn't cotton to her much," he admitted. "Said she was a climber."

Brewster waved a hand. "Quite. And it was Mrs. Grafton's complaint that Margery had let her down by engaging herself to a bookseller's assistant."

Again the furrow of thought appeared on George's forehead. "Look here, Brewster," he said, "I don't see much difference between a bookseller's assistant and an assistant in a motor shop, do you?"

Brewster shook his head.

"It's not what I see that matters; it's how it looks to your stepmother. You are no discredit to the family in her eyes. She knows that motor-cars are things which interest the 'best' people."

"That's right, anyway. We've got Lord Carrick's son in our sales department," George agreed, "to tackle the swells."

Brewster got to his feet.

"But you can't see him behind a counter trying to sell, say, Margery's new book, can you?" Then as George's fleeting smile dismissed the absurd suggestion Brewster added: "It's my notion Margery's book is at the root of Mrs. Grafton's fear."

"Fear?" George echoed, looking up.

"Oh, just that Margery's name will get mixed up with the murder of old Dodsley, I mean. She thinks the papers will fasten on the coincidence that young Dodsley's fiancée is the author of a murder story published three days before old Dodsley is himself murdered."

"Yes, that's queer," George agreed.

Brewster glanced at his watch. "You'll be rather late at the garage this morning," he suggested.

"Not due till eleven. I worked late last night," George explained, his thoughts obviously elsewhere.

"Well, I must get on with my work," Brewster yawned, stretching himself, as George put out a hand and drew the *Daily Post* towards him.

"Look here," he said quickly. "You said just now that Dodsley has been murdered. But is that certain? This paper doesn't say so."

Brewster's arms were still at full stretch while George spoke. He kept them at full length for a second before replying.

"I was assuming the worst," he said, "which is what Mrs. Grafton would do. A mere suicide will cause less sensation, you know, and that will mean less chance of—well—Margery's name coming out."

The explanation satisfied George. He pushed the paper away and rose.

"Yes," he said in a tone of dismissal, "it's all just fudge on her part, although she may not know it. The only real thing about it is her fears of anything that might damage herself in the eyes of her new swell friends." George paused suddenly and put his hand on the other's shoulder: "Why, come to think of it, I came down Charing Cross Road myself just about the time the police found the man. There's another coincidence for you. Brother of the sister to whom nephew of the dead man is engaged, seen in Charing Cross Road about the time the fatal shot was fired."

When George laughed at his own flight of fancy it seemed to be Brewster's turn to lay a hand on his shoulder. He was even shocked by such laughter at such a moment.

"Shh!" he breathed, casting a look at the ceiling. "Your father is still asleep. Remember he must need rest after last night."

BOOK II

CHAPTER I
Police in Consultation

ON THE MORNING FOLLOWING THE DISCOVERY OF THE body of Richard Dodsley there was nothing in the exterior appearance of the shop to advertise the fact that murder had been done within its darkened interior. All his neighbours and such of the public as had noticed the stop-press item in their papers knew of course that he was dead. But to the average loiterer at the door and window boxes in the street's numerous bookshops that meant little, since Mr. Dodsley did not come into contact with their type of buyer. For one thing, though his principal business was in second-hand books, he did not deal in the cheap sort which could be exposed for sale in exterior boxes and shelves. And though a few second-hand rarities were set in the window, the front shop was entirely devoted to new books, a department managed by his nephew, with the help of two female assistants.

Mr. Dodsley's own concern was with the treasures housed in the inner apartment, for dealing with which had an expert male assistant in Mr. Cyril Carter. As for Mr. Dodsley's fellow dealers in the street, their assumption was that he had shot himself in a moment of depression, an act which they could quite understand, for things were very bad just then in the second-hand book business, as none knew better than themselves. How much worse must things be with Dodsley who had once been the envy of the street! For if there had been a falling off in the cheap stuff trade, his high-class market was practically dead. And Dodsley had more capital locked up in half a dozen rare volumes in that back shop of his than would have sufficed to buy up the whole of an ordinary dealer's stock, with the premises thrown in. Yet with things as they were in this country, and with the American export trade at a standstill, Dodsley, they knew, could have no prospect of selling at even a quarter of the price at which he had bought.

The other booksellers of the street had never really liked Mr. Dodsley. Envy is not a soil on which love thrives; but now that he was dead, a kindlier fellow-feeling prevailed, and more than one rival in the book business passed the shut door and the drawn blinds of the shop with softened emotions, and more than a touch of regret for things formerly said about Dodsley and his manners and methods.

Behind the drawn blinds, however, there had been much activity since the early hours of that morning. Just inside the closed door a lanky, young constable stood on guard, and at a small table over on the right, burly Sergeant Barrett as rosy of face as the other was pale, sat, attentive to any call which might summon him to the inner room where the two Yard men were still in consultation.

But time hung heavy for the two officers at the door. Behind the sergeant's chair a brown Siamese cat crouched in a state of obvious perturbation, his round blue eyes alert and distrustful. The Siamese was at no pains to hide his dislike at the presence of these strangers. He stolidly ignored all the sergeant's blandishments, moving stiffly away out of range whenever a caressing hand was extended, and then turning to watch the door for the reappearance of some one belonging to his own every day circle of friends and acquaintances. The constable's yawn turned into a smile as he saw the cat reject his superior's blandishments.

"Got up on the wrong side this morning, he has," the sergeant remarked. "Somebody trod on one of his corns, eh?"

"Offside foreleg is what he's lame on," the constable remarked.

"Ah, that'd be Roberts last night. Put him out of taste with the uniform," the sergeant said.

Sergeant Barrett abandoned his advances and instead took to drumming with his fingers on the table. He did not know what progress had been made with the case, but there had been much coming and going in the past two hours, and from the superior knowledge his long service had given him he was in a position to awe his young colleague by whispering the identity of each official as he passed inside. And Constable Copping, who had heard of most of them, from Dr. Vines, the pathologist, to Chief Superintendent Spiksley, and Freely the fingerprint expert, was so impressed that it looked as if his jaw might have dropped but for the helmet strap sustaining his chin.

After eight o'clock, however, there came a lull in the proceedings, and the two officers in charge of the case, Inspector Mallet and Detective-Sergeant Crabb, had been left in there to get on with it alone.

Sergeant Barrett, who had spent the night on duty but who had not, like Roberts, been given a rest, began to feel weary as soon as the material with which to astonish his young subordinate failed him. He yawned heavily. Copping, hands behind back, stood idly scanning the titles of the books on the shelf level with his face. As if reassured by the silence, the cat relaxed his vigilance and sitting up, slewed round his head to attend to something disturbing on his back.

Copping wheeled round abruptly.

"Well, I don't believe it," he announced with decision.

The sergeant stopped drumming his fingers on the table.

"That should settle it," he said. "But what don't you believe, Joe?" he added as a kind of afterthought.

Copping nodded at the shelves of books, all in their new and brightly coloured jackets.

"What they said about the old man leaving his nephew in charge of all them books."

"Why shouldn't he?"

"Well, they're new, ain't they? And them others in that other room which they said the old chap looked after himself are all old, ain't they? If that's true there's something more than meets the eye in this business."

Barrett sat back to stare quizzically at the constable.

"D'ye mean you've got *your* eye on it, Joe?" he inquired. "My godfathers, we'll soon see you at the Yard if you have."

Copping's sallow complexion flushed.

"Well," he said, "I've just been thinking, standing there with nothing better to do," he remarked defensively, as if thinking might otherwise be an offence against the police regulations.

Sergeant Barrett nodded assent.

"I get you. You've been standing wrapped in thought while those two sleep-walkers from the Yard, who've unfortunately been put in charge of this case—"

"Oh, cut it out, Sergeant, I didn't mean it like that," Copping pleaded.

"Out with it then. Out with what you see is fishy or it may be too late," Barrett said with affected eagerness, tapping the table in a way that made the Siamese suspend operations on his back and look up in open-eyed alarm. Copping cleared his throat as if to gain time for more thought.

"Come on, Joe," the sergeant encouraged him. "Why do you find it hard to believe the old man took charge of the old books?"

"Well, it ain't natural, is it? If he really was the master you'd expect him to be handling the new books, wouldn't you? Unless, that is, the poor old fellow was quite under the young un's thumb."

Barrett bent forward.

"You think he did this job then?" he whispered hoarsely.

"Well, maybe we can't go as far as that yet. But in my opinion it's worth the looking into," Copping added with a knowing nod.

"Because the old man was the one who looked after the old books?"

"Well, it ain't natural, if he was the master. Stands to reason, don't it? If it was your shop, do you see yourself mucking among the old trash in the back shop and letting another sell the nice clean new stuff out 'ere in front?"

The angry, querulous tone in which Copping propounded the question verged on insubordination. His sergeant, however, did not seem to notice this.

"You think the old books worth so little?" he suggested. "You are a fool, Joe Copping. You're arguing as if old books are on the same level as old clothes. I'm surprised at you, not to know that old books fetch double the price of new. I am surprised," the sergeant repeated.

Copping was surprised himself. He knew his sergeant

well enough to be aware that this time Barrett meant what he said. And Copping, who had received his education at a school in which all books were provided at the public expense, attached but little value to books, whether new or old. He could hardly believe his ears.

"Double the price," he repeated, incredulously.

Sergeant Barrett beckoned him over to his table.

"Seeing's believing," he said. "Come 'ere, my lad."

On the table lay two catalogues of books which an hour ago Inspector Mallet had put into his charge. From one of them he was now in a position to impart some of his own recently acquired knowledge about the book trade.

"This here is what's called a catalogue," he explained, "and that means a price list. The old gentleman hadn't just finished making it when he was done in. Now look at that—appears to be a crime story, so it's in our own line." His finger went to an entry and Copping, with a hand on the back of the sergeant's chair, bent forward to read:

Moore, George,—*Drama in Muslin*, spotted, but otherwise fair copy; first edition pub. 7/6, offered at 30/-

Copping whistled his amazement.

"*Coo!*" he breathed. "Talk of old clo'es. If only my old trousers went up like that!"

Copping's amazement gratified the sergeant. He had found new material with which to astonish his subordinate.

"That's nothing," he remarked, turning over to another entry. "You look at this one, which is also a crime story, as you can see, of a long time back."

Shakespeare,—*The Rape of Lucretia*, 1624. 12mo. Blue moroc. t. c. g. Fine. £75.

Sergeant Barrett, disappointed when the expected gasp

did not sound in his ear, looked up to see Copping frowning thoughtfully at the entry indicated.

"That's not as much as he'd get for it today," the constable said at length.

"Not—*what?*" the sergeant cried. "What in thunder do you mean, Copping?"

Copping's forefinger went to the spot.

"Well, that '12 mo.' is short for twelve months, ain't it?"

Barrett's eyes narrowed in thought.

"Yes," he said. "I suppose it is. Hard to see what else it can mean."

"Funny to set down what he got for it," Copping remarked.

The sergeant rubbed his chin. He had not seen this. But it would not be good for Copping to let him know it. Then the explanation seemed to dawn on him.

"Why," he said, "it's plain enough, isn't it? He set it down here to show what they gave for that sort of thing in 1624."

"Just what I say," Copping nodded confidently. "At the Old Bailey he'd 'ave got not months but years for an offence like that today."

Barrett's eyes slowly traversed the entry again. Copping was getting above himself. It was not good to see a junior like Copping so uppish, he thought as his eyes reached the last words in the entry.

"Well," he said, "twelve months wasn't *all* he got for it, was it?"

"What else?" Copping demanded.

Now the sergeant suspected there was something here more than he understood. But it would never do to let Copping see that. So Barrett's blunt forefinger pointed boldly to the figure with which the item ended. Copping bent to read.

"Oh!" he almost gasped. "I thought that was the price. *Fine £75.* That means over and above the twelve mo.?"

"Of course. And mind you, Joe Copping, £75 was a lot of money in these pre-war days." He shut the book with a slam.

"I didn't think they fined as well as gaoled, except motorists, I mean," Copping explained.

Barrett felt master of the situation once more.

"Perhaps not," he snapped, "but I dare say there's still a few things in the criminal history of England what you're not aware of yet. Now you just get back to that door and leave the detective side to them as has the gift for it."

But, if the sergeant could have seen into the room in which the two Yard men sat he might have been doubtful about that gift. Inspector Mallet was one of the old school. He had come to the Yard after years of service in a Division in which his natural shrewdness had developed through contact with the various types of tricksters and confidence men who flourish on the credulity of the country cousins and colonial visitors. Indeed, on the street he might himself have been mistaken for a farmer up from Somerset, until, that is, you met his eye. Indeed, his assistant, Detective-Sergeant Crabb, with some twenty years less service to his credit, had the police officer far more clearly stamped on his figure, expression, and bearing. Meeting Crabb one would have guessed his usual wear was a uniform, although he had served a very short time in the uniformed branch; but one could never have associated Mallet with a uniform. One would set him down as a countryman who had put on his Sunday suit for a holiday in town.

As, however, Mallet and Crabb considered the murder of Mr. Dodsley on the scene of the crime, both officers seemed perplexed and worried to a degree that would have surprised Sergeant Barrett and probably pleased Constable Copping.

"Yes, I see what you mean," Crabb was saying. "A shop murder *is* different. There was that one in the Avenue—"

"Yes, but that was done in an empty shop. Yet we never got the man."

"You think that made it easier—the fact of the shop being empty?" Crabb suggested.

"Naturally. There were only one or two who'd business at that shop. Not a stream of customers as here. That's what makes it worse than if it had been done in a house. In a house you can narrow down your possibles."

Crabb hesitated.

"Well," he ventured after a moment, "we're fairly sure as to the time it was done; and there'd hardly be a stream of customers at that hour."

Mallet looked across good-humouredly.

"That's the point, boy," he nodded. "It's obvious somebody did come at that hour, somebody who found him here at that hour. And if you can tell me what Dodsley himself was doing here at two o'clock in the morning my opinion of your new police college will go up ninety-nine and a half per cent."

The young detective-sergeant, however, rack his brains as he might, found no suggestion with which to raise Mallet's opinion about the new police college.

Mallet got to his feet and began pacing about as if seeking a reply for himself. Crabb's eyes went to the diary found in the dead man's pocket. They had spent an hour over the entries in that little brown leather book, and so far only two items in it looked worthy of more than momentary attention.

The first entry, however, which was not in the dated section but on a blank page headed *Memoranda*, only attracted their attention because it was unintelligible, no more in fact than an arrangement of numerals set out in two lines. It was an entry that might mean anything or nothing. The other entry interested him much more. In the square allotted to *March* 30 appeared the words:

Consulted Mr. F. MacNab.

Crabb could not think why his superior puckered his eyes so intently over this, for the "consulted" led him to infer that Mr. F. MacNab must be either a doctor or a dentist.

"I wonder if it wouldn't pay us—" Mallet said, half to himself, and then stopped.

"Yes, sir?" Crabb encouraged.

Mallet turned.

"When did you tell the others to attend?"

"The nephew and the assistants?"

"And the charwoman, Mrs. Headcorn."

"Ten o'clock was fixed to allow us a margin," Crabb responded.

Mallet pulled out his watch.

"That leaves us rather more than an hour. Yes, I think we can't spend it better than by consulting him ourselves," he added, putting up his watch again. "It may yield us something to go on before we have the others in."

"You—know him then?" Crabb hesitated.

"I've heard of him—from Inspector Snargrove, who found him useful in a particularly difficult case."

"Not—*not* one of those private detective fellows, sir?" Crabb gasped. Mallet, who was filling his pipe, glanced up and, catching the look of horror on Crabb's face, smiled indulgently. His young subordinate's use of the word "fellows" was by itself enough to indicate that he belonged to the new school, and he well divined that Crabb had been horrified by the notion of "consulting" an outsider.

"Ah, Crabb," he nodded, "you're very young yet. When you're as old as I am, when you come within hail of your retirement and, like others, begin to think of keeping on as a private inquiry agent—as you will do if you've the love of the work in you—you'll think different." Letting this prophecy sink in while he went on stuffing his pipe, he added, "As for consulting this man, the notion of which made you jump, what else are we doing with the charwoman and the assistants and the nephew?"

"But they don't pretend to be detectives," Crabb protested.

Inspector Mallet stiffened up.

"Pretend," he said sharply. "Who's pretending? Here's a man murdered. No pretence there! And here are we with no more in our hands than three cigarette ends and a woman's broken hair-slide as possible clues till we come on this entry which shows us that two months ago the murdered man had occasion to consult a detective."

"A private detective," Crabb interjected with what was almost a sneer.

Mallet retorted heatedly.

"And does that suggest nothing to you? *Why* didn't he come to *us* you ask. There was something he wanted to find out, of course. Then why not go to the official police? Is the answer that he was afraid some one might be implicated whom he, through fear, or for family or business reasons, did not wish to see in the dock? I don't know. But as I haven't your nice and delicate feelings about the source from which I may get the answer, I don't care whether this man is a private detective or a public lavatory attendant."

Crabb looked crushed.

"Yes, sir," he admitted. "I appreciate that. It does look as if he must have been frightened of something or somebody, against whom he didn't want action to be taken."

"Maybe," Mallet snapped as he recovered his breath and got the match to his pipe. "Now find his number and ring him up. If he's at home ask him to come here."

Then when his colleague got busy with the directory, Mallet sat down and with his pipe going well gave his undivided attention once more to the dead man's diary. And Sergeant Crabb, waiting with the 'phone at his ear, seeing his puckered frown, thought how exactly he suggested a stout farmer of middle age puzzling over a railway timetable after being persuaded by his wife to attend the distant funeral of some distant relative from whom he himself had no expectations.

CHAPTER II
Books Are Silent Things

DETECTIVE-SERGEANT CRABB, INSIDE THE NEXT half-hour, was supplied with another example of how little a man can look his part when Barrett ushered in MacNab. The man, he considered, looked more like a doctor than a detective; but he was younger, much younger, than Mallet had somehow led him to expect.

Inspector Mallet, after a brief exchange of the usual commonplaces, came at once to the point.

"We find your name in his diary," he said. "He seems to have consulted you about something on the 30th of March."

"Quite correct," MacNab agreed. "He called on me at the Adelphi, about the disappearance of certain books from his shop."

"Ah, yes. And did you gather the reason why he went to you, and not to the police?" Mallet inquired.

Crabb liked both the question and the manner in which it was put. No offence, however, appeared to be taken.

"Mr. Dodsley told me why he came to me, but I don't think it was the only, or even his chief reason."

"Yes?"

"He said he came because I was a customer of his, and had some knowledge of books."

Mallet smiled.

"Meaning that the police had not?"

"Meaning, I think, that the thief knew much more about those particular books than most people," MacNab corrected. "You see, it was no case of petty pilfering, but a sustained disappearance of valuable books, one by one, over a period of weeks. So I began my investigations by going round the bookshops."

Mallet looked startled.

"What? All the bookshops in London? Some job that! But you charge by time, I suppose. *We* could have circularised them in a single day."

"Only the second-hand bookshops," MacNab explained. "And among them only such dealers in rare books as were in a position to offer the price this particular thief had shown himself to be aware they were worth."

"Yes," Mallet conceded, "I suppose that does narrow it down."

"To about a dozen—in London. But I met with no result. So the conclusion was that the man had either disposed of them outside London, or was holding them up. And, of course, if he were a private collector the books might never come on the market at all."

Mallet nodded appreciation. He was interested, for the moment at least. All this was new to him, his experience having made him more knowing about bookies rather than books.

"Quite," he said, "a police circular would do nothing to meet that case."

"Well," MacNab went on, "our next move was to tempt him into the open. I argued that, whether he was holding up these books as a collector or for higher prices, such a man would be one who kept his eye on the market. So I advertised in the trade journals for one of the books I knew he had, offering eight hundred for it."

Mallet sat up.

"Eight hundred what?" he cried. "Not pounds, surely? You don't mean that?"

"Oh, yes, but we didn't propose to pay anything, you understand. Eight hundred was about three times what the book would fetch."

"But your fish didn't rise to it?"

"He did not. Others did. We had two offers of the book which we declined on the score of their poor condition, after Mr. Dodsley, on inspection, saw that neither was his copy. And there," MacNab added, "so far as I am concerned, the matter rests."

Mallet, leaving his chair, began to pace about. The movement looked instinctive. It was as if the other man's admission of failure had subconsciously induced him to some kind of activity on his own account. The other man, Crabb noted from his corner, sat at his ease, apparently unperturbed by his failure. On hearing that admission, Crabb had cleared his throat with a significant little cough. But it was the other man alone who seemed to have overheard Crabb's inarticulate comment. He looked over at Crabb curiously, as if he had for the first time noted his presence in the room. Suddenly Mallet surprised Crabb by an unexpected question.

"Whose idea was it to offer thrice the book's real value?"

But the question seemed to please the private detective. His face lit up.

"Ah," he said. "I appreciate that, Inspector. I warned him it was more than likely to rouse the man's suspicions. But Dodsley insisted. Said he knew what he was doing. And as that chimed in with a suspicion I had that he knew more than he had told me, I gave way."

"You suspected the thief might turn out to be some one he might not wish to prosecute?"

"Exactly; that being his only obvious reason for employing me rather than you."

Mallet, hands behind his back, nodded his assent.

"Yes," he said. "Yes; it seems a fair inference. He would of course have had to tell us more than he need tell you."

"And have to pay me when he could have had you for nothing," MacNab added with the ghost of a smile.

But if Mallet saw any humour in this he was too eager to give any indication of it.

"Yes, that seems to make it conclusive: he did have something to hide," he declared. "All this strengthens the possibility of a connection between his death and the theft of the books." Sitting down close to MacNab, he began to twiddle his thumbs rapidly. Crabb had become familiar with Inspector Mallet's little idiosyncrasies in manner and gesture. He knew that when he paced about with hands behind his back like a handcuffed prisoner, he was at a loss. He knew that when he sat down and began to twiddle his thumbs, so that the one seemed to be in pursuit of the other, he felt himself to be hot on a good scent.

"Now," he went on, "this man was shot dead exactly where I'm now sitting at four minutes past three, the discovery being made at three-sixteen by the constable on his rounds. From your knowledge, can you suggest what Dodsley was doing here, or why he should be here at all, at such a time?"

Surprise appeared on MacNab's face.

"You know the time he was shot?" he asked. "The *Record* only gave the time at which he was found."

Mallet made a gesture which Crabb understood. He crossed to the table.

"We have his watch. The glass, when he apparently threw out his arms in falling, struck the edge of the desk and was smashed. What is more, the hands were so dented in that they pressed against the dial and stopped the works."

MacNab at once recognised the watch Crabb exhibited. He had noted it on Dodsley's wrist as being in harmony with the man's natty and even dandified appearance. Of smaller size than men usually affect, it looked on his thin wrist just as completely his as the neat little pointed grey beard on his chin. The watch beyond doubt was Dodsley's, and as he saw, it had stopped at precisely four minutes after three.

"Bit of luck for us, that," Mallet remarked with a chuckle of satisfaction. "Doctors never are sure of the time of death within an hour or two. As for death by shooting, he might have been dead soon after the shop closed, for all we'd otherwise know. And here was he, throwing out his hand and giving us the time to a tick. Why, if he'd written it down on his desk, he couldn't have done it better."

"Quite," MacNab agreed, "provided, of course, his watch happened to be working at the time."

Mallet looked taken aback. The possibility was new to him. His thumbs ceased to revolve.

"You mean showing the correct time?"

"No, I meant if it was going at all. Slow or fast wouldn't make much difference, for it's unlikely it would be more than a minute or two one way or the other."

Inspector Mallet breathed again, the thumbs accelerating.

"Well," he said, "that's what any watchmaker can tell us. Whether, I mean, there's any other cause than the bent hands responsible for the stoppage. We can leave that till the watch is examined, and go back to the question I put. Supposing the watch was working, can you suggest why Mr. Dodsley should be here at about two in the morning?"

A psychologist would probably have been interested in noting MacNab's reactions to Mallet's question. Crabb, seeing him get to his feet and begin to move about in that restless fashion, judged the question to be one that left him at a loss. For Crabb was accustomed to see Mallet behave like that, with the difference that Mallet held his hands behind his back, the left wrist clasped firmly by the right hand, whereas this man moved about, with both hands thrust deep in his trouser pockets as if groping deep for something he knew was there although uncertain in which pocket the thing he searched for might lie. At length he turned to the patient Mallet.

"Well," he said, without removing his hands, "I can only suggest he was here waiting for some one he somehow knew would come. If that watch is not out of order no other explanation is rational. But beyond that there are these facts in support. First, I hadn't been on the case long before becoming, as I've said, certain that he knew more about the disappearance of his books than he told me. Then, after I had put in much time in the shop itself, watching the customers, it became clear to me that only some one with an intimate knowledge and special access could carry out these thefts."

Mallet nodded his appreciation. His thumbs revolved thoughtfully; but MacNab's hands remained in his pockets.

"A bookshop is a first-rate place for unobtrusive observation," he continued. "One can remain in it an indefinite time, dipping into one book after another, all over the place. Well, in a few days I got familiar not only with the assistants and their routine of duties but, after the first two weeks, I was able to distinguish the casual looker-in from the habitual caller who knew where to go for the kind of book he was after. Now the really valuable books were kept locked up in the glass-fronted case where they could be seen. In fact, you yourself, Inspector, could see them now from where you sat if you hadn't moved this desk."

Mallet's eyes opened.

"How did you know we'd moved it?" he asked. "We found it had been moved to one side and put it back to the centre to find why."

"It always stood to this side. And if you'll put it back and look through that little window, you'll see why," MacNab said.

With Crabb's help he lifted the table to the side nearest the door, and Mallet, having placed the chair behind the writing table, sat down expectantly.

MacNab indicated the window.

"Look!" he said.

Mallet's eyes went quickly to the window, through which he could see right down the length of the shop. Almost instantly he picked up the significant object: a glass-fronted bookcase standing to the right side against the wall which divided the back from the front shop.

"Yes," Mallet said. "Yes, I see. With the table where it is now, he had the case continually in his line of vision."

"Whereas," MacNab added, "if he had kept his table in the centre, he would have a clear view through the doorway into the front shop."

"So the case was kept not only locked but constantly within his sight as he sat here."

"Exactly," MacNab agreed. "That was his display case. The contents were changed at intervals from the highly valuable books he kept in here." He pointed to the cases which lined the back wall of the office, and Mallet swivelled round his chair to stare at the shelves behind him.

"Well," he remarked, "except for the fact that they're all behind glass, and each shelf is marked by Roman figures, I'd never guess these books had much value. Yet, of course," he added, as he wheeled round again, "it isn't always the best dressed man who has the most money in his pocket."

"Well," MacNab continued, "you see how any one standing in front of the window would block his view."

"Yes," Mallet said musingly. "If the thief had a confederate as well as a key it would take only a second to whip out any book whose position he saw through the glass."

"It could be done like that."

"But you don't think it was?"

"Well, no—o," MacNab admitted.

"Will you tell me why?"

"I have no evidence. Is what I think important?"

"It may be. Look here. About what that watch can tell us—don't you see that the same blow which broke the glass may also have damaged it internally? Suppose the watchmaker finds a broken hair spring or a displaced pinion, there's nothing in that to tell us whether the watch stopped at two in the afternoon or two in the morning."

MacNab, who had listened with his gaze on the carpet, looked up.

"Very well," he said with decision. "I'll tell you what I think if you allow me to verify it afterwards by seeing what that watch may have to say."

Mallet in his surprise looked first at MacNab and then, as if to see if he had heard aright, over at Crabb. Catching sight of his assistant's lifted eyebrows he sat back again in his chair.

"Agreed. Go ahead!" he said, full of curiosity. "What I'm after is to find a motive strong enough to account for his being here in the middle of the night." Then he leaned forward over the table and astonished Crabb by saying in an impulsively excited fashion: "If you can establish a motive for his presence here at that unusual hour, I may tell you that two small clues we have in our hands will become things of vital importance."

Crabb, of course, was aware of the two clues to which he alluded. His surprise was due to the discovery that Mallet could become excited and impulsive. The other man, busy formulating his thoughts, appeared not to notice.

"I think," he said at last, "he must have come here last night to confront the person he by this time knew to be responsible for the thefts. My impression now is that he knew the man's identity not less than a week ago, for it was on the Tuesday of last week he sent me a note to say he had no further need of my services. On the Monday I think I convinced him that the books were being stolen by some one in possession of a key to the shop as well as to the case. What influenced me most was that a daylight theft needed not one but two confederates. You see a confederate who blocked Dodsley's view by standing in front of that window could hardly do so by looking in at Dodsley. That would have drawn attention. He must stand with his *back* to the window, as if unconscious there was a window there. But then Dodsley, finding his view cut off, might make for the door without himself being seen, and so surprise the actual thief whose own back would necessarily be towards the office door as he faced the bookcase. Thus another observer would be needed to watch the door from right in front, perhaps from behind the open bookshelves nearest the door. There being no glass in those shelves and no backs to them, he would only have to remove a volume to have a perfect peep-hole. But of course such a method was too elaborate and risky."

"*Damn!*"

The expletive was forcible enough in itself and did not need the bang of Mallet's fist on the table which was its accompaniment.

"Why?" MacNab said. "What's—"

But Mallet had risen and taken his arm.

"This way, and I'll show you," he said. "It's going all wrong."

He led the way to the door and lifting the curtain passed through. Just outside he stopped and pointed to the shelves facing them. These shelves, projecting from the walls, stood about seven feet high and were double. That is to say, each shelf was wide enough to hold two rows of volumes, one row facing them, and the other facing the second set of shelves parallel to them.

"Look at that," Mallet said pointing.

MacNab easily perceived not only what he indicated but its significance. From a shelf somewhere about eye-level a book was missing. But the blank would not have been so noticeable had not the book on the other side also been missing, for the two missing volumes made a blank space by which one could see right through to the shelves of the farther row.

"There's your peep-hole," Mallet cried. "A man *was* on

the watch. These two books weren't withdrawn by a chance reader and laid down elsewhere. They were put down on the floor, and more than that, both were together on the floor, showing that the book on this side had been drawn through from the other side."

MacNab rather disconcertedly agreed that Mallet was right. The volume withdrawn from the side at which they looked could have been removed for no other purpose than to allow the person behind the shelves to see through. It could not have been taken out by one desiring to read, since from where he stood on the other side its title would not be visible. Yes, it looked as if, after all, there might be no connection whatever between Dodsley's murder and the disappearance of the books. The thefts had ceased while he himself had been frequenting the shop. But he felt sure it was not because of that fact that Dodsley had dropped him. As a private detective, MacNab had become quite familiar with the client who dropped him at the most interesting moment. He was perfectly familiar with the symptoms, and however much variation there might be in the excuses offered, he always knew the real reason to be that the client had some good reason for not wishing to prosecute. This, of course, was a side to the profession known only to the private detective.

But it was through his experiences in such disappointing cases that, far better than Mallet, he could feel assured that Dodsley knew who was robbing him. Yet, the question now arose: did he know how many were in it? And if he did, was it likely he would lie in wait for them alone in the shop at that hour? But if the thefts were carried through at night there was no need to have any watching confederates at all. And if it were a night raid, was it likely the thieves would be content to carry off one book at a time? Why not clear out the whole case?

MacNab's head swam with all these contradictions and possibilities. He turned from where he leant against the door to see Mallet and Crabb with their heads together some way up the shop. Mallet beckoned him over. The inspector's mouth had a curious twist as of self-derision or pity or perplexity, and as MacNab approached, his hand went out to a point at the next wing of shelves.

"Look there," he said. "What do you make of that?"

Staring at the shelves, MacNab saw that what looked like a peep-hole had been contrived there also, in similar fashion, by the removal of books from each side.

"And this other too," Mallet went on, indicating the remaining wing. "The fellow behind this lot must have wanted to hear as well as see." He laughed. "Might have stuck his head through," he went on. And MacNab saw that from the last set of shelves not two but several volumes were missing from both sides, and so exactly opposite as to make a wide opening.

"What in thunder does it all mean?" Mallet sighed. Then, as no reply came, his right hand went round his back to grasp his left wrist and he stood staring with narrowed eyes at the big gap in the shelves. As for MacNab, he soon became certain that the gaps had been deliberately made: it was too improbable a coincidence that from each of the three sets of shelves books standing exactly opposite each other had been removed for any other purpose. But Mallet was mistaken in supposing the three peep-holes implied the presence of three watchers. Each in turn might have been made by one person in stealing forward towards the door of Dodsley's office. That this door was the objective MacNab had little doubt after going over to inspect the corresponding set of shelves on the other side of the room, where he found not a single gap in the serried ranks of vari-coloured bindings. When he returned, Mallet momentarily dropped the wrist to sweep his hand towards the thousands of books which crowded shelves and walls from floor to ceiling.

"My God," he sighed in a whisper, while his eyes went circling round, "if only these books could speak!"

But books, though full of words, are silent things: they have no tongue.

CHAPTER III
Something That Spoke

Detective-Sergeant Crabb felt both amused and annoyed by MacNab's next action. He had some justification for both these contradictory emotions.

For when MacNab, following on Mallet's outburst, produced a magnifying glass and went down on his knees to examine the floor between the shelves, the act became a reflection on both Mallet and himself. Did he suppose they had neglected that obvious duty? Or did he think he could come on something they had overlooked?

"You'll get nothing there," Mallet said with conviction.

"I hope not," came the reply from the floor.

The two others exchanged a glance as if to see whether they had heard correctly. For a moment they watched him moving about with the glass within an inch of the thick brown linoleum. Then Mallet, thinking MacNab could not have understood his assertion, put it in another form, with a trifle of impatience in his tone.

"Hoping to find something?"

MacNab got to his feet.

"No," he said, pocketing his lens; "hoping to find nothing."

"Looks as if you've got it then. Not even dust on your knees." Mallet nodded with a sly wink to Crabb, which, however, MacNab chanced not to miss.

"Yes," he replied dryly. "Yes, this seems one of those rare cases in which it's better for you to find nothing rather than something."

While Mallet narrowed his eyes over this, Crabb half turned away, his disdain reviving. This was the sort of thing one would expect from a private detective—words that looked astute but really meant nothing. But Mallet, it seemed, wasn't going to allow him to cover up his failure like that.

"Look here," he said briskly, "there *was* something to find on the floor. We got what there was to find, unfortunate though that may be."

A little rift of irritation seemed about to develop. Mallet's professional dignity had no doubt been wounded on seeing the other man go down to look over a floor he himself had already examined, and, on the other side, MacNab may have been moved to get something back for the wink he surprised on its passage to Crabb. But now, just as he was making for the office to retrieve his hat, he turned to face the two officers.

"The two clues you spoke of, inspector, did you find them on the floor?"

"Oh, I don't mind letting you see them before you go," Mallet said amiably.

"But you got them on the floor?"

"Why, yes, just where two of those spy-holes were made among the books." Leading the way into the office he went on: "But neither of them looks like establishing a connection between the thefts and the murder."

From a drawer in the writing table he extracted two match-boxes, and shoving one open he exhibited a metal hair slide such as women use to keep a strand or tress of hair neatly in position.

Mallet touched it over with a finger.

"Pin catch gone, you see. Dropped out of her hair."

Taking up the other box, he slid it open. It contained three cigarette ends and two spent matches.

"And that's all you found?"

"Well," said Mallet defensively, as he shut the box, "a man got hanged not long ago who wouldn't have been but for one spent match he left behind." As MacNab took up his hat Mallet added, "So three fag ends and two match ends ought to be enough to catch a mere book thief."

At the door MacNab turned with a wave of his hat. "But these belong to your case, not mine, Inspector," he said.

"What?" Mallet cried. "You mean to say—" Then seeing Crabb politely holding the curtain aside he burst out: "Here, one moment."

"It's nine-thirty now, sir," Crabb reminded him. Mallet impatiently waved this remonstrance aside.

"Oh, let them wait. I've got to hear why he's so sure these things apply to the murder."

MacNab came back, Crabb reluctantly following.

"If it were only a matter of curiosity, I'd still want to know," Mallet explained. "Hang it all, after an assertion like that you can't bolt and leave me no chance to prove you wrong."

MacNab put his hat on the table.

"That's what you want to do, of course."

"Of course," Mallet smiled. "Who wouldn't? You were so cock-sure, you know."

MacNab's good humour returned.

"And yourself," he said, "weren't you equally cock-sure about something when you saw me on my knees?"

"Well, you prove me wrong about that then," Mallet retorted his eyes alight.

Half seated on the table, MacNab indicated the two match-boxes.

"You say these were the only clues you found on the floor?"

"There certainly was nothing else; the floor was as bare as my hand. Why, man," Mallet laughed, "you didn't even have to dust your hands when you got up."

"Ah, you noticed that, did you?"

Catching the other's smile, Mallet laughed encouragingly. Crabb well understood that particular laugh. He had heard it before when the chief inspector happened to be putting a nervous or reluctant witness at his ease. He sat forward, stretched out a hand and pulled Crabb closer up. "We both noticed it. Why, we'd need to have the dust in our own eyes not to have seen there was none on the floor, eh, Sergeant?"

"Well, and wasn't that just the clue you missed?" MacNab asked in such a way that Crabb's smile of assent faded while forming itself.

"You did say you were looking for nothing and had found it," Mallet agreed in a changed voice.

"Look here," MacNab said, "the people who were here last night had nothing to do with the book thefts. These cigarette ends alone are enough to prove that. The book thieves knew what they wanted and where to find all they wanted. Besides, you can't see any of them loitering about smoking while they looked through books on the cheap shelves, leaving that case untouched. Now—"

"One moment," Mallet cut in, holding up his hand. "One moment, please. You say last *night*. You say they were here last night. How do you get that?"

"Because if you like to put it so, I got no dust on my knees just now. Why, you ask, was there no dust on the floor after a whole day's coming and going of customers? I've seen as many as thirty at one time moving among those rows of books. Yet that floor hadn't a sign or symptom of that traffic. Why not?"

Mallet's fist came down.

"It had been swept," he said.

"Or washed. The charwoman can settle that point. Now the next—"

"No, no! We'd better have that settled at once," Mallet interrupted. "The woman is due here now. Fetch her in, Crabb." Then as Crabb left he added, "I might tell you we would have seen all this for ourselves after we'd seen the charwoman, but I won't. Such a simple thing to miss too." Stooping, he pulled out a drawer and extracting a bundle of papers selected one which he passed over to MacNab.

"If you think these are clues bearing on the murder," he said, "I'd be glad if you looked through that; it's the statement of the officer who discovered the body."

MacNab was touched.

"As for missing the obvious," he said, "it's the obvious that's apt to get missed. Don't I know it! And, you see, I had the advantage of you, for after haunting this shop as I had been doing, I knew what it looked like at the end of a day. Why, I've even *heard* the dust and grit under my shoes as I moved about among those shelves."

Mallet did not seem to hear: his mind was forging ahead towards the deductions to be drawn from the dustless floor. So MacNab took up Constable Roberts's statement. But before he had got very far, Mallet interrupted.

"If you're right about the charwoman," he said quietly, "it follows that these cigarette ends, and the books left on the floor, were put there after the cleaning up was over. And I suppose we can take it that the woman, in the usual way, did her work after the shop was shut for the night. Therefore, the smoker was some one who entered later, some one who stood inside the bay formed by the protecting shelves, out of sight if the shop was in darkness; and he stood long enough in one spot to smoke three cigarettes. Yet, if the shop was in darkness, he was not there to read, nor, the assistants being gone, to buy, nor to steal, or he would not have lingered so long over the job, among the less valuable books. So this person was—" Mallet broke off suddenly, looked up, and unclasped his hands. "Good Lord!" he cried, aghast.

"Well?" MacNab urged, startled and impatient.

Mallet regarded him almost woefully.

"Why, don't you see—this hair slide in one place, the cigarette ends in another—it's that damned charwoman; the real explanation is that they are all *hers*."

MacNab was shaken. Mallet must be right. Here was something he had himself missed which should have been as obvious as his own dustless floor.

"You'll see it's that," Mallet nodded as Crabb's purposeful footsteps became audible. But Crabb entered alone. Mrs. Headcorn, it appeared, had not yet arrived, although all the others except the dead man's nephew were in attendance. Mallet, annoyed at the charwoman's absence at such a moment, sent Crabb back to get her address confirmed by one of the assistants so that the constable might be sent to compel her attendance.

"After all," he said, when Crabb re-entered, "after all, even if these things are hers, they don't explain those spy-holes, do they? She didn't drop her hair slide and then pull out a couple of books to see if it was on the other side." Then as if this suggested more, he came over quickly to open the box containing the cigarette ends. Staring a moment at the contents, his face brightened and he thrust the box under Crabb's nose as if he meant him to smell: "Three cigarettes and two matches—what do they suggest to you, Crabb?"

MacNab laid down Roberts's statement to listen. But Crabb knew he was not expected to apply his nose to the box: the elation in his superior's tone somehow told him he was expected to use not his nose but his eyes. He stared and thought hard.

"Two matches to three cigarettes," he murmured. "One match for the first. Second for—no, can't say whether he lit the second from the first one or used the second match for the third cigarette."

"Still, there was an interval between either his second or third smoke," Mallet suggested.

"Yes," Crabb agreed. "Yes, he had to use the second match between one or the other." His voice quickened as he saw more. "The unfinished one is the one he smoked last."

"Marvellous!" Mallet cried. "But what makes you so sure?"

"Well, sir, he wouldn't throw away one to begin another, would he, unless the others were more to his taste, which can't be the reason here, since all three seem the same brand."

"Are they? Why then is the unfinished one flat and the others round?"

Crabb seemed to think this rather too elementary. He smiled faintly.

"Some one trod on it," he said. His face brightened and he went on quickly, "To put it out of course, because—well—the man had been there some little time anyway; the interval between his smokes tells me that. Then he gets tired and starts a third, but—"

"But why do you assume it was a man? Don't women smoke?" Mallet insisted.

"But women use either a lighter or those flat packets of matches, not wooden matches."

"All right, let that pass. You were saying—"

"I was going to say that before he got half-way through his third, something happened that made him drop it and put his foot on it."

Mallet shut the box dexterously with one finger of the hand in which it lay.

"Exactly," he said. "He was waiting and watching. The cigarettes witness to the waiting, and the openings made among the books witness to the watching." He turned to his assistant. "But if you're right about the wooden matches, Crabb, there's a woman in it as well, for though a woman may not carry a box of wooden matches, no man carries a hair slide. Still, of course," he finished with a sigh, "to be sure on all these points we have to wait for that infernal charwoman."

MacNab pushed across Roberts's statement and got to his feet. Mallet, who now sat at the desk with his fountain pen going full speed, did not look up.

"Well, what do you think of it?" he asked.

"That officer's statement is very interesting," MacNab replied.

"Yes," Mallet agreed. "We'll be putting him through the mill presently."

MacNab felt a little sorry for Roberts. There were things in his statement which looked like boding the constable no good when the time came for Mallet to take him through it. But as for Mrs. Headcorn, he had little doubt as to what her evidence would be; for leaving the cigarette ends out, he knew that the hair slide had fallen out of no woman's hair. With the catch gone by which the pin was held in position, it never could have held itself in place, much less a strand of hair. Yes, it looked like turning out a case full of interest. He would like to hear more of it. Dodsley's death, however, had no connection with the loss of the missing books; even if it had, Dodsley himself had dismissed him. MacNab once more took up his hat, then hesitated as he regarded Mallet.

"There's just one thing I hope you won't mind, Inspector," he said, tentatively.

Mallet stopped writing and raised his eyes.

"Yes?" he responded sitting back a little.

"That diary in which you found my name."

Mallet sat right back.

"Yes," he nodded.

"If I had a look through it, there might be something—I mean my association with Dodsley might suggest—"

"Might make it suggest more to you than to us. Yes, I quite see that." He motioned Crabb with his pen, and Crabb produced the diary. So while Mallet continued constructing the questionnaire for the approaching examination of the waiting assistants, MacNab retired to a corner with the little book.

CHAPTER IV
The Dead Man's Diary

THE EARLIEST ENTRY MACNAB FOUND WHICH COULD refer to the theft of the books was that on February 8th. This ran:

Yet another missing this morning.

That implied books previously missed. Then on March 30th appeared the entry relating to himself. In between those two dates a number of notes on books occurred, but they appeared to refer to specially interesting purchases such as that on May 15th.

Acquired the A. L. collection for D. G.

The only entry of books sold appeared to be those specially valuable ones taken on credit by known clients for whose money he had to wait.

MAY 20,—Stout took first Alice for £5. This time promised payment tomorrow. Maybe!

But Dodsley's pessimism seemed not to have been justified by Mr. Stout, in this instance at least, for under the date May 21, only two days before his own death, Dodsley had scribbled:

Note by hand D. G.

Apparently Mr. Stout, whoever he was, had in this transaction resolved to give the mistrustful Dodsley a pleasant surprise, since he had sent D. G. to the shop with a fiver for that first edition of *Alice in Wonderland.* Then MacNab remembered having seen the initials D. G. already. Hunting back he came on the entry under February 10, and had to revise his inference in regard to Mr. Stout's wish to give the bookseller a pleasant surprise. It must, he now saw, have been Dodsley who sent D. G. to collect the money, not Mr. Stout who sent D. G. with it. Evidently this D. G. acted for Dodsley in some capacity, since it was through him the A. L. collection had on that date been acquired.

MacNab's absorption in the little book attracted Mallet's notice, and his questionnaire being finished he came across to the corner where the silent MacNab and the watchful Crabb were seated.

"Got something?" he asked hopefully.

"Nothing definite," MacNab reluctantly admitted. "All the same, something might be got out of this D. G. who seems to have done work for him."

MacNab was quite conscious that there was no more than the barest possibility that anything of value would result, but, having shown Mallet the entries, he was quite unprepared for the burst of laughter his suggestion evoked. Even Crabb was moved to mirth, though it was very restrained, not loud and explosive like his chief's.

"You'll forgive me," Mallet said after a little, "but really, you know, that was too funny. Even at such a moment," he added soberly. Wiping his eyes he used the diary to point at Crabb. "It was he who solved the mystery of D. G.," he said. "Well up in Latin, he is."

"Latin?" MacNab echoed coldly. "What's that to do with it?"

Mallet bent forward, his forefinger at the last entry.

"Of course I spotted a thing like that. 'Note by hand D. G.' I say to myself—two days before the murder. What was that note about, and who is this D. G. I ask myself? And who is this first Alice who's taken by Stout the day before? Where to? I ask. And for £5. It all seemed—well—queer enough to be worth looking into. So I put it to Sergeant Crabb here. And he blew it all sky-high in one breath, as you might say." Mallet turned the page right way round for MacNab to read. "Why, don't you see, Dodsley didn't mean any *person* by that. This Mr. Stout the day before bought some book for £5, and Dodsley, it seems, wasn't too hopeful about getting the cash for it. But Stout sent a fiver the very next day, and Dodsley is so surprised that he makes a note of the fact, adding the letters D. G., which, as Sergeant Crabb says, are Latin, and stand for—" Mallet looked round—"What words did you say, Crabb?"

"*Dei Gratia*," Crabb explained.

"Which meant *By the help of God.* You see, being a pious old fellow, though a bit distrustful, he thinks he'd never have got his money so soon out of Stout but for divine help."

MacNab sat staggered. It was quite true. Dodsley might

have so used the initials. But all doubt vanished when Crabb clinched the matter by pointing out the entry under February 8.

"In fact," he remarked, "you can tell when he considered he'd made an exceptionally good deal by his use of these initials. *'Acquired the A. L. collection by D. G.'*"

"Quite right," Mallet affirmed. "I had an old aunt who was pious in the same way. I ought to have remembered it. She never wrote a letter without putting in D. G. about everything that happened—or was it D. V.?"

The question remained unsettled, for before Mallet could decide, a knock came, and Sergeant Barrett put his rosy face inside to announce the arrival of Mrs. Headcorn. At a nod he stood aside to allow the lady to enter.

Mrs. Headcorn, diminutive, hatless, bare-armed and excited, looked as if Copping had pulled her away from some floor. But if she had no scrubbing brush in her rugged hand, neither had she, as MacNab observed, a slide in her hair.

Clearly possessed of a mind of her own, she did not seem the sort of witness to be cowed into docility.

"Sorry you didn't find it convenient to attend at the hour appointed," Mallet said, as soon as she was seated before him.

"Well, I got my livin' to get," she nodded defiantly back at him. "I'm not one as gets it by settin' on a chair."

But Mallet knew how to handle her.

"You didn't realise, perhaps, that you were our most important witness," he remarked, taking up his pen and pulling a sheet of paper towards him.

"Me?" Mrs. Headcorn's eyes lost their wrathful glint as they opened wide.

"Oh, we couldn't possibly get on without you," Mallet asserted.

The taut muscles around Mrs. Headcorn's mouth melted.

"Fancy that," she simpered. "Really! I—I—don't know what to say."

"Oh, the answers to a few most important questions is all we want from you, Mrs. Headcorn," Mallet said encouragingly.

"Anything I can do to help, I'm sure."

"You were here at work last night, weren't you?"

"I'm here every night. Nice place it 'ud be if I wasn't with the sort o' folk who come in here—all too busy getting things into their heads to have time to knock the dirt off their feet. Why, if only you—"

"You do your work after the shop is closed, of course?"

"That's right. I 'as to have the place to myself. Why, if only you—"

"Yes, yes," Mallet said sympathetically. "I'm sure it's hard work. No doubt you have to take a rest sometimes and—perhaps refresh yourself with a cigarette."

"What me? Not much! I leave that to the young 'uns what's taken to the trousers, same as I saw at Southend last Bank 'Oliday. Why, if I was to tell you—"

Mallet pushed the open match-box across the table.

"So," he said, "if these cigarette ends were found on the floor I can take it you did not leave them there?"

Mrs. Headcorn after a stare looked up.

"You got them on the floor?"

"Between the shelves, about five o'clock this morning."

"Well, all I can say is they got dropped there after I'd left last night," she declared.

Mallet soon satisfied himself that she had not in the dark missed observing the cigarette ends. As for the suggestion that Mr. Dodsley himself might have dropped them while looking at the books after she had left, this was a notion she called really ridiculous. For one thing Mr. Dodsley didn't smoke, being, she declared, much too mean to waste money on tobacco; and for another, in too much of a hurry that night to stand about reading books.

Mallet pricked up his ears.

"And what was he in a hurry about?" he asked.

"To get rid of me, of course."

"You knew he wanted you gone?"

"It 'ud be funny if I didn't, the way he kept coming out and looking to see how far I'd got. That made me take my time, that did. Did me work proper. That's how I know about there being nothing left anywheres on the floor last night, see? Well, after a bit he got real shirty, and started all of a sudden to cuss at me something shocking."

"So you left in a hurry, I suppose?"

"Not me. I don't get upset by language. It only made me feel as if I was doing my own floor. But I'd be sorry if my old man was to use such language the night before he was took."

Mallet pushed the second match-box towards her.

"We thought you must have left in a hurry," he said, exhibiting the hair slide, "because you dropped this."

Mrs. Headcorn, after a glance, shook her head.

"I don't use them things at all," she said, "but if I did, I'd not have them yeller, my coiffeur being dark."

"Oh we thought you might have used this to pin over your shawl," Mallet explained.

"Don't wear a shawl. Never did and never shall. Shawls is low class," she snapped.

Mallet's smile of satisfaction on hearing this pronouncement may have been mistaken by Mrs. Headcorn for agreement with, and approval of, the strong view she held about shawls. But the gilt hair slide might have been made of something much more precious than gold from the care with which he replaced it in the box.

"Am I to take it, then, that there was no one else there when he began to use violent language?"

"That's right, Mr. Carter being the last to go on account of having the sales to do up for the day."

"Then Mr. Dodsley himself must have locked up the shop?"

"Of course, there not being anybody else to do it."

"You saw him lock up?"

"I didn't actually see him turn the key if that's what you mean, but he must have done the locking up himself, if it was done at all."

Mallet nodded assent.

"Of course. How stupid of me! But you did see him leave, I take it?"

The question roused scorn in Mrs. Headcorn's eyes.

"D'ye see me turning round to say good-night to the likes of him after the way he swore at me?" she demanded. "Not much! I'm not the sort to cheapen myself so. D'rectly I was done I walks straight out with my nose in the air, same as any lady would."

Mallet nodded.

"Thank you, Mrs. Headcorn; I quite understand." He hesitated for a moment. "You didn't see any one loitering about as you left? What I mean is, we have reason to believe two people whom we are anxious to interview, entered the shop after you left. If Mr. Dodsley did not want you to see them, that might account for the way you were treated by him. Just take a moment, and try to remember."

But Mrs. Headcorn shook her head with finality.

"I looked neither right nor left," she declared, "and if the Lord Mayor 'isself 'ad been standing on his head in the gutter I'd not have seen it."

After Mrs. Headcorn left, Mallet sat thoughtfully regarding the two match-boxes which held his two possible clues.

"A man and a woman in it," he said at length. "She's at least made that fairly certain. But we're as far as ever from fixing the time."

Crabb was impelled to speak.

"It looks as though he did leave the shop, sir," he said. "The three cigarettes smoked indicate some one waiting inside."

"Yes, but they don't tell us just when the waiting was done," Mallet said. "And I'd like to be a little more sure of that before seeing any more of these people. If Dodsley left after Mrs. Headcorn, and some one entered to await his return, as the cigarette ends suggest, that person must have not only been aware Dodsley intended to return, but also have had a key to the shop. Now it will be simple to ascertain who had keys, but if only we could fix the time to within an hour or so, the testing of any alibi offered us might yield results."

Crabb hesitated, a suggestion on the tip of his tongue. But it was so obvious that he feared to put it forward. Then he ventured it diffidently, in the form of a question.

"Isn't Dodsley's haste to get rid of the charwoman a pointer to the time?"

Mallet looked up.

"You mean it shows he expected some one he didn't want her to see."

"Well, yes, sir, suppose he meant to stay behind and catch the book thief." Glancing across at MacNab, he remarked:

"You believe from the way he dropped your services he had now a suspicion as to the thief's identity."

Mallet twisted round impatiently.

"But the cigarettes—found where they were, show us some one there passing a time of waiting, and that wasn't Dodsley, since we know he was not a smoker."

"He must have left and returned later," Crabb suggested.

Mallet snorted contempt.

"And how long did this book thief wait in there to get caught?" he demanded. "He must have turned very repentant, surely. And he must have known Mr. Dodsley intended to return. Then when Dodsley did return he somehow lost both his patience and his penitence and shot him out of hand, I suppose."

"Oh, sir!" Crabb protested.

"Pass me the diary," Mallet snapped in a tone that made Crabb almost jump for his case. "And the watch," he added.

There was that in his voice which, after Crabb had placed both the little book and the watch on the table brought MacNab from his seat to stand beside the expectant Crabb. Mallet's excitement escaped neither of them. His fingers flipped the pages over till he found the memoranda page on which certain numbers had been entered. MacNab's examination of the diary had been confined to the dated section. Crabb had not considered it worth while to draw his attention to this particular entry. And now from the position in which he stood, facing Mallet whose head was bent over the book, he could see only certain numerals upside down.

"No," Mallet said at last, "it's too far-fetched. But I thought I had a hunch about the time." He pushed the book over to MacNab. MacNab examined the figures.

VIII 45 IX 23 X 16
I 54 II 32 III 16

"It was that VIII 45 that I remembered, after she'd told us she usually left at 8.30," Mallet explained. "Made me wonder if it was the time of an appointment he'd set down."

Crabb came round to stare at the diary. The Roman numerals might refer to the hours, since none went higher than twelve. And, for the matter of that, the smaller figures might equally stand for minutes, not one of them exceeding the number of minutes in an hour. MacNab looked up.

"And this 'III 16,'" he said, "that was the time at which Roberts came on the body, wasn't it?"

"Oh, within a minute." Mallet's short laugh was harsh with disgust. "Good enough guess on Dodsley's part if he meant it for the time at which the constable would find his body."

"But *was* it Dodsley who made this entry?" Crabb hastily interjected.

The suggestion startled Mallet. He sat back as if some one had struck him.

"Ye—s," he whispered after a moment. "Yes, that's true. We don't know it's his—only that it's in his diary."

"The 'II 32' may then stand for the time he actually was shot," Crabb suggested. "I've heard one of our lecturers say this sort of thing is sometimes done by a certain type of criminal out of mere bravado. One instance he quoted—"

"What do you think?" Mallet put the question to MacNab. The reply did not come at once.

"I don't know what to think. It's not easy to see how the figures can mean anything at all," he confessed.

Mallet protested.

"Oh, come; they may not mean as much as Crabb surmises, but they *must* mean something. No man not imbecile makes pointless entries in a diary."

"Look at the figures again."

Mallet, thus challenged, picked up the diary. After his eyes had narrowed over the book for a moment Crabb saw them suddenly dilate.

"Why," he said, "both lines are simply the figures one to six in a different order."

"Except the last," MacNab agreed. "You expect that number to be reversed like the others to make 61; but instead it repeats the 16 of the first line."

Mallet threw down the diary, and rising took a step or two away.

"Well, it's no timetable anyhow," he said disgustedly. "Nobody could fix up a series of events so as to include hours and minutes in that order."

Crabb, who had taken possession of the discarded diary, ventured a comment.

"Of course, sir, if it had any reference to the clock, 'III 61' would be set down as 'IV 1.'"

"Exactly," Mallet snapped in his disgust. "It's impossible even to guess what such an artificial arrangement of numbers can refer to." He sat down again heavily, and after rather gloomily staring for a time at the surface of the table, looked up at MacNab. "Well," he said, "we needn't detain you longer. Much obliged for your help," he added, as MacNab got to his feet. "And if there should, after all, be a connection between the thefts and the murder I hope we may consult you again."

CHAPTER V
Inspector Mallet Makes the Watch Speak

As soon as MacNab had taken his leave Mallet, being anxious to fix the time of the murder before holding any more interviews, turned to Roberts's report on the finding of the body. Foiled so far in establishing the time of the murder, he now turned back to the report and the notes he had made when both Roberts and Sergeant Barrett were questioned earlier that morning.

"You know," he said, "that festive young man bothers me. I wonder if he was as fancifully drunk as Roberts said."

"The sergeant corroborated on that," Crabb reminded him.

"Yes, but Barrett admitted he saw him only for a minute or two."

"You mean that if he was not drunk he could rely on the story he told about the door opening and shutting?"

"Not quite," Mallet rejoined. "Drunk or sober, I'm not sure I could exactly rely on that young man. But if I knew he was play-acting I'd feel fairly certain he knew more about the crime than I do."

"And Roberts and Barrett were both sure he was not."

"So they are, Crabb, so they are. But consider this. They neither of them, till we began probing, thought that incident of the drunk young man had any connection with this affair. They thought of him as merely a man in a condition which their night duty made them quite familiar with. But suppose in this instance they were wrong, and then follow what happened. Roberts says his attention was first attracted by the sound of feet running towards him. He stepped away from the doors he had been inspecting and stood under a lamp till the man arrived. As soon as the man caught sight of him he pulled up. As soon as he speaks Roberts sees his condition. He babbles incoherently about a door up the street which had opened and shut of itself. Then the sergeant arrived on the scene." Mallet's forefinger tapped the table with a decision familiar to Crabb. "But *where* had the young man come from?" he asked. "If he was running and Barrett was walking, he must have passed Barrett higher up the street."

"Unless he came from somewhere between Roberts and Barrett?"

"Certainly," Mallet agreed, "that's just my point; this shop is in that position."

Crabb pondered over this for a time. Aware that Mallet was using him as a whetstone to his own wits, he knew his function at the moment was to discover flaws in his inspector's reasoning.

"There was the cigarette," he said at length. "He told Roberts he went into the doorway to light it. He may have been there some time and never passed Barrett at all, though he ran towards Roberts."

But Mallet shook his head.

"No," he declared, "that won't quite do. He reached Roberts with an unlit cigarette in his hand. *Where* did he get it?"

Crabb was swift to take the point.

"You mean he dropped the case higher up the street than this?" he said.

Mallet stared for a moment at the table between them.

"Let's make the positions visible to the eye, Crabb," he said. With that he first pushed forward the diary to the centre of the table. To the right, at a foot's distance, he set one of the match-boxes, and on the left, at about eighteen inches, he placed the dead man's watch. Then with the three articles now in a straight row he extended his hand across the table and set the second match-box close to Crabb's right hand so that it stood opposite the first box. Then his finger went back to the first match-box.

"This," he said, "is where Roberts stopped the running man, just before Barrett arrived on the scene in his wake. He tells a story, which seems ridiculous, about having seen a door being opened and shut by itself, or by a cat. They try to persuade him to go home, but he betrays all the talkativeness and incoherence usual to a man in his condition, and stays on. In the end he takes Roberts right past Dodsley's door up to Allom's shop." Mallet's finger passed over the diary and came to rest on the watch.

Crabb emitted a soft whistle.

"Led him up the garden, eh?" he breathed.

"Maybe." Mallet nodded thoughtfully. "It's a sure thing, anyway, that whether by design or accident, he led Roberts, who was trying all the doors and locks as he came along, right past the door of the one shop in which murder had been done. More than that," Mallet continued, "after Roberts had examined Allom's door and found everything normal, observe how the man still kept Roberts's attention fixed on himself. The officer was even drawn away out of his own division by crossing the street, and was kept standing there in talk—" he nodded at the box near Crabb's right hand—"as Roberts admits, for another fifteen minutes."

Crabb found what he thought was a sound objection to all this.

"Roberts also said he very nearly arrested him," he remarked. "That would have been more than awkward for the man later on if he were implicated in the murder."

"Yes," Mallet admitted with reluctance, "that is true. I can't imagine a guilty man, drunk or sober, taking that risk with a police officer. On the other hand, there's that unlit cigarette. Actually, if he went into any doorway at all to get it going it was Dodsley's. But if it was Dodsley's doorway then the case out of which he got the cigarette ought to have been found somewhere between this shop and the spot lower down where Roberts stopped him. Instead of which, Roberts finds it up the street beyond the door in the opposite direction."

"You assume the case was his?"

"Till the contrary is proved, since Roberts tells us the man felt his pockets for his case, and could not find it." He stretched out his arm abruptly. "Crabb, that case holds ten cigarettes. When found, it had six left in it, five on one side and one on the other. So when we add three to the one he carried in his hand, that accounts for its full capacity. What would you say if we had found not three but, say *four* cigarette ends on the floor?"

Crabb's reply was prompt.

"One at least couldn't have come out of the case," he said.

"Whereas," Mallet murmured half to himself, "all we found could have. Rather a queer festive night his must have been too," he continued. "Lots of drink but very little smoking, evidently, since all night he had used but three."

"A heavy smoker would carry a larger case," Crabb suggested.

Mallet looked across at him.

"Yes," he agreed, "that may well be true. And of course at a party the smokes would be provided by the host. You know," he went on more rapidly, "in some ways I wish we could rely on his story. If that tale of his is true, it would give us exactly what I want to know—the time at which the crime was committed. You see that, of course?"

Crabb did see it.

"You mean the murderer was still in the shop when this man went to the door?"

"That's it. Roberts tells us he said the door opened and a cat looked out and seeing him there shut it in his face. But Roberts afterwards saw that cat outside, playing with the cigarette case. So the person who opened the door must have got away a few minutes later while Roberts stood round the corner over the way, attempting to persuade the poor young gentleman to go home quietly."

"Yes," agreed Crabb, "that would give the time if the chap wasn't raving or lying."

"If he wasn't. But about that we can't be sure."

Almost mournfully Mallet regarded the murdered man's watch lying where he had placed it to mark the position of the other bookshop farther up the street. An oblique segment of its glass face still remained in position, covering the section from 4 to 9.30, the hands in the section in which the glass had disappeared being pressed flat to the dial at four minutes past three o'clock. And Roberts had found the body twelve minutes later. If he could only be sure the time on the watch was right, it would go far, Mallet knew, to corroborate the young man's tale of the door that opened and shut. Would he come forward when the news of the murder was published? Even if he did not, that could not be taken to imply any complicity in the crime. For, as Mallet knew from experience, it was seldom a man would come forward to volunteer evidence which, when published, would make him cut an unheroic or, as in this instance, a ludicrous figure.

Inspector Mallet felt at a loss. If only he could, before beginning his interrogations, have been sure as to the exact time of Dodsley's death! He stared resentfully at the watch with its broken glass lying before him on the table.

Sergeant Crabb saw Mallet's face harden suddenly. His left hand went out to seize the watch while the fingers of the other hand were fumbling in his waistcoat pocket. But it was not till Mallet extracted a pair of forceps that Crabb comprehended. Mallet heard the sharp indraw of his breath.

"Crabb," he said, with the watch on the table before him and the forceps in his hand, "can you swear to it that the hands of this watch were in their present position when we removed it from the wrist?"

"Certainly, sir," Crabb replied. "It is on the record."

Mallet nodded.

"That will be enough; it's now essential to know whether it was in working order when the glass got broken."

Crabb half rose to lean over the table while Mallet began to use his forceps. For he knew what the first tick of the watch would mean. But Mallet was taking a big risk. He might be destroying rather than securing evidence. And he had difficulty in releasing the hands. Either the forceps were not strong enough or the fingers that held them were nervous or clumsy. Several times the forceps slipped off with a sharp little click. Mallet was certainly taking a risk. Crabb held his breath, expecting the hand to break and fly off the watch. But Mallet seemed to appreciate this danger too, for giving up his attempts to lift the hands, he pushed his forceps between the small hand and the dial and, with infinite care, levered it clear. Then when the minute hand was also up, his ear went down to listen. Crabb had no need to stoop. In the silence of the room the tick-tick-tick was quite audible.

Mallet stood up.

"That settles two questions," he said with a nod. "Dodsley was done in at four minutes past three precisely. And it also explains the mystery of the door which perplexed the young fellow Roberts stopped some fifteen minutes later."

"Yes," Crabb agreed, "it certainly looks as if that young man wasn't as Roberts supposed, so fancifully drunk after all."

CHAPTER VI
Three Assistants

MISS JENKS FELT ILL AT EASE SITTING SO LONG IDLY IN the shop in which she usually had too much to do to sit for more than a few seconds at a time. She had nothing to do, that is, except stroke the Siamese cat which had sprung on to her lap the moment she sat down. Miss Jenks had been, as usual, the first of the three assistants to arrive. The tragedy had not taken her unawares. She had read the news in the paper it was her invariable custom to buy on the platform at Finchley while waiting for her train.

Life for Miss Jenks had been so long a matter of changeless, uncoloured routine that this abrupt incursion of the unexpected shook her nerve. But for all that, while she sat waiting in the shop, no outward symptom of her inward commotion was visible—at all events to the eye of Sergeant Barrett. She was not his type. He liked them fair and fluffy. But Amelia Jenks, with her sallow skin, black, lank hair, with horn spectacles on a nose so short that it revealed too much of her nostrils, looked even more than her thirty years. True, she had fine dark eyes which suggested that despite the meek, subdued expression normally there, a fire might be slumbering within. But her eyes were more than offset by the mole above her right cheek, close to the ear. To some faces a mole in the right place adds piquancy; but Miss Jenks's mole was more than a minor defect; it was a tragedy, for it was large and black. Well aware of this, Miss Jenks, acting on a friend's expert advice, did her best to cover it up by dragging down a strand of her thick black hair which, with more or less success, she held in position over the black mole with a hair-slide.

But Sergeant Barrett brightened up when Miss June Preedy appeared. To his mind she was, in the words of a song he knew, "a little bit of sunshine on a dark and stormy day." Watching the two exchange their greetings, Barrett stroked his moustache with full appreciation of the fair girl's charms. And as Miss Preedy's practised eye soon made her aware of the fact, time passed less heavily for them than for Miss Jenks of the downcast eyes and the unimpressionable Constable Copping.

Unlike Amelia Jenks, June had no horror of the police. She was too familiar with their uniforms, as shown on the screen, for that; and thanks to the cinema, which had fortified her nerves by many a gangster film, she faced up to her own part in this Dodsley affair with a quite pleasurable thrill of expectancy.

"Gee," she whispered, "ain't it just too awful?"

She stared at Barrett, her blue eyes round with innocent wonder, rather like a baby taking its first look at a strange animal. She had a lisp that added emphasis to the baby look in her eyes. Both the lisp and the look were those of her favourite screen heroine, and the look had been achieved after long practice in front of her mirror. If it failed when she tried it on Dick Dodsley, it was too much for the sergeant. He bent forward to pat her arm gently:

"There, there!" he murmured soothingly.

"I just can't get on to it yet," she said shakily, the *can't* being spoken in a way only to be heard in this country inside the cinema.

Amelia Jenks moved restlessly in her chair. She liked Americans when they came into the shop, liked their frank friendliness and their breezy volubility, which was so far beyond her own capacity as to seem an ideal. But she loathed Miss Preedy's imitation American, and to hear her "right now's" and "I guess so's" and "d'ye get me's" made her squirm. Not that Miss Preedy habitually used such forms of speech while at work in the shop. For her the ideal life was that which she saw reflected in the pictures of her screen idols. For the dull, monotonous life of the shop the dull, colourless English language was adequate enough. But the great exciting moments, when life rose towards the screen level—that was different, whatever Amelia Jenks might say. Both girls, indeed, had attended the same elementary school at Finchley, but it was to the local picture house that Miss Preedy owed most of what she knew and practised.

"My, it's jus' terr'ble—terr'ble, bat ah gotta get used to it, I suppose."

This time it was her knee the sergeant patted gently.

"Now, now," he said. "After all, this is London, you know."

His reminder, from the manner in which he sat back and threw a chest, meant that London was a place in which the unexpected always happened.

A knock sounded, and the sergeant with a nod sent Copping to the door. After a brief exchange through a narrow aperture, Copping opened the door just sufficiently to allow Mr. Carter to slip inside. Mr. Carter's eyes had a scared look, and he was rather breathless, as if he had run all the way from Hammersmith.

He sank into the nearest chair, which happened to be that from which Copping had risen to let him in. Miss Jenks flicked her eyes in a hasty look at him, and then resumed her slow, thoughtful stroking along the full length of Saka's quivering spine. Sergeant Barrett noted how the young man's eyes went not to Miss Jenks but straight to Miss Preedy.

"This your usual time?" he asked sharply.

Mr. Carter's head slewed round to stare at him for a moment.

"I wasn't coming at all today," he said. "I—"

"Yes?" The sergeant sat right up when Mr. Carter failed to complete his sentence. He had put his question merely to impress Miss Preedy, but now it looked as if he might be about to light on something.

"Well, I was due to attend an auction in Birmingham today." He fumbled in his breast pocket and, evidently thinking Barrett to be in charge of the case, extracted some papers. "These are the items Mr. Dodsley instructed me to bid for." Rising, he offered the documents to the sergeant. But Barrett hurriedly waved him back. Constable Copping emitted a slight but significant cough.

"All in good time," Barrett snapped at Mr. Carter, adding as he looked across at his subordinate, "Seem to be feeling the draught, Copping."

Copping moved away from the door to take his stand behind Mr. Carter's chair. Mr. Carter's mind was evidently perturbed. Copping could not help observing that. His eyes were always seeking for Miss Preedy's who had eyes only for Sergeant Barrett. They were talking with lowered voices

over there, and Copping saw that Mr. Carter was straining
to overhear what happened. Mr. Carter seemed to have
ears designed to catch what other people did not wish to
be overheard, for they were not only large, but stood well
out from his temples. When, however, the sergeant indicated the Siamese on Miss Jenks's lap, Mr. Carter sat back
as if in relief. The Siamese had eyes as blue as Miss Preedy's
own, but that fact had never established any fellow-feeling
between them, Miss Preedy somehow regarding it as a liberty on the cat's part to have eyes like her own.

Of the three shop assistants, Miss Jenks alone liked the
Siamese. Mr. Carter merely tolerated the animal as a necessary adjunct to a shop in which mice could work such
havoc on valuable bindings. Miss Preedy said Amelia Jenks
liked the cat simply because there was so much of the cat in
herself. But that was after the cat had rejected the advances
she herself had made on perceiving Saka was also a favourite of young Mr. Dick's. Amelia Jenks knew all about that
rebuff. June Preedy thought she could make her blue eyes
even more melting than any Siamese, anyway. And for one
brief moment she thought her goo-goo orbs had done the
trick. Miss Jenks had found her eagerly turning up the dictionary in the back shop. To find Miss Preedy so eager over
an English dictionary so surprised Amelia that she pulled
up to inquire about it. In the act of whirling the pages, June
whispered that Mr. Dick had just called her vapid, and she
wanted to know what the compliment meant. It happened
to be a word with which the cinema had not made her
familiar. And Miss Jenks, glowing with the knowledge of
what Miss Preedy would find, moved on to hide her smile.
But not so quickly as to be out of hearing the book banged
angrily down when Miss Preedy found what she sought.

It took her a whole month, however, before she recovered sufficiently to find consolation in Mr. Carter. And Mr. Carter cherished, as Miss Jenks knew, ambitions of his own as well as admiration for Miss Preedy. He had his own ideas as to how a bookshop should be run, and one day when he had made enough, he meant to have a shop of his own. He had even begun to accumulate stock for it in a quiet way. And long before Miss Preedy ceased to make him writhe with jealousy over Mr. Dick, he had perceived what an attractive assistant she would make when the lucrative American trade revived. It was only because things were bad in America that book prices were bad in England. But that was his opportunity, to build up and hold a stock against the day when the Americans would be buying once more! And when they did return, wasn't June just the one to make them feel completely at home? He knew how to make full use of her gifts, if the Dodsleys did not. Of course the old man was dead now. Mr. Carter's gaze went round the serried rows of books. There was not so much in new books, the big money was in the rarities. And now it was only himself who could really run that department. Young Dick knew nothing about that side of the business. He had been jealous of Dick at first. And then, finding there were no grounds for the jealousy, he became rather annoyed with Dick for his insensibility to June's charms.

Mr. Carter's pleasant day-dreams about his immediate future were only broken when Mrs. Headcorn emerged from the inner room. Mrs. Headcorn looked satisfied with herself. They all read the sense of self-importance showing on her face. She had been up before the big men. On her way to the door she paused, rearranging her skirt.

"'Tain't so bad as you might think for," she reassured

them. "You've no call to be quaking—not if you stand up to 'em, like I did."

"Now then!" Barrett cut in. "That's enough." He waved his hand at the door which Copping held ajar.

"Just fancy making us wait for a dame like her," Miss Preedy protested as the sergeant resumed his seat.

Barrett leant forward.

"It's not for me to complain about that," he murmured.

But the heavy gallantry was lost on Miss Preedy. The pout she gave him was entirely her own, not Miss Ginger Rogers's.

"I'm not used to being stood in a corner like this," she burst out. "And if they're figuring to make me the last in the procession—well, the longer I'm kept the less they'll get."

The policeman in Barrett was as much shocked by the outburst as the man in him was hurt.

"Come, come, miss," he protested, "you can't mean that."

"That's me," she snapped.

Barrett, glancing round to see how the others were affected, noted that Mr. Carter seemed distressed. As for the other young lady, though she did not look up to stare like Mr. Carter, her hand lay motionless on the cat's back as if abruptly stopped in the middle of a stroke. After a time— long after the little white hand had resumed its caressing rhythm—a thought came to the sergeant—a thought born of his long experience of street processions, though it was suggested by Miss Preedy's use of the word "procession" But it took him several minutes before he was able to formulate his thought into words, and fit it to the situation. Then he turned to Miss Preedy with confidence.

"Ever seen a procession?"

She stared back at him.

"Sure," she said. "What are you getting at?"

"Did you ever see the really important people head any procession?"

"No, never," she responded promptly; "it's always the police who stick themselves in front."

Barrett frowned heavily. His carefully thought out argument seemed to be going wrong. And he wasn't sure whether the snigger had come from Mr. Carter or Copping himself. Then he saw how to get his argument back on the rails again.

"The police," he said, "aren't part of the procession at all. They are simply there to protect it, to clear the streets of any obstruction. And," he went on impressively, "it's the really big people who come last, the least important coming first."

Miss Preedy's face brightened.

"I got you," she said. "You mean it's the same with us here right now?"

"Certainly. And you can safely take it from me that the longer you are kept back the more important you are to us. It's really insignificant people who are first called."

Sergeant Barrett had every reason to be satisfied with his argument. He had smoothed down Miss Preedy's ruffled feelings as successfully as Miss Jenks had smoothed down Saka's ruffled fur. Still, he had something more to say, something calculated to smooth the way for the two Yard men engaged on the case. Voices in the back shop, however, brought him to his feet, and he held it back until MacNab— apparently the second figure in the procession—passed out. Even then he did not get on with what he wanted to say, for in turning he caught a certain look of mystification, or it might have been perturbation on Mr. Carter's face.

"Know him?" he asked.

Carter hesitated.

"Well," he said, "I do and I don't. He's been hanging around the shop quite often lately."

"Customer then?"

"Well, I don't know. He's never bought anything to my knowledge, that is."

Miss Preedy moved restlessly in her chair. She didn't like this diversion of interest from herself.

"Oh, cut him out," she said impatiently. "He don't count. He's only one better than the charwoman."

Barrett lifted a pointing finger.

"That reminds me," he said. "Let there be no keeping back of what any of you know just because you're kept waiting. You keep in mind what I told you; in my experience it's the people they think really important who're taken last."

As he finished they heard footsteps coming from the back shop. Detective-Sergeant Crabb appeared in the opening. He glanced at the sheet of paper in his hand. Then he looked up.

"Miss June Preedy—this way, please."

This time Constable Copping's cough brought no remark from the sergeant. Possibly that was because this time the constable had remembered to put his hand over his mouth.

CHAPTER VII
Miss Preedy and
Mr. Carter

IF SERGEANT BARRETT COULD HAVE READ MISS PREEDY'S mind as she passed up the shop to appear before Inspector Mallet, he would, to his surprise, have seen he had done his work better than he knew. For Miss Preedy faced Mallet determined to let him see she was not so unimportant as her place in the "procession" suggested. Mallet, in good humour over his work on the watch, perceived Miss Preedy's annoyance, and judged that in a girl of her style the cause might be wounded vanity. He got up and himself placed a chair for her as if she had been a duchess. At least that is how Miss Preedy subsequently described his actions to a girl friend.

Miss Preedy, mollified but certainly not less resolved to let this nice man see he had made no mistake about her importance. Crabb slid on to a chair against the wall directly behind her and got out his notebook.

"Well, Miss Preedy," Mallet began, "let me first assure you that any information you give us at this stage will be treated as confidential. And I'm sure you will do all you can to help us, won't you?"

The tone and manner still further restored Miss Preedy's self-esteem and she responded with frankness.

"Search me," she promptly replied. "I'm here to put you wise all I can—right now."

Sergeant Crabb's notebook nearly escaped his grasp. But it was a reply that told the detective more about Miss Preedy's mind, outlook, tastes, values, and habits than Miss Preedy could have dreamed.

"Thank you," he said. "You see, we want to hear what you have to say so's we can check up on what the others tell us later on."

She beamed a smile across at him.

"I got you. That's how I figured it out myself, though that red-nosed boob out there let on—"

"Quite," Mallet interrupted. "Now what we want to get at first is; what possible reason Mr. Dodsley had for being here at two in the morning."

Mallet hardly expected she could settle that question. But it was his shrewd inference that if he began with a question beyond her she would be all the more ready with full details on such points as were within her knowledge.

"I can't be dead sure about that," she said, "but I guess you might get a lead to the answer if you knew the inwards of that rumpus between him and his nephew."

Mallet sat up.

"They had a row? You are sure?"

Miss Preedy narrowed her eyes at him.

"You asked me; I'm telling you."

"Did you know what it was about?"

"Sure, and without plastering an ear on the keyhole neither."

She nodded at the glass-fronted bookcases. "Old man Dodsley had been missing some of his tomes."

"Yes," Mallet said encouragingly.

"Well, when a young fellow's kept short, and has a girl to trot around, you don't want to be told any more, do you? If he's not just a bum he must have some dough to do her well. Mind you," she added, "I'm not saying he did. No more did old man Dodsley, if it comes to that. They just had a set-to about the keys of the shop. That was the old man's point. There being only two keys, one he kep' himself, and the other young Dick had. And it seems the old fellow had been having the shop watched while business was on, though none of us knew it, and—well, there you are."

Inspector Mallet did not think they were quite there yet; but he was nevertheless impressed. The girl had not got this from some film story—anyhow not that part about the missing books. It was possible that Dodsley, having become certain about the time the books were being taken, had remained on in the shop to catch the thief red-handed— with fatal consequences to himself.

But if the thief was the nephew, it seemed unlikely that Dodsley would speak about it to him, much less make a row over it, before establishing his guilt by catching him in the act. Yet, if as appeared certain, the thefts were carried out after the shop was shut, it must be the nephew, unless some other person had a duplicate key. Mallet made a note. Then he looked up.

"Your work was confined to the new books side of the business?" he inquired.

"That's right."

"But I suppose you sometimes lent a hand in the second-hand department, when they were busy there?" he suggested.

Miss Preedy smiled.

"They never were what you'd call hot and hasty in here," she said; "but I have sometimes helped Mr. Carter with his packing up. That's when I heard the row in here between the old man and his nephew and got fired when he came out and saw me here."

Mallet looked surprised.

"You were under notice then?"

"Yes. He told me I didn't fit in."

"The second-hand business was in the hands of Mr. Carter?"

"Except when he was away at auctions. Then Miss Jenks took over here." She paused, and then burst out: "She fitted in all right. Looks as much second-hand as any of the books, she does."

Mallet sat back.

"Well, thank you very much, Miss Preedy," he said with a smile. "If anything turns up later I hope we can count on you."

"Oh, anything to oblige, I'm sure," she said, getting to her feet.

He motioned to Sergeant Crabb.

"Now we'd better see Miss Jenks."

Miss Preedy paused, looking dissatisfied.

"You won't get much out of her. Close as a clam, she is."

Mallet's wave of the hand was half a leave taking and half a reassurance to Miss Preedy.

"That in itself might tell us a lot," he said. Then, as the sergeant escorted her to the door, he added as if it were an afterthought: "Oh, by the way—just as a matter of routine, you know—there's one question I have to put to all concerned, and I may as well include you."

She turned round to face him.

"Yes," she said, and waited.

"After you left here last night how did you spend your time?"

"Spend my time?"

"Yes. You went home to do some sewing, I suppose?"

"Nope. I had a date with a friend last night."

"And I'm sure he gave you a good time."

Miss Preedy cocked her fair head knowingly.

"What d'ye think?"

"He took you to a picture house, I bet."

"You'd have to part then. Last night I had to go out to Hackney to see him in a show his club put up for the sick kids' hospital out there. Sick enough it made me too." She shuddered at the recollection.

"Yes, and after that?"

"Well, after that to get the taste of it out of the mouth and seeing it was over by ten and we all dressed up and nowhere to go, we took a taxi back, and went to the *Cynara* to get in touch with real life again."

"That's the night club in Bell Street round the corner?"

"You got it right. It's got a real elegant dance band. Lots of smart folk tumble in."

"And you saw no one there you knew, I suppose?"

Her blue eyes narrowed till he couldn't tell their colour.

"Now, jus' what makes you say that?" she demanded, her chin going up.

"Oh," Mallet replied hastily, "from what you said I gathered the place was new to you."

"That's a miss anyway! I saw Miss M. G. G. there dancing with a young fellow who was not young Dick. But that's telling," she laughed.

Mallet looked puzzled.

"But who is Miss M. G. G.?"

"Oh, I forgot. You wouldn't know. It's the girl Dick runs around with—Miss Grafton. You should know her. She does crime stories."

Mallet's wide open eyes spoke for themselves, and Miss Preedy indulged his curiosity. "Dick got to know her by her books. I don't read any of them myself. Guess you don't somehow want to read books when you're handling them all day. But she and he clicked over the counter, I've heard."

Mallet sat down to make a note.

"And this young fellow she was with," he asked before he had finished, "what's his name?"

"Ah, there you have me stalled," Miss Preedy admitted.

"What was he like?"

"Real swell. Dark and dazzling, and not too tall to give your head a rest on his shoulder. Just the sort of guy to go out with when you're feeling a bit hot and hollow."

"They were alone all the time?"

"They were there when we drifted off."

"Did she see you?"

"Did she see me?" Miss Preedy sniffed. "Did she see me? Would she have seen me even supposing I'd been in my shop outfit? I reckon not."

"And when exactly did you leave?"

"Along about 2.30."

"Sure? Think again."

The exhortation surprised her. She straightened up to stare at him.

"I've no call to. Honest to God, I remember hearing some clock strike when I was dropping inside the taxi."

"All right. Now do you mind telling me who you were with?"

Miss Preedy did seem to mind. She took a few moments to consider her reply.

"Well," she said thoughtfully, "I guess it won't hurt any to tell you now he's dead."

"Dead?" Mallet echoed.

"Old man Dodsley, I mean. It was Mr. Carter who took me out las' night. He'd get fired if the old man knew he did any buzzing around the clubs. But he's got more fun in him than you'd think from his face."

"Thank you, Miss Preedy," Mallet said. "We'll have a look at his face presently. But," he added gallantly, his head on one side, "I hope we haven't seen the last of your own face."

Miss Preedy returned his arch look with interest, her fair head cocked to the other side.

"Oh, you can count on me," she said. "I'll skip around any old time you say."

As soon as she was gone Mallet turned to Sergeant Crabb. "How's that?"

Crabb's pencil went up to scratch his chin. After a moment he shook his head.

"Search me," he said.

Mallet smiled.

"That's how I feel myself, Crabb. But do you think there's something in it?"

Crabb hesitated.

"I was struck by the questions you avoided putting, sir," he said.

"Such as the number of drinks they had, and whether Mr. Carter let her go home alone after the clock struck two?"

"That kind of thing, sir."

Mallet shook his head.

"Going too near the bone, that would be. You saw how

she hung fire when I pressed for the time they left the night club. We must first let Roberts have a look at Mr. Carter, who has, as she puts it, so much more fun in him than you would think from his face."

"Then you don't think she's in it?"

"Of course not."

"But there was a woman in it, if that hair clip means anything."

"Well, boy, I think you said there's a woman with a hair clip waiting out there, didn't you?" He pondered for a little. "No, let's have the man first," he said.

Mr. Carter, after depositing his bowler on the floor at the side of his chair, looked up to find Inspector Mallet fixedly regarding him. Mallet somehow could not see Mr. Carter as a frequenter of night clubs, except, perhaps, such early closing ones as were associated with Young Men's Mutual Improvement Societies connected with some chapel in the remoter suburbs. He looked such an earnest young man. He had regular habits stamped all over him. You knew he rose at the same hour every day, caught the same train or bus, sat at the same A.B.C. table at his lunch hour, and caught the same bus or train or tram home, and went to bed each night at the tick of half-past ten. He looked a teetotaller and a non-smoker, if looks mean anything at all, Mallet thought. And though the rather prominent Adam's apple in his throat did work up and down several times as he sat facing the man from Scotland Yard, his features otherwise revealed no trace of any nervous tension.

"Sad business this, Mr. Carter," Mallet said.

"Yes, indeed," Mr. Carter agreed. Then, after a moment's silence, while he waited for the inspector to continue, he blinked his eyes and put emphasis into his agreement by emitting a heavy sigh. Mallet was thinking that but for Miss Preedy's testimony he never would have guessed Mr. Carter's facial muscles ever had relaxed in mirth.

"Well, Mr. Carter, you and I must put our heads together to see if we can bring the criminal to justice," Mallet remarked. Then, as if to indicate that this might be a lengthy process in which some aids to memory would help, he produced, flicked open and held out a cigarette case. "Try one of these," he suggested.

Mr. Carter looked at the little gold case which showed nine cigarettes, five on one side and four on the other— looked at it long enough to have counted its contents. He shook his head.

"Thank you, but I don't smoke," he said with decision.

Mallet's eyebrows went up in astonishment.

"Not at all?" he asked.

"Well—er—not in business hours," Mr. Carter amended. Glancing round the serried shelves of books, he remarked, "One couldn't, you know, at any time in a place like this." His tone could not have been more decisive had some one offered him a fag during service in his favourite chapel. Mallet, almost abashed, repocketed the case. But Miss Preedy had been, he noted, so far trustworthy: clearly there were some things Mr. Carter would do at one time and not at another. He got to business.

"Mr. Carter," he began, "could you suggest any reason for Mr. Dodsley coming here, and remaining here in the middle of the night? We simply can't account for it, you know."

Much to his surprise Mr. Carter could easily account for it.

"Why, yes," he said, "the catalogue kept him here; it always did."

"The catalogue?" Mallet repeated, mystified.

Mr. Carter leaned forward to explain.

"It's clear you are not in the book trade," he remarked, going on to explain what making up a sale catalogue involved; the selection of each item from stock, the examination of its condition, the fixing of the price according to its rarity, and so on.

"And you think it possible he came here for that last night?" Mallet asked.

"More than possible," Carter replied. "I think it most probable. Almost a dead cert, in fact. You see," he added hastily, as if realising that his last words were as much out of place in business hours as cigarettes, "there was extra pressure just now, as he was most anxious to have the printing done in time to catch the American mail for the reviving trade in the States."

"And he always did this work himself?" Mallet asked, somewhat knocked out by what he had just heard.

"Well—no, not always," Carter said with a little reluctance.

"Who assisted usually?"

"His nephew invariably."

"And why not now, when there was this extra pressure?"

Mr. Carter's reluctance was more obvious. His face looked pained.

"Well…" He hesitated. "I suppose it's my duty in the circumstances to—to—tell what I know."

"It certainly is." Mallet was very decided. There was a snap in his eyes as well as in his words. The Adam's apple rose and fell several times.

"I much regret having to say it," Carter began, "but for some time now there's been trouble between that young man and his uncle. 'His heart's no longer in the business,'

Mr. Dodsley once said to me. Not, mind you," Mr. Carter said, "that I ever saw any serious neglect on Mr. Dick's part. But, as you know, my job was in the rare books side; and it was only Mr. Dodsley who knew the state of the business as a whole. But business had been bad in my department as well. The falling off of the American market, you know, due to general trade depression out there. It would perhaps astonish you to know how widely spread is the taste for rare books in America. I remember—"

"As briefly as you can," Mallet cut in. "Keep your memories for your autobiography, Mr. Carter."

"Well, as I was about to say," Mr. Carter went on hurriedly, "the bad trade conditions probably accounted for the old gentleman's irritation. He had to find a vent for it. In fact, none of us escaped. He has even discharged Miss Preedy. And the climax came two days ago, when young Mr. Dick, whose own nerves seemed to me affected, said he was going away for a couple of days."

"That was on Tuesday last?"

"On Tuesday last," Mr. Carter nodded assent. "He told me himself he meant to leave that night on his motor-cycle, put up at Brockenhurst, and do a couple of days tramping in the New Forest."

"One moment," Mallet interrupted. "What exactly made you suppose his nerves to be affected?"

"Why, for one thing he was so jumpy. For another the fact that he had overlooked the catalogue, clean forgetting all about it."

Mallet waved an appreciative hand. "Go ahead."

"Mr. Dodsley came up behind us as he was telling me this and overheard. Mr. Dick fairly jumped when his voice broke in to suggest he'd better take the printer for company, and let the catalogue go to the devil. But when he offered to stay on Mr. Dodsley said he must not think himself so indispensable, he would carry on alone, even if it took him all night."

"Meaning last night?" Mallet asked.

"Meaning last night."

"And the young man left according to plan?"

"He did."

"Well, Mr. Carter, he never arrived at Brockenhurst."

This was a surprise for Mr. Carter.

"You—you know that for a fact?"

"Oh, yes. We phoned up the hotels when his landlady told us where he had gone."

"His number is XLA 3001."

"Yes, we got that on his registration book in his rooms," Mallet said, "but so far he hasn't been picked up."

"Well, I can tell you this," Carter said. "Before he went round for his motor-cycle he told me he would probably return on the Friday night to take over work on the catalogue. He was very upset really, and counted on his uncle's irritation to have died down by then. That was after I had reminded him that as I was due for the auction in Birmingham on that day his uncle would have been all day alone, except for the two girls, before his night work began."

If ever Detective-Sergeant Crabb, when the time comes for him to retire from Scotland Yard, sits down, as the manner of some have been, to write his reminiscences, he will certainly say of Mallet that as a detective he was remarkable not so much for the questions he put but for those he avoided putting. At this moment there were three questions clamouring for answers which Crabb saw, but which Mallet did not put. First there was the question as to whether Carter knew about the theft of the most valuable books; next there was the question as to when and where Carter had parted from Miss Preedy; and lastly Crabb wondered why Mallet had not probed into Mr. Carter's unwillingness to speak of the bad relations between uncle and nephew. For if Carter, suspecting the nephew, yet did not want to bring him under suspicion, why did he volunteer information about Dick's intention to return to take over with the catalogue? For that was information that instantly focused suspicion on the nephew—although it was volunteered by Carter as a fact standing to the nephew's credit. In other words, in seeming to do his best to excuse Dick, Carter had, in reality, done his best to accuse him.

But Mallet did not follow up the lead given, if indeed Carter meant it for a lead. Instead he produced Dodsley's little diary.

"You've customers of all classes, I understand," he said, while turning the pages.

"Yes, in the rare books side especially, we do business with very distinguished people."

"You know many by name, I take it?"

"*And* sight," Mr. Carter added, "from seeing their portraits in the press."

"Well, here's an entry you may help us with. Yes, here it is, May 15." His finger went to the spot: "*Acquired the A. L. collection by D. G.* Can you tell us who this A. L. is?"

For the first time Crabb got a hint of that hidden capacity for fun in Carter to which Miss Preedy had testified. But the smile was of the briefest, with more in it of contempt than of mirth.

"'A. L.' isn't a person," he explained. "'A. L.' stands in our business for autograph letters."

"Autograph letters?" Mallet echoed in mystification.

"Letters in the handwriting of famous people are always in demand," Carter explained.

"I see. Yes. And Mr. Dodsley dealt in such letters?" Mallet asked almost humbly.

"Naturally. There's big money in it. Even a short note from Bernard Shaw about a cold in his head fetched twenty pounds the other day."

"Dear me," Mallet exclaimed. "But they do say there's a lot of idle money about just now."

"There's always money in the right stuff—if you can get your hands on it," Mr. Carter declared. In the confidence born of his superior knowledge, a tincture of condescension, if not contempt, was perceptible in his attitude. For the first time Mr. Carter took note of Mallet's clothes. One could not be in any awe of a man wearing such a sloppy suit and a green and yellow tie.

Mallet shut and shoved the diary out of sight as if it had been an indecent book. He seemed rather at a loss what to say next. Mr. Carter helped him out.

"Lucky for Mr. Dick Dodsley he didn't turn up here last night."

"Lucky, why?" Mallet asked mildly.

"What I meant was, if he had, he would have been here last night instead of Mr. Dodsley."

Mallet stared for a moment.

"But surely that isn't the only bit of luck for him, Mr. Carter."

Carter's eyes opened.

"What else?" he inquired.

Mallet swept a hand in the air.

"All this shop, stock, lock, and barrel. Doesn't he inherit?"

"Well—yes. There's no one else I know of. I hadn't thought of that."

"Oh, one can't think of everything, Mr. Carter," Mallet said lightly.

There was another short pause.

"Queer how things turn out," Mr. Carter sighed. "So, after all, he'll now be able to stock Miss Grafton's novels."

Detective-Sergeant Crabb cocked a most expectant ear at this. It seemed obvious that Mr. Carter had something he wanted to get out in connection with Miss Grafton. But Mallet did not give him the lead he seemed to expect.

"Yes," he murmured almost absently. "Yes, I suppose so." Then looking up he said, "Queer I didn't know what 'A. L.' stood for, isn't it?"

The apple in Mr. Carter's throat did a few gymnastic exercises.

"Of course it was rough on Mr. Dick who naturally wanted to help his young lady," he said. "But Mr. Dodsley definitely refused to have her books in the shop."

"Dear me, are they as bad as all that?"

Carter's hand went to his breast pocket as if this was what he had been waiting for.

"Well, I've never read any of them myself—not my type of literature—but here's a notice of her latest, *Death at the Desk*, which I cut out of my paper coming up in the train."

Mallet laughed the long slip of paper away.

"No, no," he said, "I never read detective stories; they are all so clever they kill my self-confidence. But there's my colleague behind you, he does not share my weakness."

Carter turned with alacrity to hand Crabb the *Daily Record* slip. Carter had been too long conscious of that silent man at his back. Of Mallet he was now in no real awe.

Mallet looked more like a stout, slow-witted farmer than a detective, and a middle-aged farmer at that. But this other man was as young as himself; and, apart from that, there was something unsettling in knowing that behind one's back there was a motionless watcher, who listened to everything and never himself uttered a single syllable. Mr. Carter, searching later on for a word to describe his experiences to Miss Preedy, told her he could call it nothing but creepy. You didn't know, as he remarked, what he was thinking, nor whether he believed you or not. It was a relief to the nervous Carter to feel that Crabb's keen eyes were now fixed on the cutting, and not on his back. And Mallet's words increased that feeling.

"Now, Mr. Carter, only two more questions, and we have finished with you—for the present, anyhow," he added playfully.

"Yes?" Mr. Carter did not return the smile.

"The first is this. You see this is a crime which does not appear to have been done for the sake of robbery. So far as we know nothing has been taken—not even his watch. Now you have been daily associated with Mr. Dodsley. Can you recall any visitor to the shop with whom he had a quarrel? Did he ever refer to any business transaction which might involve him in trouble? Did he ever show signs of apprehension—that sort of thing? Just cast back in your mind and see."

Mr. Carter for quite a time thoughtfully studied the floor, his brow furrowed with concentration. Finally he shook his head with decision.

"No," he said, "I can recall nothing like that. Of course I've often seen him lose his temper. I've even heard him use language which made me glad the shop happened to be empty at the time. As for apprehension, he wasn't the sort to be afraid of anybody—too domineering and masterful, you know. In fact, among ourselves it was only young Dick who stood up to him, as I've already told you."

Mallet passed to his second question.

"Very well," he said, "here is my last question. Do you think Mr. Dodsley could have left the shop door open when he came here last night?"

"Certainly not." Carter spoke with conviction. But Mallet persisted.

"Not in a moment of abstraction, Mr. Carter? Or worry over the catalogue and the need for haste of which you spoke? Have you never yourself forgotten to lock your door?"

"Well, I've often forgotten my key," the young man replied very seriously, "but I never forget to lock my door. And," he added, "even if I had, Mr. Dodsley never would."

Mallet was piqued by the intense assurance of this pronouncement, and asked Carter what he meant. After fidgeting about on his chair for a little, Carter was able to formulate his meaning.

"He was a man full of the pride of possession," he declared. "He kept a watchful eye on customers, and did not trust his own staff as he might have. If we arrived early we had to wait outside till Mr. Dick or himself appeared. Mr. Dick I have known to come without his key, but the old man never."

"Yes," Mallet said as he rose to his feet. "Yes, you are probably right, Mr. Carter. He does not seem the sort of man to leave the door unlocked."

Mr. Carter retrieving his hat from the floor, turned expectantly to Sergeant Crabb as if to recover his cutting from the

Record. But Crabb stupidly misread the outstretched hand, and in response took it in his own, shaking it in the most friendly fashion. And Mr. Carter, after a moment's hesitation, departed without his cutting.

"Well, what do you think?" Mallet asked when they were alone.

"A most helpful young man, sir," Crabb replied.

Mallet smiled.

"So that was why you shook his hand so warmly."

"Not quite. He expected me to return that *Record* cutting, and I didn't wish him to know how much I wanted to keep it."

Mallet's smile was replaced by quite another expression as Crabb, diving into his pocket, produced the slip of paper.

"But we could easily have got a copy of the issue from the office," he said as he took over Carter's cutting.

It was Crabb's turn to smile.

"It wouldn't have been the same," he said in a way that sent Mallet's eyes narrowing over the slip in his hands. Crabb waited. He hoped Mallet would miss it. It would be something to have seen a thing Mallet missed. But he noticed Mallet wasn't reading the words. He knew of course it couldn't be the words, since the words would be the same in every copy.

"Ye—s," Mallet said eventually. "Ye—s, I see what you mean, Crabb. If he had been a draper he could have done it."

Crabb nodded.

"That's it. Said he cut it out coming up in the train. Then he must have carried scissors, and the train that carried him must have been a mighty sight steadier than the one that rocks me in from Hendon."

Mallet examined the edges.

"You're right, boy," he said. "And they must have been

an outsize in scissors too. Look where the snick ends and the next cut begins. But why should he lie about a thing like that?"

Crabb, pulling gently at his chin with finger and thumb, tried for the explanation.

"You know, sir," he said at length, "I somehow can't see a fellow like that with a gun."

"Oh, I can," Mallet asserted. "What I can't see him with is a woman, and a woman with a hair clip there certainly was in this." As he spoke he sat down at the writing table and lifted the 'phone. "I'll get the Yard to send a man to find out about Miss Preedy and Mr. Carter, and the time they reached home last night," he said while he waited. While the connection was being made, Crabb gave himself to a re-reading of the *Daily Record* notice of *Death at the Desk*. But he had not quite finished before the receiver was replaced.

"And now," Mallet said with decision, "I'd like, before we call in that young woman with the hair slide, to have a look at what we've got."

CHAPTER VIII
The Scratch on the Hand

INSPECTOR MALLET, PUTTING BOTH ELBOWS ON THE table, and propping his chin on his clenched fists, looked across at his young assistant. Crabb had his chair tilted against the wall and, with his heels on its crossbar, sat waiting for Mallet's reconstruction of the crime.

"Who knew Dodsley would be here late last night?" Mallet abruptly demanded. This was not exactly what Crabb expected, but he was familiar enough with Mallet's methods not to be taken aback.

"Young Dodsley and Carter," he promptly returned.

"Who had a quarrel with him?"

"Dick Dodsley."

"Who benefits by his death?"

"Dick Dodsley."

"Who besides himself had a key to the shop?"

"Dick Dodsley."

Mallet, his chin still on his fists, narrowed his eyes.

"Yes," he said thoughtfully. "Yes; but it isn't quite so simple as all that. Most of it is based on what Carter had to say about Dick. We haven't yet heard what Dick may have to say about Carter."

"Well," Crabb ventured, "he's not exactly rushing in to say it, is he?"

Mallet said nothing. He did not appear to have heard. After a moment or two he unexpectedly asked for a cigarette. Crabb knew what would happen to the cigarette; it would be more chewed than smoked. But just as he was holding the match thinking how out of place the little white cylinder looked against the big, rubicund face, Mallet spoke.

"As far as opportunity goes," he said, "both Dick and Carter are almost in the same boat. And as for motive, what if Carter is the book thief for whom Dodsley was waiting last night?"

"But would he have taken a revolver with him or used it to cover so paltry a theft?"

"For all we yet know the weapon may have been Dodsley's. And as for a paltry theft, the value of the books approached a thousand, I'm told, and many a murder has been done for less."

Crabb had no difficulty in playing the part expected of him. He had still a few objections up his sleeve with which to clarify Mallet's theories.

"But Carter would scarcely take a woman with him," he said.

"Why not? We know on her own admission he had a woman with him within an hour of the crime. We also know that same woman had been discharged by Dodsley. And, mark this, Crabb," Mallet cried, warming up, "this same woman, if we are to infer what is relevant to a crime of this nature, was one whose obsession for the cinema must have made such a crime seem very small beer compared to the gangster mass-murders she habitually saw on the screen. And don't these gangster pictures always feature, as they say, a dashing, heroic and lovely young female accomplice?" Crabb rather staggered, wavered for a few moments. He could still adduce the fact that Carter possessed no key while Dick Dodsley did. But he knew what the reply would be: Carter might have got temporary possession of one or other of the two keys; and to take a wax impression was an easy job of not more than three minutes.

"Well," he said, "Carter is here and the other man is not."

"Carter was here last night and the other man was not."

"As far as we know," Crabb corrected.

"Agreed. The only man known to us actually on the spot was the man Roberts talked with."

"And Carter of course."

Mallet hesitated. Crabb thought he had caught him out.

"If Roberts's man wasn't just silly drunk, I would say he was in it too," he remarked. "And we did conclude he wasn't, didn't we?"

"But," Crabb objected, "that would mean there were three in it."

"Would it? Think again."

Carter did think hard for a few moments. Then he looked up to notice that Mallet also seemed to be deep in the same occupation.

"You don't mean—"

"Yes, that's what I do mean," Mallet said.

"That the man Roberts met was Carter?"

"Or young Dodsley," Mallet nodded. "It's the one thing that fits the known facts." He sat forward. "Listen! We know a man and a woman came into this shop last night. We know they passed some time in it, presumably waiting for

Dodsley's arrival. They knew he was coming. He did. He passed them where they were hidden in the dark, between the shelves, and entered his office. If he had come to get on with his catalogue they didn't give him time even to begin, for one or other of them crept in and shot him before he began. They were not there to rob the shop, since they could have done that, and got away, before he appeared. The motive may have been revenge, but most probably they were after something Dodsley was known, or supposed, to carry about with him. For they didn't clear out at once. That is the essential fact established by what the wrist-watch tells us. Dodsley was shot at 3.4 and found by Roberts at 3.16. That is to say, if Roberts had not been held in talk by that young man, the discovery would have been made nearly twelve minutes sooner. No great difference that would have made, any one might suggest. But mark this, Crabb, this is the circumstance that now impels me to believe Roberts's young man was an accomplice. It is the fact that if he had not detained Roberts, and diverted his attention, Roberts would have taken the woman red-handed."

"The *woman*!" Crabb ejaculated.

"Why, yes. Who else was there?" Mallet said. "As I see it, the man had left her with Dodsley—to get out of him, alive or dead, whatever it was they were after. He had gone outside to keep watch, leaving her to get on with it, the door unlocked, of course either to permit his return or her to leave. Now Dodsley was shot at four minutes past three, and Roberts tells us he heard St. Martin's clock strike three while somewhere near the bottom of the street. At the same time the sergeant was somewhere near the top, having turned in from St. Martin's Lane, a little farther away. But, of course, for all that he was out to watch, the man's real concern was in what he expected to happen inside. He would hear the shot all right, though it did not reach Roberts's ears, muffled as it would be, away back here in the depth of the shop. But the sound would make the man look about him rather anxiously, I'll swear, and in doing that he either saw or, more probably, heard Roberts trying all the shop doors as he came along.

"What happened next? Did he push the door ajar to give a warning, and find the frightened Siamese cat trying to get away? Then he makes off up the street, away from Roberts. But almost at once the sergeant comes into view. He stops short, knowing that the woman is now between two fires, pretty well certain to be caught. What is he to do? His first thought is to go on, to assume the unconcerned, natural air of a man walking home. He takes out his cigarette case to suggest a man with nothing to fear, or to give Barrett a valid reason for his sudden stop on sighting him. But just as he is about to light up, he perceives the woman's danger is now doubled. At any moment she may come out, and now she cannot come out without being seen. Even if she doesn't, he has left the door unlocked, as Roberts will discover. He thinks of a better way. He drops the cigarette case and runs.

"He runs back, past the shop door, drawing the sergeant after him. Then, well aware that this action will lead to questions and raise suspicion, he pretends to be silly drunk before he comes up to Roberts, and carries it off with both of them. The sergeant goes his way. He has been got safely past the door. But Roberts still remains. And he does not know whether the woman has got away or not. So he leads Roberts, in his turn, past the door by telling him a partly true story about another door higher up the street."

"Yes," Crabb admitted, "it looks like that; but I can't see that man Carter with all the nerve and quick wits needed for it."

"Not on his showing this morning," Mallet conceded, "but that Preedy young woman claimed for him more than he let us see."

Crabb looked up at Mallet quickly.

"But surely Preedy would have kept mum about that if she herself were in it?"

Mallet shook a doubtful head.

"I don't know. She is such a fool, I can't be sure. Her frankness might be mere bravado, imitated from some gangster film heroine she's seen."

"Anyhow, it must have been a woman in close enough touch with the shop to know that Dodsley would be here last night," Crabb argued, "and so far, of the two who fill that part, we have seen only one. Quite a different type this other," he added half expecting a snub.

Mallet gave way.

"All right, call her in," he said.

A glance at Miss Amelia Jenks as she entered was in itself enough to show the inspector she did not belong to Miss Preedy's type. But the same glance suggested to him that Miss Preedy was probably correct when she called her as close as a clam. A certain rigidity about the mouth which contrasted so strongly with the facile, pearly smiles affected by Miss Preedy, testified to Miss Jenks's natural disposition.

Mallet studied her carefully from beneath half-closed eyelids as she took her seat before his desk. Although he already held a certain theory about the case, he preserved an open mind on it, ready to perceive anything new that came his way, and it was not for nothing that he kept Miss Jenks waiting so long for her turn. He noted with satisfaction her steeled and strung-up attitude in the chair. He read apprehension in that upright attitude, and in the manner in which she stared at him through those large horn spectacles. Even her over-prominent nostrils seemed to be staring at him, questioningly, like two marks of interrogation.

"I see you keep a cat at home, Miss Jenks," he said with a nod as he sat back easily.

Whatever Miss Jenks had expected it was not this. She almost jumped.

"A—a cat," she stammered, her glasses rapidly reflecting blink lights as her head shook.

"Yes," Mallet said. "You've got a scratch on your right hand. I'm not a detective for nothing, you know," he added as she stared down at the back of her hand.

"Oh, yes," she said. "Yes, I see."

"Done last night too, I notice."

Miss Jenks covered the scratch with her left hand. The action was instinctive, Mallet noted, as if she feared how much he could read in it.

"Yes," she said. "I—I startled him by touching him suddenly in the dark."

"Indeed—in the dark? But aren't cats supposed to see in the dark?"

"I—I bent down to pick up something I had dropped, and stepped on his foot."

While Mallet appeared to be pondering over this, Crabb observed that Miss Jenks began to get rather breathless. From where he sat he saw little more than her shoulders, but as he did not take the symptoms for anything else than extreme agitation, he judged that she, like himself, had suddenly foreseen what Mallet's next question would be.

"And I suppose he made a mighty hullabaloo when you trod on his—which foot was it?" Mallet inquired; "one of his front feet, I suppose, as he approached you."

But if the young woman had any dread of a particular question it was not this one.

"Oh," she said promptly, "I couldn't tell that, you know—not in the dark." Then she added, as if pleased with the chief inspector's concern for her pet, "He's all right this morning, anyway."

"Good," Mallet said heartily. "Perhaps, after all, it was not his foot you trod on but the thing you had dropped—a hair clip, wasn't it?"

Miss Jenks' hand went up to the hair slide near her ear as she stared blankly at him.

"Now how *could* you know that?" she asked in what looked like genuine amazement. Then, almost instantly, the surprise was replaced by a puzzled expression, as if it had suddenly occurred to her to wonder why Mallet should keep on talking about her cat at such a moment.

"Oh, well," Mallet said as his hand went down to open the drawer in the desk, "it's really quite simple. Such things, I believe, are constantly being dropped. The one at your ear I notice doesn't look very secure." He produced the matchbox. "And perhaps I had hair clips in my mind," he admitted, "for here is one certainly dropped here last night." He held the clip out to her on his extended palm. "You'll notice too it's broken as if some one had stepped on it."

This compelled her to rise and approach the table.

"You found that here?" she said, her head lowered to examine the broken hair slide.

"It was dropped among the book shelves last night, Miss Jenks."

"How—how strange?" she breathed.

Mallet shot a glance over the bent head at Crabb who now sat forward, watching intently, from his chair against the wall.

"Yes," Mallet agreed. "Yes, it is odd; but what's odder still is that the cat here seems also to have got his toes trodden on."

Miss Jenks straightening herself, shook her head.

"Oh, nothing odd about that," she said. "Poor Saka, he's always getting among the customers' feet." Then she pointed a finger at the hair slide. "Something odd about that, though."

Mallet looked a trifle startled.

"What do you mean?" he asked.

"Well, the catch has gone; the pin couldn't hold."

"Oh, we know that," Mallet said impatiently. "Why, what—"

"But it can't have been in any one's hair for ages; it must have been used for something else," she declared.

Mallet's impatience vanished. He shifted in his seat before speaking.

"Well, my girl," he said, looking up at her as she stood at his table, "perhaps you'll explain that. What makes you think it has not been used for its normal purpose?"

She put her finger down.

"Oh, any woman could tell that," she said; "it couldn't hold itself in position. Besides—" she hesitated.

"Yes?"

"Well, the catch for the pin looks as if it had been broken off long ago, doesn't it?"

He picked up the hair slide. As he examined it closely it came to his mind that they had not found the broken-off catch on the floor. True, the catch was probably not more than a small loop of wire, soldered on to the back of the slide; but their search on the floor had been almost microscopic, and they ought to have come on it.

"Yes," he said, "I see what you mean: that catch was not broken yesterday. And yet it was carried here," he added, half to himself. "What for, I wonder?" He lifted his eyes to Miss Jenks who had gone back to her chair. "Would you mind letting me have a look at your own hair clip?" he inquired.

In the act of rising, Miss Jenks removed her spectacles, unclasped the slide near her right ear, so that the strand of thick black hair fell over the right eye, revealing the disfiguring mole. With her head tilted to one side, the strand of tousled hair floating in its new position, a flush of dull red dyeing her cheek, she seemed somehow to have parted with her previous staid, rather old maidish appearance for something rakish and frisky, the large dark mole suggesting a bruise recently received in some bacchanalian carousal. Mallet was deeply interested. But he took over the metal slide she offered and set it on the table beside the other. It was much shorter, and less broad in the blade. He turned it over to examine the pin. A glance told him that he would not have missed finding the broken off clasp of this smaller clip had it been anywhere on the floor. The pin, too, went home with a resilient click impossible for the loosely jointed hinge of the other, which had long since lost its power to hold even the lightest strand of hair in position. And yet it had been carried about in some one's pocket, as its bright condition suggested. Why hadn't it been thrown away? The thing had no intrinsic value. Mistaking his thought, Miss Jenks broke in.

"You can buy them in assorted sizes on a card at Woolworths," she remarked.

With a slight gush of exasperation, he hit the table.

"Yes, yes, but what I'd like to know is why any one should keep a broken and useless trifle like that," he said, shoving her own slide back across the table to her.

Miss Jenks, while replacing it in her hair, regarded the broken slide thoughtfully.

"Well," she said, "I have seen one just like that used to cut the pages of a book."

"As a paper cutter?" Mallet cried, surprised and doubtful.

"Oh, yes, indeed," she assured him when she had finished patting down her hair.

"By a woman, of course?" he said.

"Well, yes," she admitted, adding defensively, "but it's less damaging to a book than the forefinger I've seen some men use."

He swiftly considered this possible use for the hair slide, and what it might imply. Then he shook his head.

No, that was not the purpose for which it had been used last night. It had been found among the old books whose pages had long ago been cut. Besides, whoever lay in wait last night to surprise Dodsley would scarcely be in the mood for reading books, even had there been enough light by which to do it. And yet, now that he considered the thing before him with new eyes, he could see that it might have been used as a makeshift paper knife. While the two clips were lying before him together he had observed that this one differed from Miss Jenks's not only in size but also in shape. For the smaller clip was arched, whereas the one found on the floor was as straight as the pin behind it. Originally he had supposed it had been flattened out by some one treading on it. Now he was not so sure that it had been trodden on at all. Any one who put a foot on it in the dark would have known where it was, and could have picked it up at once.

Baffled to extract anything from the hair slide, Mallet took a cast back in his mind and began to reconsider Miss Jenks herself. It was doubtless true that women dropped their hair clips all over the place at every hour of the day and night, especially at night, and it was probably a fact that multitudes of London cats got their paws trodden on every day, especially their front paws. All the same, it was curious that this young woman should have a connection with two such incidents on the same night. She broke unexpectedly into the line his thought was pursuing.

"Have you read Miss Grafton's new book?"

It sounded like a question she had been almost bursting to put and could no longer restrain. This was not mere literary chatter: it was a collapse of self-control under the pressure of an overlong, pent-up desire. Mallet's practised ear was quick to appreciate the difference.

"No," he said quietly, and waited.

"Well, you should," she said with a nod that sent the lights flashing from her spectacles.

"Dear me, is it as good as all that?"

Miss Jenks, breathing quickly, almost stamped her foot.

"Good!" she cried with a sniff, "it's almost as bad as it can be."

Mallet bent forward negligently, placing his left elbow on the table with his chin propped on his hand, regarded her with a smile.

"It's what they call a detective story, isn't it? Well, I don't read 'em—good or bad. My interest is in real, not imaginary crimes."

It has been said that Inspector Mallet had been misnamed

by Fate. Mallet was a name that would have fitted Crabb, for Detective-Sergeant Crabb had all the impetuosity and impatient directness of youth, whereas Percy Mallet favoured the side-way approach to his quarry. Possibly Mallet had developed his method as a consequence of the effect produced by his personal appearance. Looking so much like a rosy-faced farmer from one of the remoter Western counties, he knew how to play the part of a simpleton, and it had served him well in handling many a self-confident London rogue. For, although this indirectness, which beguiled his man into thinking him far away from the vital point, induced amusement at first, it usually produced exasperation in the end. And it was Mallet's experience that one got much less useful or reliable truth out of wine than out of this same exasperation.

So now having replied blandly to Miss Jenks's question, he was quite sure she was ready to blurt out something she had previously determined to withhold. Yet she did hesitate a moment after his complacent assertion that imaginary crimes held no interest for him. He read the hesitation easily enough, recognising it as the sort of moment in which one is confronted by a step from which, if taken, there is no going back. When she looked at him with a sudden upward jerk of the head, he knew she had burnt her boats.

"You're trying to find out who shot Mr. Dodsley, aren't you?" she demanded.

"And what do you know about it?"

"I've seen what's in the papers for one thing; for another I'm pretty good at putting two and two together."

"We'd like to see the result, Miss Jenks," Mallet said. "It's more than we can do, so far. We're not sure whether the two and two make four or twenty-two."

"Then you read *Death at the Desk*," she said with slow significance.

Mallet was startled—too much startled to speak at first. But after a swift whirl of thinking he recovered his grip.

"Oh, come, Miss Jenks," he expostulated. "What possible connection can there be between an imaginary crime and this actual one?"

"By M. G. Grafton." Miss Jenks uttered the words as if she were merely adding the name of the author to the title of the book she recommended, but her words sounded more like an accusation.

Again Mallet's thoughts took wings. The salient fact appeared to him to be that they certainly held evidence of a woman's presence there last night, a fact which could not be within the knowledge of Miss Jenks, unless she herself was in it. And it flashed to his mind that Miss Jenks, alarmed by his prolonged interest in the scratched hand and the dropped hair slide, was now seeking to divert suspicion on to another woman.

"You know Miss Grafton, I suppose," he said.

"Of course."

"When did you see her last?"

"Yesterday morning. She came here with a young man she called George. She wanted to see Mr. Dick."

Miss Jenks's replies were now so prompt that it became clear she intended to keep nothing back.

"But," Mallet objected, "I understood the young man had left for somewhere in the New Forest last Tuesday. Didn't she know?"

"She did not. They had quarrelled on the Monday."

"Do you happen to know the cause?"

Miss Jenks's smile at the question was as bitter as it was brief.

"There were several causes—more perhaps than I know about. Last week there was one on the day her book came out. He said it couldn't have happened like—the murder in the story, I mean. He hated saying it. Any one could have told as much from his voice. But she lost her temper and—"

"One moment," Mallet interrupted. "Do I understand all this occurred in your presence?"

Miss Jenks hesitated.

"Well, no," she said, more slowly. "Not exactly. You see—"

"Yes?"

"Well, you see in a way it was an accident. They didn't know I was there. Usually she came about one, when the others were at lunch, and Dick and I were in charge. When she did come, he either took her out to lunch or sent me out. And as I didn't always—" she hesitated again, and Mallet helped her out.

"Didn't always care to be disposed of like that."

"Didn't always want lunch just then," she corrected. "Especially as I was sure it was her suggestion. I've even seen her give him a nudge to get rid of me."

"Quite so. Well?"

"Well, last Friday when he brought her into the back shop when I was dusting, I got ready to go and leave them there together. But an important customer entered, and I stayed on in the front to attend to him. That did sometimes happen, though business was usually *nil* at that time."

Mallet nodded an impatient assent. Though he noted the bias against Miss Grafton, he was all ears to hear what passed between the pair who did not know they had an eavesdropper.

"But when Mr. Kendrew was so long in deciding which book on roses—"

"Mr. Kendrew is the name of the customer?"

"Yes. He's an M.P. And he took so long in making up his mind that afterwards it didn't seem worth while for me to go. I simply couldn't help hearing what passed. Well, she flung out at him so when he said no murder could have been done as she'd put it in the book. Of course he didn't like saying that, but it would hurt him more to see her getting made fun of by the book critics in the papers. Being her father's daughter that put her back up."

"Her father—you know him then?" Mallet asked.

"Well, who doesn't these days?" Miss Jenks in her turn inquired in a way that made Mallet sit up.

"You don't mean David Grafton?"

"Of course I do. I'd have thought everybody knew that."

Mallet was really startled. His hand upraised to signal her to proceed, remained for a moment motionless. Then he waved her on.

"Go ahead. Did he specify what exactly was wrong?"

"He said the time of the murder was, and the place, and the murderer's talk with a policeman after he'd left, and the taxi, and the way he removed the body."

Mallet glanced past Miss Jenks to see how Crabb had been affected. But this was the moment for a young officer to exhibit self-control, and Mallet read no emotion on his face, though Crabb's body muscles had gone suddenly taut at the mention of the talk with a policeman after the crime.

"And of course," Mallet suggested, "Miss Grafton wouldn't have been her father's daughter if she'd taken this lying down."

"She did not! What she said was that every detail had been thought out, and she'd allowed the murderer to make only *one* mistake, which, she said, was necessary if the crime was ever to be detected."

"Did she say what the mistake was?"

"No, only that if a murderer never made a mistake he'd never get caught, and so there would be no story. After snapping that at him she went back on to some earlier dispute they'd had about Mr. Dodsley."

"You mean his uncle?"

"Yes. I'd heard them at it before, and also Mr. Dick and his uncle on it too." At the remembrance Miss Jenks sighed. "Poor Mr. Dick, he did have a time between the two of them. Jealous of each other they were. No wonder he cleared out for a rest all by himself. The old man going on at him for neglecting the business, and getting himself mixed up with the Graftons."

"What?" Mallet interposed. "Surely he didn't think Mr. David Grafton unworthy to be—"

"Oh, he didn't think much of him," Miss Jenks in her turn cut in, "and maybe a bit less of the daughter, she being a woman as well as a Grafton."

"He didn't like women then?"

She smiled wryly.

"You'd know if you'd been one, and worked here."

"And the dislike was not quite one-sided, I take it," Mallet went on.

"That it wasn't. Not with one like her! Why couldn't he break with his uncle, that's what she kept on at him about. She had broken with her father because of him, she said."

"You mean because of her association with Dick?"

"Yes, it was on his account, she said, she'd left home, and why couldn't he do the same for her, an uncle being less than a father. She always kept saying that; seemed to take it that it proved he cared less for her than she did for him."

"Now come to yesterday," Mallet said.

"Yesterday she came in, hurrying and excited, just after one. She takes a look round, and then asks me for Mr. Dodsley. Of course I knew well enough which she meant. She always called him that, not wishing, I suppose, to hear his Christian name on our lips, and afraid we'd leave out the Mr. in front of it."

"You say she was excited?"

"Yes, she was—breathless, anyway. So I told her Mr. Dodsley was in the office. Why not? How was I to know she didn't know Dick had gone away for a couple of days?"

"You know where he went to?"

Miss Jenks nodded briefly.

"New Forest somewhere. Well, I didn't think she'd be long in there with old Mr. Dodsley. But that's where I was wrong. It was a good half-hour before she came out. And not with a flea in her ear, as I expected, but looking quite well pleased with herself. She took my breath away by giving me a smile as she passed. It took me a time to get over that smiling good-bye, and to realise it was old Mr. Dodsley, after all, she had called to see."

"And there had been no quarrel between them?" Miss Jenks looked straight back at him.

"That doesn't follow. She may have got the better of him, or seen how she was going to."

It was impossible to miss the innuendo conveyed in the last six slowly spoken words. But Mallet ignored the hint, so far at least as to let it pass without comment or question. As for Detective-Sergeant Crabb, inwardly he was thrilling with the perception that the Dodsley murder might turn out to be a case destined to result in newspaper headlines that would startle the country. His pleasant dreams were broken into by Mallet.

"Just two more questions, Miss Jenks, and we'll let you go," he began. Crabb smiled covertly. Mallet always ended like that. He could not see as far as the press headlines; he could see ahead no further than the next two questions.

"This man George you spoke of, what do you know about him?"

"Nothing, except that I've seen him with her once or twice. He looks about twenty-two, and was well-dressed the first time he came to the shop. She called him George, but I never heard his surname. They seemed on a very friendly footing with each other."

"And the other times you saw him, what was the difference?"

"Oh, that was yesterday. But he didn't come in. I saw him hovering about, waiting for her outside. He looked like a workman—very grubby and untidy, with a smear of dirt on his face."

"But you would know him again?"

"Oh, yes."

"All right. Now for my last question. Have you a copy of Miss Grafton's novel in the shop?"

Miss Jenks's face lit up at the question.

"There was one. Dick's copy, if he hasn't taken it with him," she said. "I think I could find it."

Mallet answered her expectant, almost eager look with a wave of the hand.

"If you'll be so kind," he said.

When she had gone, he looked at Crabb.

"You read detective stories, don't you, Crabb?" he said. And when Crabb admitted he did, Mallet went on, "Well, if you ever try your hand at writing one, call your murderer Dick, and no one will ever spot him. Dick!—it is the name that stands for all that is frank, honest, open, manly, and English." He took out and began to fill his pipe. As if pleased with his fancies he looked up. "Tell me, Crabb, did you ever hear of a criminal named Dick?"

Crabb strove hard.

"Well," he said after a time, "there was Dick Turpin."

But Mallet was so lost in his own thoughts that he did not seem to have heard.

Out in the front shop Miss Jenks had some trouble to find Miss Grafton's book. As she explained to Sergeant Barrett, it was a private copy, kept on a shelf behind the volumes exposed for sale. And its position appeared to have been changed. Sergeant Barrett assisted her by lifting out the volumes by the armful. Eventually they came on the wanted book.

"*Death at the Desk*, eh?" The sergeant looked at the cover with curiosity.

"A detective story," Miss Jenks explained; "they want it in there." She nodded at the office for which she was already making.

Sergeant Barrett rubbed his chin in perplexity as he stared after her. Copping ventured on a solution to what seemed to mystify his superior.

"Must have woken up—those sleep-walkers in there—and want something to pass the time," he said, as soon as his yawn permitted.

CHAPTER IX
Inspector Mallet Goes West

AFTER MISS JENKS LEFT, MALLET STARED FOR QUITE A time at the scene depicted on the jacket of *Death at the Desk*. In its essential details it corresponds so closely to what he himself had seen in the early hours of the morning. It was not, of course, remarkable that there should be a similarity in the room's furnishings and fittings, since desks and office chairs are all more or less of a pattern. But that there should be a resemblance, not only in the pose of the body on the floor and the position of the wound in the head, but also in the facial appearance of the dead bookseller to the imaginary bookmaker, did touch Mallet's imagination. He stared, indeed, continuously at the prostrate figure on the jacket while Crabb read aloud the notice in the *Record* which Mr. Carter had cut from that paper.

"Yes," he said when Crabb finished, "it does look like an imitation."

"That is what Miss Jenks suggested," Crabb pointed out.

"There's this man George she spoke of too, I'd like Roberts to have a look at him."

"Well, sir, on the face of it, the one murder seems a parallel to the other."

"You think so?"

"I do." Crabb spoke with confidence. "Whoever did for Dodsley was familiar with the contents of this book. If he wanted to demonstrate the—well—practicability of the crime, he couldn't have followed it more closely. And the book was hardly in circulation before the murder."

Mallet looked up.

"Why not say *she*, Crabb? You're hinting it was the author of the book herself, aren't you?"

"Oh, no, sir!" Crabb protested. "That would depend on a number of things not yet within our knowledge."

"Such as?"

"Well, for one thing I'd want to know just how much Miss Grafton takes after her father. Whether, I mean, she, like him, goes straight for what she wants."

Mallet regarded his assistant with interest.

"*H'm.* Crabb, that's telling me the type of newspaper you read—straight for what he wants."

"That's what the papers do say about him."

"Yes; and they all agree—at any rate they do today—that he usually gets what he wants; but few of them would agree that he goes *straight* to get it."

Crabb appeared to think that this strengthened his case.

"Well, sir, if that's right and the daughter takes after him, she must have what she wants by hook or by crook!"

"And what did she want?"

Crabb shifted slightly in his chair. Here was the catechism again!

"Young Dodsley, for one thing. But the old man stood in the way, as we know from Miss Jenks."

"And for another?"

"Well, supposing she made up her mind to clear the old man out of her way, it would be natural for her to do it in the same way as she'd put in her story, especially since the writer in the *Record* and young Dick himself said a murder couldn't be done like that."

Mallet shook his head.

"Ah, Crabb," he said with a sigh, "this is what comes of reading detective stories. No plot is too far-fetched for that type of fiction. Give 'em up, Crabb: it's a bad habit that may ruin your career," he added as he slipped *Death at the Desk* into his pocket.

"Well, sir," Crabb said defensively, "you agreed there's a woman in it. I take it that you yourself concluded the murder had been done by a woman, while the man in the case watched outside."

Mallet got up as if to brush this aside with more vigour.

"Yes, yes, we have good reason to believe there's a woman in it. We also know that a man, here as in the story, after the murder talked in the street with a constable. We are aware that, as in the story, the crime was committed when the criminal and his victim were alone, in the early hours of the morning, and in the murdered man's office. But if you're going to tell me, Crabb, she risked her neck in order to justify herself after a jeering notice of her book in a newspaper—well, all I'll say is that your taste for this class of fiction is perverting your judgment by inflaming your youthful imagination." Mallet stabbed at the table with a stiff forefinger. "Things like that don't happen, Crabb," he declared, beginning to pace about like a man disturbed and annoyed. "My godfathers," he fumed, "things have come to a pretty pass for the police if a young woman in her position can murder her lover's uncle just to prove his nephew wrong about her book."

Crabb kept silent while Mallet paced about in thought, head downcast, hands clasped behind his back. He easily fathomed the cause of his superior's mentally disturbed condition. Such clues as they had were conflicting. At the start everything pointed in the direction of young Dodsley. He knew his uncle was to be alone that night in the shop; and there had been a quarrel between them. And of the two keys to the shop, the nephew had one and the uncle the other. In addition, the nephew had disappeared. But then, just when young Dodsley seemed the man to go for, the indications began to point in another direction. It seemed clear, even from the notice of the book supplied by Carter, that there was a connection between it and the actual murder. Whoever had done the murder had read the book. And that book had been published only three days previously. But it seemed highly improbable that young Dodsley, who had declared the crime to be impossible as set out in the book, would be the one to demonstrate its possibility in actual fact. And as for his disappearance, Mallet could attach little weight to that, for a guilty man is usually well aware of how such a movement on his part draws immediate attention to himself. Besides, had he meant this absence to provide him with an alibi, he would hardly have destroyed it by telling Carter he would return to help the old man with the catalogue on the night which proved to be the night of the murder.

"Of course," Mallet broke into Crabb's thoughts, "all that tells against Miss Grafton comes to us from Miss Jenks."

"Just as what tells against young Dodsley comes from Carter."

"Yes," Mallet agreed, "that is so. Still, that woman Jenks made it clear she had no liking for the other woman."

Crabb's response was quick.

"Well, I didn't gather that Carter cared much for the other man," he said. "He told us of Dick Dodsley's intention to return last night, obviously, as he thought, to incriminate him. And, after all, she had been associating with other men in his absence."

"You mean Miss Grafton?"

"Yes; the man she had with her at the night club, and this man George, Miss Jenks spoke of."

"But look here, Crabb, there's—" Mallet paused as the 'phone whizzed off. His next words were spoken with the receiver at his ear. "*Yes, Inspector Mallet speaking… Oh, they've got him? Where?*"

The reply took some time, and Crabb, hearing nothing but a deep-toned inarticulate, rumbling voice, was reduced to watching Mallet's face.

"*I see,*" Mallet said at last. "*Yes, that would account for it. Eh?… Oh, no, not at all. We're on another clue now.*" He laid down the receiver gently, a look of disappointment replacing the pleased surprise with which he had begun to listen.

"That seems to clear young Dodsley anyhow," he said, half to himself.

"He's been found then?"

Mallet nodded absently, like one whose thoughts were elsewhere.

"Yes—in the hospital at Lymington. Had an accident on his way back to town last night. Concussion—doctors won't say what his chances are."

Crabb thrilled.

"Then he's ruled out."

"For the time being; but I'll want to know precisely when the accident happened. Anyway, he'll keep while we look elsewhere."

Crabb had now no doubt as to where that elsewhere would be, and when Mallet, extracting *Death at the Desk* from his pocket, once more began to stare at the prone and gruesome figure depicted on its cover he felt sure his superior had fixed his attention on the most probable suspect. But Mallet's next remark took him aback.

"Wish I knew how much we can rely on that woman Jenks."

"You don't think she's in it?"

"It's that alleged dispute as to the practicability of such a murder I have in my mind. She clearly has a strong bias against Miss Grafton; probably cherishes a secret passion for the young man herself. Was that tale of the quarrel a clumsy invention to put us on the wrong scent after she got frightened by our talk on hair clips, and the scratch on her hand?"

"Stevens will find out whether there is a cat," Crabb said.

"Yes, no doubt. But that won't take us far. There's a cat in most homes, and as to Stevens finding out whether this one is lame or not, you remember her saying it was all right this morning. Yet this cat in this shop is still lame this morning."

Crabb pondered this.

"There was this Mr. Kendrew she said had detained her—a member of Parliament," he suggested.

Mallet's face brightened.

"Yes, that's an idea. I've no doubt he was in the shop, but was it at the lunch hour? If it wasn't, she's lying, and if it was, he may have at least heard voices in the back shop."

But though the 'phone directory yielded them the name

of Mr. Kendrew's club, it was not so easy to get into touch with him. A call to the club gave them Kendrew's home address, and a through call to Kent only brought the information that the squire was supposed to be on a week-end visit to his friend, Commander Male, near Buckler's Hard in Hampshire. Then just when the persistent Mallet was trying to get through to Kendrew, a call came from Stevens at the Yard with the result of his visit to Miss Jenks's Finchley home. Stevens's report at once made it unnecessary to pursue Mr. Kendrew any further. For not only had Stevens established the fact that Miss Jenks's home did possess a cat, but also that Miss Jenks's mother, as yet unaware of the tragedy at her daughter's place of employment, vouched for the fact that her daughter had not left the house after her return from business last night, and so could not have been a witness of the Belisha-crossing accident about which Stevens was inquiring.

As afterwards appeared, however, Mallet, even had he got through to Buckler's Hard, would not have established contact with Mr. Kendrew, for at the time he and his friend, Commander Male, were in the sailor's seven-ton cutter, tacking down the Beaulieu river, making for the Solent, confident of finding in the fresh winds of the Needles the reinvigoration both sought after the long hours of spent air in the House of Commons.

It was on the stroke of two that Mallet touched the bell at Mr. Grafton's pleasant little house in Charles Street. In spite of himself he was just a trifle stirred and excited. The case looked like developing into the sensational category, involving people of a class far above that in which most of his experience had been gained. And Mallet, annoyed to find that quickened beat of his heart, replied brusquely to the superior parlourmaid when informed that Miss Grafton was not at home.

"Perhaps you can find me some one who can tell me where she is," he insisted.

And when the haughty damsel, after looking him up and down and appraised him to her own satisfaction, was about to shut the door, Mallet produced his warrant card. It did him good to see the abrupt change effected by the sight of that card.

In the morning-room he stood waiting at the window, looking out on the park, with all his customary self-control. But when a slight sound from the door behind him made him turn, he was surprised at the sight of the woman who stood still grasping the handle while she regarded him. The maid had undertaken to find Mrs. Grafton, and for the moment he thought this young woman must be Miss Grafton herself.

"Yes?" she said, "what is it you want?"

Mallet detected some anxiety in her tones. It was only after he had explained himself, telling her he had come to seek some information from Miss Grafton that she let the door handle go and came towards the window. Then he saw she was not quite so young as he had supposed.

"But why do you come here? Miss Grafton does not live here," she said.

Mallet, noting she did not inquire about the nature of the information sought, told her he had already been to Miss Grafton's Bloomsbury rooms, and failed to find her.

"Well," she said coldly when he had finished, "my step-daughter goes her own way. We know little or nothing about her here. She follows her own tastes, and makes her own friends."

Then as she glanced at the door, obviously expecting

him to go, he said: "You know I am a police officer, yet you do not ask me what I want to see her about."

He saw the mouth harden.

"When a girl leaves her home to associate with people out of her own class, the less her own family know the better for their peace of mind."

Mallet laid his hat on the table.

"Now, Mrs. Grafton," he began confidentially, "believe me, we quite appreciate your point of view. But possibly Miss Grafton feels she has to mix with all sorts to get material for her novels. And I have reason to believe she could be of the greatest assistance to us on the case I have in hand."

Mrs. Grafton smiled bitterly.

"Yes," she said, "she would like that. It would be sweet publicity for her. If she can't have fame, she can at least make herself notorious."

Mallet was not indisposed to glean any information about Miss Grafton, however prejudiced the source, for he believed himself capable of making the allowances necessary.

"Dear me, is she really like that?" he sympathetically inquired. Then as her tightly compressed lips seemed to be the only response she intended to make, he added. "A hunger for notoriety, and a partiality for low society, yes, if that is true—" He stressed the "if" and left his words unfinished hoping to provoke an outburst of frankness.

"True! Of course it's true," she cried. "Isn't her real place here, helping me, at my right hand, just as I am at her father's right hand, for those important social duties belonging to one in his position? Instead of which, she goes off to live what she calls her own life. And what a life! Two rooms in a low locality to write low-class novels by day, and then dancing and dining with young men in retail shops after their shops are shut! Not that there's anything wrong with night clubs in themselves. Many of the best people go there, you know, just as some of the best run hat shops in the West End; but of course nobody that counts runs a bookshop, much less a second-hand one." Working hard, her tear-ducts produced two small witnesses to the extremity of her vexation. The fragile handkerchief went up to dab her eyes. "And now," she said, "to crown all, you come here seeking her, and I at once know her father's name is going to be dragged through the mud."

"Oh, that doesn't follow," Mallet protested. "At present I am only seeking for information she may be in a position to supply."

"I foresaw this," she went on unheedingly. "I foresaw what would happen as soon as I read the papers this morning. You didn't have to tell me why you are here."

It occurred to Mallet that he was wasting his time.

"Perhaps," he suggested gently, "if I could see Mr. Grafton himself, he might be able to tell me how to find her."

The heat with which the suggestion was met astonished him.

"No! I make it my business to shield him from such worries. He knows nothing. Besides," she added more quietly, "he's over-tired this morning, still in his room, exhausted, after his triumph last night." Her eyes went up to the ceiling for a moment, and then, turning towards the detective she added in a hushed, confidential voice: "It would be too ghastly to see one who had brought down a government brought down himself by his own daughter, wouldn't it?"

Mallet, however, was not impressed. Partly this was because of his anxiety to make a good show in this particular case. He was quite aware the Dodsley murder would not have been put into his hands had there been even a suspicion it could lead him away from the common type of robbery with violence criminal he knew. But who could guess that a shop murder in Charing Cross Road would lead him not south to Kennington but west into Kensington? And Mallet had the fact forced on him that, after all, women were, under the skin, much more alike than men. Had he been in Southwark interviewing the wife of some wanted confidence man, or cat burglar, she might have called him a rosser instead of an officer, and she would have been shrewish and even blasphemous in denying all knowledge of her man's whereabouts, but the same defensive instinct would confront him in both women.

Mallet lifted his hat from the table. He picked it up in a way that made the act seem somehow ominous.

"Well, madam," he said quietly, "it looks like being an unfortunate affair for Mr. Grafton. I'd very gladly keep his name out of the newspapers if it could be done. But you see how it is. Miss Grafton, who you say has been mixing with these people, probably can give us useful information. We've got to see her. And if her friends cannot tell us where she is—well, we must put our own methods into action."

"What methods?" she demanded.

"I'm not at liberty to say," Mallet replied, with grim decision.

"But they mean publicity?"

"Undoubtedly," he said. "If the young lady has a fancy for that, she'll get enough of it inside the next twenty-four hours."

Mrs. Grafton shuddered. Mallet saw the convulsive quiver, and it was enough for him, even though he could not guess the temperature to which her blood had dropped. Neither could he see how, at his words, her mind had flashed over all the consequences to her social ambitions likely to follow this publicity. Her hand thus forced, she gave way.

"Well, there's Mr. Brewster, of course," she said weakly.

"Who is he?"

"Mr. Grafton's secretary. He's on friendly terms with Miss Grafton and also with—well, with the young man Dodsley. He might at least be able to tell you how to get in touch."

"Is he in the house now?"

"He was half an hour ago. I'll go and see."

But Mallet stopped her.

"If you don't mind, would you ring for him?"

It was an order more than a request. She was furious. But this was only part of the indignity she had to suffer on Margery Grafton's account. In silence she acquiesced, and going over, touched the bell.

When Brewster appeared, Mrs. Grafton explained the visitor in a tragic I-told-you-so tone.

"Inspector Mallet of Scotland Yard. He's searching for Margery in connection with Dodsley's death." Brewster's stare of incredulity passed swiftly to the detective.

"For Margery?"

Mallet hastened to explain.

"Oh, we think she might help us," he said. "We're most anxious to get in touch with such persons as knew the Dodsleys. And Miss Grafton, who as an author, has no doubt a keen eye for different characters, is likely to be of great use."

"Yes, I see," said Brewster uncertainly.

Mallet put the position to him. They had failed to find Miss Grafton at her Bloomsbury address, nor could her landlady suggest where she could be found. A call too had been made on her publishers, but they could only supply the address in Bloomsbury.

"But," Brewster cut in, "what about Dick Dodsley? He is the man to ask."

With his eyes on Mrs. Grafton, Mallet replied to his suggestion.

"He had an accident—last night, near Lymington."

"What?"

The exclamation came not from Mrs. Grafton but from Brewster. Mallet turned to him.

"Thrown off his motor-cycle. He's in hospital with concussion."

"That accounts for it," Brewster said, half to himself.

"Accounts for what?"

"Queer if uncle and nephew were both to go on the same night," Mrs. Grafton murmured, almost hopefully.

"Accounts for what?" Mallet insisted.

"Well, for the fact that he didn't turn up last night as arranged. We—well—we couldn't account for it at the time," Brewster said half absently, his mind obviously busy with the events of the previous night, which Mallet's news had put in a new perspective. But when the inspector urged him to explain, his words came briskly: "It was last night at the *Cynara* Club. In the afternoon I'd run across Miss Grafton in Bond Street. She appeared in great spirits. I knew she and Dick had had a bit of a dust-up over the—well—poor opinion he held about her new book. But they'd made it up—that morning, after a letter from him. We had tea together at Brooks, so that she might tell me all about it. She had just been to see old Dodsley, with whom Dick had fallen out, to tell him she'd heard from Dick, and that he wasn't to worry over the catalogue, as Dick would take it over himself. The old man, she said, seemed so pleased she had come round to tell him that he even patted her shoulder when she left. She was to meet Dick at the *Cynara*."

"Did she say when?" Mallet asked.

"Oh, yes—about 1.30, after he'd finished off the new catalogue. Said he'd called that his act of reparation and self-denial. She then suggested I should turn up to join in the celebration. But that I couldn't undertake to do—not with my duties at the House with Mr. Grafton, you know."

"So you didn't go?" Mallet said disappointedly.

"Oh, yes, I did. She urged me so when we parted, that I promised to turn up if I could get away. As it happened, there wasn't much just then for me to do, and in fact I left Mr. Grafton reading Margery's novel. When I got to the *Cynara*, it must have been nearly two, and I expected to find them together. But Dick hadn't yet arrived."

"Go on, please, Mr. Brewster," Mallet said. "This may be very important."

"Oh, I've little more to tell you. We waited on, danced, talked, had a soft drink or two, you know, expecting every moment to see him come in. I stayed on, knowing Mr. Grafton wouldn't need me unless the unexpected happened. All my real work had been done already, of course. But I couldn't miss his amendment to the ninth clause, you know—not even for Margery's sake."

"So you left before he came?"

"Yes. About two-thirty, that was."

"And was that the last time you saw Miss Grafton?"

"It was."

"Now, Mr. Brewster, I gather that up till two-thirty, Miss Grafton and you were all that time waiting for Mr. Dodsley."

"Of course."

"Did it never occur to the young lady to go round to the shop to see if he was there?"

Brewster apparently took this as a childish question.

"Certainly it did," he said impatiently. "But she feared he might come while she was away, and take it that she had refused the appointment he had made at the Club."

Mallet nodded.

"Quite. That's understandable. So you left Miss Grafton still waiting at two-thirty, and that was the last time you saw her?"

"It was."

"But, perhaps, sir, you can suggest how she can be found?"

"Well, Inspector, if I were seeking for her, naturally the first place I'd now expect to find her would be Lymington."

"But she hasn't yet heard of the accident."

Brewster's eyes opened wide for a moment.

"You are sure? How can you know that?" he asked.

"Because she hasn't turned up there, for one thing. For another, by the time her address and his identity was established by a letter found in his pockets, she had disappeared."

Brewster shook his head.

"In that case, I'm afraid I'd just have to wait till she reappeared," he said.

"Like the rest of us," the long silent Mrs. Grafton interjected.

Mallet turned to her impatiently.

"Yes, madam, but that is what we can't wait for," he said. "We must find her at once." And the emphasis he laid on his two last words was born of the knowledge that Miss Grafton had been left at 2.30 by Brewster, and the dead body had been found by Roberts at 3.16. What more likely than that, left alone, she had changed her mind—or was it taken her chance?—and gone to the shop! A woman, as the dropped hair slide testified, there certainly had been in the shop that night. And a man had been with her. Miss Preedy's story tallied exactly, so far as it went, with what he had just heard from Brewster. Then a name Miss Jenks mentioned came back to Mallet. He looked up.

"Do you happen to know an acquaintance of Miss Grafton's—a young man named George?"

The swift stare exchanged by Brewster and Mrs. Grafton rather startled Mallet. He had thought the question scarcely worth putting, since, from Jenks's description of the young man's appearance, he belonged rather to Miss Grafton's underworld, and not at all to the world Mrs. Grafton would know.

"George," Brewster murmured thoughtfully. "It's a very common name."

"No, no," Mrs. Grafton interjected quickly. "He had better know. George can do no harm. And the inspector has promised to save us all the nasty publicity if we help him." She turned to Mallet with a forced smile. "Isn't that so, Inspector?"

"As far as I can," Mallet agreed.

"Then I rather fancy George must be her brother," Mrs. Grafton said. "It is possible he can tell you how to find her. He's learning the motor trade, you know, at Tophams, who is a nephew of Lord Wye's."

When Mallet left to visit the garage of Lord Wye's nephew, Brewster stepped over to the window where Mrs. Grafton stood watching the departing detective's back.

"Why did you tell him about George?" he asked. She turned to stare at him.

"Don't be ridiculous, Owen Brewster. You don't suppose he suspects George?"

"It's not George he suspects."

"Why do you say it like that?"

"George is going to be put through it, though. Last night he came home just before I did. He'd been out in the car, and from what he told me, I fancy he hasn't much of an alibi. Knowing that, I wanted to fend off that red-faced nosey parker."

"But there must be hundreds of young men in London exactly like that. And George at least had no connection with the—"

"The Dodsleys? No, but unlike the hundreds of other young men in London, his sister had."

He saw her face go white. She had to moisten her lips before she spoke.

"You don't mean he suspects...Margery?"

"That is what I do mean." Brewster spoke with slow assurance.

"My God," she said, "that would indeed put us into the limelight."

When Mallet rejoined his waiting detective-sergeant at the corner, Crabb's expectant eyes were full of questions. But not till Mallet entered the 'phone box round the corner was his anxiety relieved. Then his youthful keenness almost relieved itself in a whistle as he overheard his superior, having got the divisional office, ask that Constable Roberts should be sent at once to meet him at Marble Arch.

CHAPTER X
What Was the Mistake?

CONSTABLE ROBERTS REACHED MARBLE ARCH BEFORE the two had time to walk across the park. It was as well for Roberts's nerves that he had not to wait long. He knew now he had not handled the incident with the roysterer of the previous night with the foresight of an alert and intelligent officer. There was his blunder with the cigarette case too. He had actually wiped out the fingerprints on it in order to see if it bore the name of the owner. His mental tension mounted as in his mind's eye he read the report he had sent in on last night's events.

Mallet set his pace across the park in proportion to the amount he had to tell his assistant. As soon as they were on the tree-lined walk, he took Crabb's arm in a manner so affectionate that two nursemaids on a seat, with an admiring eye for the younger man, agreed, rightly, that he was a policeman, but wrongly, that the older man was his uncle up from the country to see the sights.

"You were right, Crabb," Mallet said, pressing his arm. "I believe you got your finger on the right party."

Inwardly, Crabb thrilled, though the thrill was not sufficient to carry the colour to his pale, clear-cut face.

"Yes," Mallet said, as he finished his account of his interview, "the secretary, Brewster, wasn't going to tell me about
brother George. Afraid of what we might extract from
George, I fancy."

"You think he was in it then?"

"Tell you that when we've seen him." Then as if this were
over-cautious he added: "Oh, this shop murder isn't going
to be a repetition of that Shaftesbury Avenue affair. I've
what Miss Preedy would call a hunch about that."

As P. C. Roberts, standing by the Arch, saw the brisk
way in which the two Yard men approached him, the bright
look in the chief inspector's rosy face almost banished his
forebodings.

"Roberts," Mallet said, "we want you to have a look at a
man in a garage near here. Perhaps you'll be able to tell us
whether you've seen him before."

Roberts was quick to understand. The last remnants of
his dread vanished.

"Yes, sir," he said. "Provided it ain't very long since I saw
him last."

"Take a good look at him. Then, if you're in doubt, don't
look at him, but keep your ear to his voice and see if it sug-
gests anything to you."

Roberts pondered this as they crossed the Bayswater
Road. Then he sidled up alongside. He was awed with
admiration for Scotland Yard. Already, within a few hours,
they had picked out from among London's millions the one
man concerned in the murder.

"And if I'm sure, sir, am I to say anything?" he asked.

"You mean claim his acquaintance?"

"How about doing it with the cigarette case?" Crabb suggested.

Mallet, after a brief consideration, adopted the suggestion. Handing the case to Roberts, he instructed him to produce the case only when he became certain this was the young man he had seen last night.

At Topham's garage they found the manager in his office. "Oh," he remarked as soon as he heard Mallet's request. "Young Grafton. Been exceeding the speed limit, I suppose. I'm not surprised."

Mallet, assuring him it was nothing of that sort but an offence of another kind on which Grafton might give some valuable evidence, asked if they could have his office in which to interview the young man.

After a slight delay, George Grafton appeared. He was in brown holland overalls, and his troubled expression suggested that the manager had been pulling his leg over this visit of the police. Motorists in these days dread the police much as burglars do, but there is this difference between the two classes of criminals: the burglars do not exhibit nervousness. And George was nervous. Recalling Mrs. Grafton's tirade of that morning, he knew that any motoring charge against the son of David Grafton would be singled out for special display by the newspapers. And unconscious though he was of having been guilty of any offence, he shared the fatalistic view of the experienced motorist, that a charge is invariably followed by a conviction.

"It's about Miss Grafton we wanted to see you," Mallet explained, noticing that as he spoke the uneasiness on young Grafton's face deepened into fear.

"My sister! Anything happened to her?"

"Oh, no. Not as far as we know. But we think she can help

us in a case we have in hand, if we could find her. No doubt you keep in touch with her, and can tell us where to find her."

Relief showed on the face they were watching as he supplied the Bloomsbury address. It looked like a good piece of acting, that lifting of fear from the young man's face. Mallet, suspicious that he was being played with, waved the information aside.

"When did you see her last?" he demanded.

George rubbed his chin. His stepmother had been right after all. Margery was going to be involved in the Dodsley case through her connection with young Dodsley. But if her disappearance meant she was intentionally keeping out of their way, he must not let her down. While George hesitated Mallet shot an inquiring look over at Roberts. But the constable's expression showed, so far, no more than doubt or perplexity.

"Well?" Mallet insisted.

"I'm trying to think," George explained.

"Oh, come; let me refresh your memory. Wasn't it last night in Charing Cross Road?"

"Charing Cross Road?" George was startled.

"That's what I said. You weren't so—well—hadn't so much liquor in you to have forgotten that meeting."

George brightened up at the question. Having resolved to lie on Margery's behalf he was glad to be able to be truthful when he thought he safely could.

"Oh," he said, "I did have a drink or two at the *Gryphon*— after I'd put up the car, of course—before going home, but not so many as to have forgotten the fact if I had met her."

"But you were in Charing Cross Road last night?"

The assurance with which the detective spoke surprised George, but he was again glad to be saved the need for lying.

"I was," he admitted. "After leaving the *Gryphon* I looked

for a taxi to take me home, and walked down towards the station, knowing I'd find one there."

"You're sure it wasn't the *Cynara*?"

"Oh, quite. I never go there. They expect you to be in dress clothes at that place."

"And you weren't last night?"

George waved this aside.

"Didn't I tell you I'd been out in the car, tuning her up?"

"And what about yesterday morning?" Mallet fired the question at him.

"Yesterday morning?"

"Yes. You were with Miss Grafton in Charing Cross Road yesterday morning, weren't you?"

George Grafton was not a good liar. Mallet's unexpected question caught him on the hop. He had been so comfortable in all he said. Up till now he thought he had done very well. His breathing quickened perceptibly.

"You're mistaken," he blurted out. "Quite mistaken. I—I—well, wasn't I trying just now to remember when I last saw her?"

"So any one who said they saw you there is lying?"

George obviously didn't like this.

"Did some one say that?" he prevaricated.

"Certainly. Some one, too, who had no reason, so far as I can see, to tell us what was untrue. Yet that person was a liar, eh?"

"Oh, I don't say that," George protested. "Not really, you know. Case of mistaken identity." The phrase pleased him. "That's it: case of mistaken identity," he repeated with conviction.

The phrase did not please Mallet: it was over-familiar to him.

"Mr. Grafton," he remarked coldly, "you didn't ask what time you were supposed to have been seen there. You don't ask because you already know when you were there."

But George thought himself equal to this.

"Oh, I didn't need to because it must have been in my lunch hour," he explained, "that being the only time I'm free."

"About one o'clock it was."

"Exactly. There you are, you see."

"Then you could have been seen there at that time?"

"Of course, if I'd been there, but I wasn't. So of course I simply couldn't have been seen there."

At this juncture a memory of his school days on the football pitch recurred to George. He recalled the assertion of the coach that the best defence was always attack, and he tried attack now.

"Look here," he burst out, "what's all this for? What does it matter to you where I was at one yesterday, I'd like to know?"

But such simulated indignation was also a feature familiar to Inspector Mallet. Recognising the forcible-feeble protest which attempts to cover up an awkward fact, he changed his tone.

"Oh, Mr. Grafton," he said deprecatingly, "no need to get hot, you know. Look at our position. We're investigating the circumstances connected with the death of Mr. Dodsley, the uncle of the young man to whom your sister is engaged. And we're all the more anxious for her assistance since learning she herself is—well—an author interested in the detection of crime." While speaking Mallet's hand went to his pocket. "There's this story of hers now," he said, producing *Death at the Desk*. "I suppose she sometimes discussed her plots with you?"

George stared at the figure of the dead man on the brightly coloured jacket.

"You see," Mallet continued confidentially, "our problem is to discover how the actual murderer gained admission to the shop, there being only two keys: one held by the owner and the other by his nephew."

The effect of his last words on George Grafton surprised Mallet. Up to that moment he had been inwardly disappointed with all he had got out of Grafton. And Roberts had not produced the little gold case. Nor from the look of uncertainty on his face was he likely to do it. But at his mention of the two keys the young man had suddenly gone almost sick with fear. Mallet knew the symptoms—the quick intake of the breath, the abruptly distended eyes and, in this instance, a glistening dampness just below the brushed-back hair on the forehead. Beyond a doubt, the young man had been badly and unexpectedly scared. Experience alone restrained Mallet from provoking the instinctive denial such a moment brings out.

In an ominous silence his gaze went through the little window. The office was no more than a booth inside the vast area of the high roofed garage, and the window overlooked a long bench against the right wall, at which a line of mechanics were busy hammering, fitting, and filing various minor parts in a car's equipment. After regarding that vista of tapping hammers, bent heads, and straining elbows he turned on Grafton.

"Well," he said quietly, "you see we know something. So you'd better tell us what you know."

"Me?" George said. "What do I know? I thought it was my sister you—"

"About keys, for instance," Mallet prompted, with a wave

of the hand at the window. "You sometimes have to make keys here, I suppose."

"Never made a key in my life," the young man declared. This time there was enough assurance and relief in his voice to convince Mallet that somehow he himself was off the scent. Yet double back as he at once did, he failed to pick up in all the talk that followed any facts implicating either George Grafton or his sister. The brother did not help the sister with her plots. He did not know where she was. Last night he had reached home some time after three. No, he could not be more exact; but it was just before his father got home from the House. He knew there had been a tiff between his sister and Dick. Brewster had told him.

All the same Mallet left the garage with no sense of frustration. Even when, going along Bayswater Road, Roberts had to admit he could not be positive about the young man, Mallet felt fairly sure of himself.

"You see, sir," Roberts said, "it's through him being in dress clothes last night and so much dirt on his face from falling about. More like a figure o' fun he was, from what he is now. And though he is about the same height, the young fellow I saw last night looked slighter built."

"He would in a dress suit," Crabb remarked.

"What about his voice?" Mallet asked.

About this Roberts was decided.

"This young man speaks slower, sir, much slower and clearer than what the man did last night, and not squeaky, not almost like a girl's as his was."

Crabb looked his disgust.

"Yes," he said. "Yes, drink does make some men gabble like girls."

When Roberts departed they took a taxi to the Yard.

"Well, Crabb?" Mallet said.

Crabb sat bolt upright, his pale, keen face very grim, his eyes set on the fringe of grey hair below the taxi-man's shabby peaked cap.

"Can't see why he admitted being in the street last night and denied he was there in his lunch hour," he said.

"You think he expected Roberts to identify him?"

"That's about it. He knew Roberts, but Roberts, silly ass, was not sure of him."

"Oh, if he wasn't sure, he was right in saying so," Mallet said. "Many a constable as young as yourself, knowing he was brought there to identify a suspect, would have obliged us on the spot. Roberts resisted the temptation and risked incurring your wrath, Crabb. He'll make quite a good officer yet."

Crabb waited a moment, then turned.

"But you think this young Grafton is in it, don't you, sir?"

"Of course I do," Mallet replied with prompt conviction. "But at first *he* didn't know he was in it."

Crabb turned right round to stare.

"Didn't *know* he was in it," he echoed incredulously.

"No. He's quite a simple youth, obviously. This sister of his has been using him. He didn't know it, though, till I mentioned the keys of the shop. Then he really got scared."

"And denied he had ever made a key, or been outside the shop in his lunch hour."

"Exactly. But we'll let Miss Jenks also have a look at him." Then, while the taxi was halted by the red lights at the Piccadilly crossing, he extracted *Death at the Desk* and laid it on his knee thoughtfully.

"After all, Crabb, don't authors of this sort usually make

us out to be fools? What more likely then that they should come to believe it. And then, given sufficient motive for murder on their own account, how naturally, with their swelled heads, any one of them might become convinced *he* would never get caught."

"In this case *she*," Crabb suggested. "But in a story there has to be one mistake or there'd be no detection."

"Yes, so Miss Jenks heard her say; but what was the mistake in this case?"

Crabb regarded the jacket.

"Seems to be a dozen or two, judging by the paper we got from Carter," he said.

"Maybe, but in the actual crime what was the mistake?"

Crabb shook his head as the taxi moved on.

"Well, sir," he said, "maybe some authors do benefit by criticism. But I'd like to read the story to see."

Mallet, however, replaced the book in his pocket.

"Not this copy, Crabb. I'm going to take a busman's holiday and read it before I go to sleep tonight."

Crabb was pleased by this surrender.

"You will?" he said with a smile.

"Why, of course. Didn't you hear me say I take evidence from anybody? With the same object I'm prepared to read anything—even the Bible itself—right through—before I go to bed."

BOOK III

CHAPTER I
MacNab Has a Visitor

THE DODSLEY CASE HAPPENED TO BE IN FRANCIS MacNab's mind when Owen Brewster was shown in. MacNab had just returned from a call on Jim Peters at the little newspaper shop in Soho. On leaving he had picked up the evening edition of the *Record* and sauntered home with it under his arm. His thoughts were on quite another case. It chanced to be one of those rare evenings in late May when the air is luminous with soft sunlight, and his thoughts turned to the river above the old bridge at Callander, and the trout that would be rising greedily to the mayfly on such a golden evening.

But by the time he mounted to his flat in the Adelphi, the dusk had deepened so much that to read his paper he was compelled to push his chair close up to the window overlooking the Embankment.

Almost at once his eye was taken by a half-column on what had come to be known as the Bookshop Murder. But though the *Record* still used splash headlines for the crime, there didn't seem to be much that was new to say about it.

Detective-Inspector Mallet had, it appeared, returned to town that morning after his visit to the Lymington cottage hospital to which, as reported yesterday, the dead man's nephew had been removed in consequence of his motorcycle accident on the night of the murder. Inspector Mallet, it was learned, had found the injured man in no condition to make a statement, and had returned to pursue further inquiries along new lines in London. It was not considered likely, however, that the nephew could throw much light on the actual crime, he being absent at the time; but the local police were in attendance at the hospital, and any information they might obtain from the young man would be immediately transmitted to Scotland Yard.

That was all. But in turning the paper over, the Late News space took his eye:

THE BOOKSHOP MURDER,—Developments of a sensational nature are expected in connection with this crime. Inspector Mallet is believed now to have evidence in his possession which removes the murder out of the class of squalid crimes to which at first sight it appeared to belong.

It was at that moment, while the paper remained still in his hand, that Janet entered with Mr. Brewster's card.

The housekeeper, it seemed, had no doubt about MacNab's readiness to see Mr. Brewster. So many queer, disreputable looking people came to see the master, and at such odd times too, that her readiness to usher in a nice-mannered, good-looking young man like Mr. Brewster was quite comprehensible. And as Owen Brewster stood, hat in hand, looking about him a little uncertainly, till the old housekeeper had retired, MacNab also liked his diffident, quiet manner. He was in some trouble, of course; the anxiety in his dark, rather mournful eyes told MacNab as much. And his hesitancy indicated that he had been compelled to come, and would probably be forced to say something he would rather have left unsaid. At least so MacNab, from his wide experience, read the symptoms. He pointed to a chair.

"Sit down, Mr. Brewster, and tell me all about it," he said.

Brewster, murmuring thanks, sank into the chair. It was an easy-chair, which had in its time accommodated many an uneasy guest.

"You won't know me, of course," he began as he placed his hat carefully on his knees, "but I am secretary to Mr. Grafton."

"Mr. David Grafton?"

"Yes, though actually I am here on Miss Grafton's behalf. It's in connection with this Bookshop Murder," he added. "I undertook to see you when I left her at Lymington."

His eyes were hopefully on MacNab's face as he spoke, and he must have perceived he had made the detective jump. It somehow gave him a more self-assurance.

"Miss Grafton is engaged to Dodsley's nephew, you know," he said. "Mrs. Grafton's much concerned too. She dreads the publicity that may result if Miss Grafton's name is mentioned in connection with the affair."

"But Miss Grafton was not called at the inquest."

"No, it was adjourned, of course; but as things now stand she may be when it is resumed. Oh," he burst out abruptly, "but Mrs. Grafton's feelings are of small importance compared with the real trouble."

MacNab settled back in his chair.

"All right. Just tell me what the trouble exactly is, and in what way my help is wanted."

"The real trouble is that the police seem to suspect Dick murdered his uncle. We know that from the way they have been questioning Margery. Not that they've said so. Their questioning has been what they would think very discreet, but any ass could see what they thought," Brewster cried with heat and scorn. After a breath or two he went on with more self-control, "We want you to take up the case, to look after Dick's interests. He's lying still barely conscious in that hospital, and you know how the police, once they've made up their minds a man is guilty, feel compelled to build up a case against him."

MacNab retrieved and replaced the hat which the young man in the heat of his indignation had unconsciously knocked off his knees. But he did not correct the erroneous notion Brewster, in common with so many others, held as to police methods.

"Is there a case against him?" he asked. "As I understand it from the newspaper this young man met with an accident down there on the night of the murder."

Owen Brewster shook his head.

"It's not so simple as all that," he said. "If it were, I shouldn't be here seeking the help of an expert. Dick wasn't in hospital at the time of the murder, nor for many hours afterwards. He ran over a bank and got smashed up at a bend on a lonely stretch of road. He was discovered down the bank unconscious by two roadmen who found his wrecked motor-cycle about seven next morning. He had put up at the *Angel* in Lymington and, as they told us at the hotel, had left about eight the night before."

"That is, on the night of the murder?"

"Yes. The garage man remembers he mentioned his intention of returning to London. But he seems to have taken a wrong turning just outside Lymington, where there is a deceptive fork in the road, and got mixed up in a network of lanes around a little place called Sway, eventually reaching the stretch of almost moorland road on which the accident happened. Now you will see where the trouble lies. The police are going to say he didn't by any means lie there so very long. They are going to say that the accident happened not on his way to town but on his way from it. We know that because we heard they were moving heaven and earth to find any one who had passed along that road any time after eight-thirty on the night of the murder. They'll agree that such an accident was unlikely to happen except in the dark, and that it did not happen in the darkness of the early hours, when he was trying to put as great a distance as possible between himself and the scene of the crime."

MacNab tried to reassure his distressed client. Going over to pick up the evening paper he pointed to the half-column which included the statement that the police did not expect the injured young man to be able to throw any light on the crime. Brewster, after careful reading, threw the paper aside.

"Mere eyewash," he declared; "it's Dick they suspect. I know that from the way they've been badgering Margery down there."

MacNab indicated the paper Brewster had so impatiently tossed aside.

"There's something in the Late News column which seems to point in another direction."

This time he let Brewster pick up the paper for himself.

"Well," he said after a moment, "I don't see that it tells us much."

"Possibly it wasn't meant to. But to me it sounds as if

some clue had fallen into their hands which has led them in a new and unexpected direction."

"You mean since this Inspector Mallet returned to town?"

"Yes, it sounds like that. But what I'm sure of," he said with confidence, "is that you can safely rely on the police. If your friend is innocent, he has nothing to fear from them."

"That he certainly is," Brewster burst in, as if resenting MacNab's hypothetical "if." "That, you in your turn, can rely on."

"Very well, he has nothing to fear from the police. Their investigations can only establish his innocence. So," he concluded, rising to his feet, "you can tell Miss Grafton she has not the slightest need of my services."

But Brewster did not rise. Nor did he seem in the least reassured. He sat quite still, gloomily regarding the bowler hat perched on his knees. Even MacNab's little cough as he stood waiting failed to get the young man to his feet.

"Now, look here." MacNab drew nearer. "Look here, Mr. Brewster. I happen to know something of this Inspector Mallet, and I'd say from what I've seen of him that he is not the sort of officer to build up a case against any suspect. He is not that type. In fact," he added, "if the type exists at all, it certainly does not at Scotland Yard."

So far from allaying young Brewster's fears MacNab's testimonial to the Yard rather increased his agitation.

"Ah, but you don't yet understand," he cried in a tone of despair. "Appearances are so black against poor Dick. Mallet can't help suspecting him, from what he knows. And, if it comes to that, he doesn't yet know all."

Little as Brewster guessed it, this was the point at which MacNab began to be interested.

"Perhaps you'll tell me just what the police know," he said quietly.

"Oh, I don't know all they know—how could I? But they know the shop was entered by a key, and of the only keys in existence, one they find in old Dodsley's pocket and the other in Dick's, when they went through his clothes in the hospital at Lymington."

MacNab considered this for a moment or two. Since there could be no doubt the premises had been entered by means of a key, things so far did look black against young Dodsley. MacNab had watched the old man's nephew just as he had studied the others while hovering among the shelves to detect the book thief. He had seemed a decent enough lad, well-spoken, pleasant without being effusive, but possibly a trifle conceited and certainly not lacking in self-confidence. How much the obvious adoration of the elder assistant, Miss Jenks, was responsible for the last two qualities, MacNab could not say, but he now thought the Grafton connection might well account for their appearance. Still, the young man must have finer things in him, qualities not obvious to the casual observer, to have evoked so deep an attachment, so profound a concern, as Owen Brewster now showed for him.

MacNab regarded Brewster thoughtfully. The young man sat dejectedly stroking the bowler hat on his knees in much the same absent-minded way as he had seen Miss Jenks stroking the Siamese cat in the front shop. But MacNab's next question arrested the hand.

"Now tell me," he said, "what is it that Mallet does not know?"

"Oh, must I tell you that?" he cried. "Surely—" he checked himself. "Well, you see, it's something nobody but myself knows."

"Go on, Mr. Brewster."

Brewster stirred about uneasily, nearly dislodging the hat.

"I'm only afraid," he pleaded, "that if you know what it is, you may refuse to do the very thing I'm here to ask you."

"I'm afraid you'll have to tell me—if you want my help." MacNab's tone was decisive.

"But it's something I haven't even told Margery herself," Brewster expostulated, his hat now held to his breast as if it were a shield.

MacNab sat down and touched the other's knee gently.

"Look here, Mr. Brewster, there may be no need for Miss Grafton to know what it is, but if you want my assistance in lifting suspicion from your friend, it's essential that you hide nothing from me."

"Yes, yes, I can see that," Brewster responded weakly.

"Very well, out with it. What is it that Mallet does not know?"

"Just this: Dick *was* in London that night."

MacNab drew back as if struck. A silence followed in which the soft brushing of Brewster's fingers on the hat was quite audible. At last MacNab broke the silence.

"You are sure of that?"

"I saw him."

The detective rose, and walked slowly away to the window. There he stood looking out, twisting the blind cord round and round his forefinger, but as little conscious of what he did as he was of the twinkling lights opposite or the gleam of the river below. And all the time Brewster's anxious eyes remained fixed on MacNab's back. At last he could stand the uncertainty no longer.

"I simply couldn't tell Mallet that, you know," he said.

MacNab dropped the cord and faced him.

"That rather looks as if in your own mind you weren't so sure of this man's innocence after all," he said.

Owen Brewster looked horrified.

"No, no," he cried. "Good God! Dick never did it. I know him, and I swear to you I wouldn't be here if I thought that. I believe in Dick. Yes, believe in him so much that I'd have to see him do it before I could believe it. It's not that. It's— it's—well—I knew that if I told Mallet what I've just told you, I'd have as good as put the rope round Dick's neck." He came a step closer. "And no one surely would expect me to do that?"

"No," MacNab admitted, "you were not bound to volunteer the information, and I suppose Mallet never questioned you on the point."

"He did not. But if he had I wouldn't tell him," Brewster declared, apparently thrilled by MacNab's concession, judging from his tone that he had won him over. And Brewster was right. MacNab's fancy was taken by the case. For once in a way his mind would be directed not on fastening a rope round a guilty man's neck but on preventing that rope from going round the neck of an innocent man.

He returned and sat down again. The almost breathless anxiety of the young man while the decision hung in the balance had brought him forward to the edge of his chair. His very attitude suggested it was his conviction that his friend's life depended on MacNab's decision.

MacNab nearly smiled at such innocent flattery.

"Very well," he said. "I'll do what I can."

Brewster sat back with a great sigh of relief.

"Thank God for that!" he said.

"Provided you undertake to assist me."

Brewster's tension relaxed: he laughed.

"Oh, I'll play Watson to you all right," he nodded.

MacNab did not laugh, but a queer sort of smile momentarily darkened his lips.

"Wasn't Watson rather a fool?" he suggested. "You'll have to do better than him if we're to clear your friend."

At first Brewster seemed to be hurt. He sat silent for a moment. Then he said rather humbly as MacNab rose to switch on the light:

"I can supply the facts: you can make the inferences."

Only when MacNab had drawn up his table and got at writing materials did he reply.

"Good," he said heartily as he began to write. "By the way, who is employing me? Miss Grafton, I suppose?"

"Yes. Sorry she wouldn't come herself: but she's down there at Lymington with Dick. What ought we to do first?"

"How is Dick?"

"Oh, better. If he hasn't had a relapse after what the police put him through."

"Well, the first thing is to go and see him. We'll give him another night's rest and go down tomorrow. Now for the facts as you know them."

Brewster undoubtedly took comfort from the other's decisive tone. Even his attitude conveyed his sense of relief. For he sat at ease now, hands clasping his knees and his chin resting thoughtfully on the top of his hat till he had made up his mind where and how to begin.

CHAPTER II
In Town That Night

THEY REACHED THE HOSPITAL NEXT MORNING SOON
after ten. Brewster's spirits had been rising from the time he
met MacNab at Waterloo. The nurse in charge made some
demur about the early hour, but gave way to Brewster's plea
of urgency so far as to go in and inform Miss Grafton, who
was with the patient.

Presently, while they stood in the corridor, Margery
Grafton herself emerged from a door on the left. MacNab,
of course, knew young Dodsley, but this was his first sight of
his fiancée. She was a girl of medium height, with fair hair, as
MacNab saw when she crossed the shaft of sunlight in passing one of the windows. And for all her sedentary occupation,
in her upright carriage as well as the quickness and ease with
which she moved, there was a suggestion of an active, outdoor
life. A smile broke over her face as she came towards them.

"So you managed to get him, Owen," she said, throwing out her left hand in an impulsive gesture of gratitude
to Brewster. Brewster took the hand in both of his, and
MacNab saw that Miss Grafton had been crying.

"Oh, Margery, they haven't been here again, have they?" Brewster whispered.

Releasing her hand to get at her handkerchief, the girl shook her head.

"No, it's not that. It's—it's just all of it," she said brokenly.

"How is he?" MacNab asked. "Do you think he can see us?"

"Oh, yes," she replied after a moment. "He's allowed to see people now, but not more than two at a time and not for more than ten minutes."

The room into which MacNab and Brewster were shown was small but bright with subdued sunlight. Dodsley, his head swathed in bandages, recognised MacNab as he stood over him by a weakly lifted hand and the ghost of a smile. Brewster, who just before they entered had whispered, while taking out his watch to register the time, that internal injuries were now suspected, stood back to allow MacNab exclusive use of the permitted time.

MacNab was ready with the questions to which he needed answers. Since Brewster left him on the previous night he had done some hard thinking, and on one vital point at least he had arrived at a definite conclusion. Holding, as he did, that there must be some connection between the murder of Dodsley and the disappearance of the books from his shop, his conclusion was that Dick Dodsley—less than any other living person—lay open to suspicion. Since, being his uncle's heir, there was no sense in stealing the books if he meant to murder him.

Against this conclusion there was, however, one possibility: the nephew might have committed the crime in a moment of sudden passion. Yet MacNab, impressed by all he had heard from Brewster about his friend, regarded this as unlikely. Brewster knew him well, and Brewster believed in his innocence, although he had seen him on a bus in town on the night of the crime. If the fact had come to the police, if that was the new evidence which, in the stop-press phrase, removed the murder out of the class of squalid crimes to which it seemed at first to belong, things looked pretty bad for young Dodsley. MacNab bent towards the white face on the pillow.

"Where did you usually put your key after you'd opened the shop?" he asked.

That Dodsley showed no surprise at the abrupt question was probably a symptom of his weak condition.

"Kept it in my pocket," he replied after thinking hard.

"Which pocket?"

"Oh, any one in my coat, you know."

"The coat you wore in the shop?"

"No, the jacket I came in, of course."

"And where did you put that one when you had your shop one on?"

Dodsley sighed as if already weary.

"Where I changed, of course, in the office. Hung the one up when I took the other down. On nail, you know, behind the cupboard door."

MacNab let him rest undisturbed for a moment. This was good enough, for it looked as if the key could be got at, though scarcely by a customer, since only assistants in the shop could have any excuse for entering the office.

"Who was in charge of the office when Mr. Dodsley went for lunch?"

"Nobody specially. But Carter was always in the back, you know—his department."

"He knew that side of the business well?"

"Lord, yes! Frightfully keen chap, Carter." A feeble smile came. "Don't say he knew literary value of the old stuff, but he did the commercial down to the last penny. Used to wonder why he didn't set up on his own account."

"Ever ask him why he didn't?"

Dodsley shook his head.

"Not ambitious enough, lacked initiative, perhaps," MacNab suggested.

"Oh, you're out there anyhow," Dodsley murmured with closed eyes. After a moment he added: "It can only be the poor chap hadn't enough capital."

MacNab lifted a chair to the bedside and, seating himself, bent forward. So far satisfied, he had now to touch on that incriminating visit to London on the night of the murder. If the police did not know about that visit already, it was certain, Brewster had assured him on the journey down, that Dick would let it out the first time they questioned him on his movements that night. He was like that, Brewster declared.

"Now about that run up to London." MacNab whispered the words like one who touches on a dangerous secret. Dodsley did not seem to hear, lying with closed eyes, quite still. The words repeated, more distinctly, caused the young man to open his eyes.

"What visit to London?" he asked.

"Why, yours on the night of the—your accident."

Dodsley's eyes left the ceiling and slewing round his head he stared at MacNab.

"What are you talking about?" he asked, almost harshly. "Don't you know I never got there? I left Lymington to get back to town, where I had an appointment; but I took the wrong turning. Then, as I'd lost so much time, I put on the pace, and of course came to a corner I couldn't get round."

"But that was on the return journey, wasn't it?"

The suggestion did more than irritate the sick man. He half raised himself on his elbow and the bandaged head nodded a vigorous denial.

"No! I didn't intend to return here. I was going home, I tell you. My time was up. I—I—" He sank back, breathing heavily.

"I see," MacNab said reassuringly. "Yes, I see." Then the nurse, alarmed by the raised voice of her patient, hurried in to protect him. Sitting back, MacNab looked over to where Brewster stood. He felt sorry for Owen Brewster. No need to persuade Dodsley to keep silent about that visit to town on the night of the murder! Young Dick's ideals were not quite so high-pitched as his friend supposed. Still, he liked Brewster all the more for believing his friend capable of reckless honesty and fearless candour. But young Dick wasn't so reckless as all that. The denial, of course, came from his perception of the danger in which that run up to town had placed him. That was all. But he must warn him of the risk to which such a denial laid him open if the police could prove he was in town that night. Others besides Brewster might have seen him. A young fool Dick certainly was, but not the kind of fool Brewster supposed.

While the frowning nurse was calming her agitated patient and smoothing down his pillow, MacNab stepped over to the window. Brewster turned from it, a deprecating, half apologetic, half imploring look in his eyes.

"He's not himself yet, you know," he murmured.

"Oh, I quite understand," MacNab agreed.

"As a matter of fact," Brewster whispered eagerly, "severe concussion often suspends, or even destroys, memory of past events."

The nurse approached with eyes sparkling and a hand pointing to the door.

"Would you mind?" she said.

Outside in the corridor they found Miss Grafton talking to a big man while another man, obviously a policeman in plain clothes, hovered in the background. Miss Grafton looked anxious and distressed. When the big man turned, MacNab recognised Chief Inspector Mallet. Mallet greeted him affably:

"Just heard you were here," he smiled. "Not still after these books, are you?"

"Something like that," MacNab replied. "You still collecting hair clips and match ends?"

"Oh, we've got beyond that," Mallet said; "it's bus tickets and keys now." Turning to Brewster he nodded along the corridor: "How did you find him today?"

Brewster shook his head in a manner that made words unnecessary.

"Oh," Mallet said, "we won't disturb him. Just want to have a look at him. Come on, Roberts." He beckoned to the other man and moved off. They stood watching till the two, after some protest from the nurse, disappeared into the room. When Margery Grafton tiptoed off to put her ear to the door, Brewster, trembling and white with indignation, drew MacNab aside.

"You see how it is," he said. "The blighters still think Dick was in it."

MacNab, who had read Roberts's report, divined the purpose for which the constable had been brought there. But he was mystified by Mallet's reference to bus tickets. If Roberts could identify Dodsley as the young man met near the shop, and if Dick persisted in denying he had been in town that night, then the case would look black indeed against him. Brewster started off to lead the girl away from the door; but MacNab stopped him.

"Let her stay," he said. "She's doing better than she knows."

Hastily he explained the danger of another denial by Dick. Brewster was quick to take the point.

"Wouldn't it be better if we told them about the visit?" he suggested. "They could see his present condition explains his denying he was in town. Later, it might be too late."

MacNab hesitated. It was quite true that if Mallet were made to realise the young man's present incapacity, his denial would not have so much weight subsequently as evidence against him. And Mallet at the moment had but one thought in his mind—to get him identified by Roberts. But he rejected the suggestion. If the worst came to the worst, the medical witnesses could protect Dodsley. And if Roberts failed to identify his man, it would be an ill service on their part to supply Mallet with evidence against a man both believed to be innocent.

Turning her head to apply the other ear to the door Margery Grafton saw them watching her. After a little she left her post and returned, shaking her head.

"I couldn't hear," she said.

"But you heard them speak to him?"

"Oh, yes, but not what was said."

She saw, and was surprised by, his look of relief.

"That means," he explained, "the officer did not recognise him at sight, and the inspector tried for his voice."

The cloud lifted from Brewster in turn.

"He won't remember that any more than his face," he said confidently. "Poor old Dick, he's not himself yet, even less so in voice than in appearance."

"And he's not likely to admit now what he denied ten minutes ago," MacNab added.

But when Miss Grafton pressed for an explanation, Brewster suggested that, as they had so much to talk about, they had better adjourn to the rooms she had in a neighbouring house. The house stood a little nearer the main road. Once in the sitting-room Miss Grafton was soon acquainted with Roberts's encounter with the young man who was suspected of some connection with the crime.

"Ridiculous," she cried, "when he was lying unconscious on the roadside at the time. And as against that all they had to go on was the fact that he was engaged to me!"

To Brewster's lifted inquiring eyebrows, MacNab replied by a surreptitious shake of the head. It would be as well if she did not know yet the accident must have occurred not on the way to but on the return from London. Brewster turned towards her as she stood looking out the window towards the little hospital.

"Shows how hard put they are," he remarked. "I've a notion they first suspected that young man to be George."

She wheeled quickly.

"Because he's my brother. Don't you see what that means? I was right: they think I'm in it too."

MacNab tried a natural explanation.

"They are working on the assumption that a man and a woman were in it."

This brought to light the detective story–writer in Margery Grafton.

"Yes," she flashed at him, "and you observe, the woman suspected remains the same, though the man varies, though he must always be some one connected with her." She laughed harshly, turning to Brewster. "Wait, Owen, you'll see! When they drop Dick, they'll be on either you or Father."

"Oh, come, come," MacNab protested. "This takes us nowhere. So far as I can judge, Mallet is right in holding old Mr. Dodsley was murdered by a man and woman acting in collaboration. He's only wrong about who they are. Our job is to get his nose on to the right scent."

After that they put their heads together in a consultation that lasted almost two hours. Ultimately it was broken up by an exclamation from Miss Grafton who had placed her chair in a position which let her see a section of the road. When the two men followed her to the window, they saw Inspector Mallet and Constable Roberts making their way towards the town. MacNab's attention went to the constable and so evidently had Miss Grafton's.

"Ah," she whispered, "doesn't he look rather dejected?"

MacNab agreed. Roberts, from his hang-dog bearing looked as if he were all too conscious of having disappointed the big Scotland Yard man.

No sooner had they turned the corner than Miss Grafton, saying she must know in what state they had left Dick, made for the door. MacNab took the chance her absence offered.

"Are you quite sure he was the man you saw?" he asked.

"Oh, quite sure—unfortunately," Brewster admitted.

"When and where was it?"

"Just before eleven. Mr. Grafton had sent me for some papers he needed, and I got back to the House while the half-hour was striking."

"That's near enough. Well?"

"I was standing just opposite Grosvenor Road, trying to pick up a taxi when I caught sight of him in a passing bus."

Brewster paused, himself startled by the way in which his words had startled his listener.

"A bus?" MacNab repeated.

"Why, yes—a bus going towards Piccadilly," Brewster said inquiringly.

"Go on," MacNab nodded.

"He was sitting in the near-side corner at the back. The bus was almost empty or I might not have noticed him. In fact I didn't till he turned his face to look out while the bus was passing a lamp. At first I thought he had seen me, and on the impulse waved to him. But of course, though he was quite recognisable in the lighted interior, I must have been almost invisible on the pavement."

"Could you tell where that bus had come from?"

"No; but I did notice it was a number 9 as it passed the lamp."

MacNab's hand thumped the table.

"Good for you, Watson!" he cried.

Brewster's jaw almost dropped in astonishment.

"Why—what—what d'ye mean?" he breathed.

"You've just shown me where to look for an alternative suspect."

This certainly did not lessen young Brewster's surprise.

"To Dick?" he almost gasped.

"Just that! A man with equal opportunity and a stronger motive for putting the old man out of the way. Listen! You heard Mallet chaff me by telling me he'd taken up bus tickets and dropped hair clips?"

"I did, but I failed to see the point."

"Never mind what he meant. I didn't know myself what he meant. But when you told me just now it was in a bus you had seen Dick that seemed to me almost to clinch the case against him—especially as Mallet himself had become interested in bus tickets."

"Quite," Brewster impatiently agreed; "but you're in this affair to free Dick, not to get him convicted."

MacNab's eyes brightened with appreciation at Brewster's hard stare of distrust.

"And when we do free him, I'll tell him how much he owes to you."

"To me? For Heaven's sake, be more explicit," Brewster begged.

MacNab, sitting back, crossed his legs comfortably.

"Here's the case. Mr. Dodsley's shop on the night of the murder was entered by a man and a woman who had possession of a key and who knew he was coming there himself. They stood between the projecting shelves of the back shop till he arrived. He passed them in the dark, entered his office, switched on the light and, sitting down at his desk, continued work on a book catalogue for which the printer was clamouring. Then the man slipped outside and the woman entered the office, possibly after some talk, while the man remained on the watch in the shop, shot him, as his watch proved to us, at 3.4 precisely."

Brewster betrayed impatience at the slowness with which his detective approached the point which would explain how he himself had been so helpful. At least it looked as if he found it hard to hide, for he rose and walked over to stare through the window. But his impatient irritation seemed to diminish as he appreciated how, after all, a detective must love to linger over the details of a case which was going well. The particularity with which the time was stated tickled his fancy, and his impatience vanished.

"Now," MacNab began after a pause, "the two big facts

so far are—one, these people knew Dodsley would come to his shop at that unusual hour, and two, they had a key to the shop."

Brewster turned.

"And poor old Dick 'answers to the description,' as the police say?"

MacNab waved an appreciative hand.

"But thanks to you, we have found another who also 'fills the bill,' as the actors say."

"I wish you'd come to that less slowly," Brewster said, returning to reseat himself, with a smile. "My vanity demands satisfaction, you know."

"You heard Dick tell me where he kept his key—in the pocket of a coat which hung behind a cupboard door in the office?" In response to Brewster's affirmative nod he went on: "Carter who worked in the back shop could get at the key."

"Yes—but—"

"One minute! You remember my asking why, if Carter was so keen and ambitious as Dick said, he didn't set up on his own account?"

"Of course I do. Especially as at the time I had an idea you thought Dick might be trying to throw suspicion on Carter."

"You noticed, then, his reply?"

"Want of capital."

"Very well. Books of enough value to set up any dealer had been disappearing from the shop over a period of some weeks."

"But is there anything to show Carter took them?"

"Nothing at all. But there was no point in Dick's taking them if he meant to kill his uncle," MacNab said quickly.

Brewster had no need to ponder over this point.

"If there is any connection between the crime and the thefts," he said.

"Good, Watson, good indeed!" MacNab said. "You've put your finger on the weak spot. In fact, so far you're a much better Watson than I am a Holmes. You see," he explained with a sigh, "I quite failed to detect even the book thief."

"But you think Carter was providing himself with capital by stealing the books?"

"No, I don't say that. What I say is that the thefts could provide the capital, and that Carter knew Mr. Dodsley would be working late that night on the new catalogue."

"But you say I helped you to make more sure of Carter?"

"Not quite that. What you did was to make me—well— comprehend why the police have become interested in bus tickets."

Again Brewster jumped to his feet. Near the window he turned: "You know you are devilish tantalising, MacNab," he cried.

MacNab liked the way his surname was used.

"Sorry," he said, "but since you yourself took on the rôle of Watson, I'm trying to play up to you in the part of Holmes."

Brewster laughed good-humouredly, as he glanced along the road towards the hospital.

"You want me to guess why the police are after bus tickets and then laugh me to scorn, I suppose? Well, I won't do it."

MacNab remained silent so long over this rebuff that Brewster, taking note of it, turned at last to see what had happened.

"Mr. Brewster," he heard in a new tone, "you saw our young friend in a number 9 bus. Do you know where that bus came from?"

"No idea."

"Hammersmith."

"Hammersmith?" Brewster's forehead wrinkled as drawn by the other's serious tone he came and sat down. "Let me see. That's somewhere on the road out of town, isn't it?"

"Yes, you pass through it going by road from here."

"Good Lord!" Brewster whispered aghast. "I remember, a frightfully congested place."

"Exactly. And just the place where it would be prudent to leave your motor-cycle in a garage and finish in a bus."

Owen Brewster bowed his head in horror. MacNab stretched out a hand and touched him gently.

"It's not so bad as all that," he said. "Carter uses the Hammersmith bus far more often. He lives there, you know."

Brewster lifted his head to stare at the man opposite.

"I suppose you're going to laugh at me for not seeing what point that has," he said. "But laugh if you like, for I'm damned if I do, since I don't see how this is going to help Dick Dodsley."

MacNab studied the flushed and angry young man with kindly eyes.

"Mr. Brewster," he said, as he looked at his watch, "your imagination does more honour to your heart than to your head. I'll explain on the way back to town. We've just got ten minutes to catch our train."

Brewster looked at him doubtfully.

"I'll have to come on later," he said. "I can't leave like this, without knowing what the two got out of Dick."

When MacNab reached the bottom of the road he noticed a man moving along the footpath on the farther side of the main road. Apart from the peculiar way in which the man stared across at him, MacNab was taken by his carriage and leisurely pace. Dropping his handkerchief, after turning towards the town, he cast, in picking it up, a momentary glance back which confirmed his guess. The man was coming back again across the entrance to the hospital road. So they were keeping the hospital under observation! Did Mallet, then, believe the young man was not so ill as he pretended to be? Did they think he was play-acting only? Well, if Roberts had, after all, identified Dodsley as the young man who had fooled him on the night of the murder, the precaution did not seem overdone. But surely the doctors or even the nurse could have reassured him as to that.

Passing down the picturesque old High Street towards the station, MacNab's thought reverted to bus tickets. If Mallet had come on a bus ticket somewhere in the shop, its significance, if it had any, ought to have pointed to Carter rather than the dead man's nephew. No doubt Mallet had established the date on which the ticket was used. But Mallet must know that Carter travelled on a number 9 or some other Hammersmith bus every day. He must try to see Mallet about this. He would go round and see him that evening, before Brewster came, as arranged, about nine on his return to town. And in the interval he would call in at the bookshop where business was now being carried on as usual under the management of Mr. Carter, assisted by Miss Preedy and Miss Jenks.

CHAPTER III
MacNab Gets Something

SOON AFTER FOUR MACNAB STROLLED INTO THE SHOP. They did not seem to be very busy. He was mildly surprised, however, to find Mr. Carter had installed Miss Preedy in the second-hand department while Miss Jenks carried on in the front, he himself moving from one department to the other, as need arose. Miss Jenks, who had the front to herself when he entered, explained the new arrangement to him as he pulled up to renew acquaintance. From the glances she cast at the entrance to the back shop while speaking, MacNab gathered that bad feeling had developed between her and Miss Preedy. Her sallow face flushed and the wisp of black hair held by the hair slide above her ear bobbed as her head nodded, her indignation growing in the telling.

"She's not fit to be there," she declared. "She's not suited."

Remembering Miss Preedy's taste in bright clothes as well as her blonde hair and highly coloured cheeks and lips, MacNab agreed.

"Well, she does look rather new, doesn't she?" he said.

Miss Jenks sniffed.

"New?" she said. "Yes, perhaps, but only as a remainder is."

He waited while she attended to a couple of customers. He was deeply interested.

"Likely to be more work for you here," she remarked darkly as soon as she returned. He saw she judged him to be obtuse.

"For me? Why, what kind of work?"

"Oh, it didn't take me long to guess what you were doing here a few weeks back."

He smiled his admiration.

"Looks as if Mr. Dodsley should have put you on the job. I was a complete failure, you know," he admitted, while watching her entering something in a ledger. "That's what makes me wonder why Miss Grafton employs me now," he added. He saw the pen stop in the middle of a word. Her eyes came up.

"*She* employs you? What for?"

He bent confidentially forward.

"For the nephew's protection. The police suspect him, you know."

"Suspect Dick?" she gasped. "She—*she* employs you?"

"In his interest," he nodded.

She was staggered for a moment.

"My God, but that was clever of her." Miss Jenks's voice was almost hushed in admiration. He smiled with self-conscious deprecation.

"Oh, I don't know. After all, I quite failed with the books, you know."

Her dark eyes flashed contempt.

"I didn't mean *you*. Only that it was clever of her of all people, to seem anxious for help in his interests."

"Oh, but she is, I assure you. I ought to know, for I've just returned from Lymington, where she's looking after him."

The quiet confidence with which he spoke exasperated her.

"It's all humbug," she said. "I ought to know, for I heard them quarrel, standing where I am now. That's why they parted. That's why he went away. That's—"

"Quarrel?" he said. "Oh, I can't believe that, Miss Jenks. Why if you'd seen how—oh, you must be mistaken."

Her next action was unexpected. Without a word she stalked to the other side of the shop, picked up a book and carrying it by the tips of finger and thumb as if it were something slimy, held it up to him.

"What's this?" he asked.

"What they quarrelled over: *Death at the Desk*."

"By M. G. Grafton!"

"Yes." She indicated the back shop. "He's got in a stock of two hundred, and we haven't sold a single copy yet."

"You mean Mr. Carter?"

"I do. He's clever if you like. About books anyway, if not about women. He's laid up fifty for sale as first editions later on when the demand comes." Seeing him standing mystified she added, "As it will with a rush whenever the book's connection with the death of Mr. Dodsley is known."

"Dear me," MacNab ejaculated, staring at the prone figure of the murdered bookmaker on the jacket. "Why it might be Mr. Dodsley himself, except, of course, that any old man with that neat grey beard would look like him."

She followed his pointing finger.

"Well, yes, now that beards are no longer worn," she admitted.

MacNab suppressed a smile.

"And he didn't smoke," he said, pointing to the cigarette case, part of which was visible near the dead man's head. "So, of course, that case must have been dropped by the murderer."

"It says nothing about any cigarette case in the story," she snapped impatiently. "If I was you I'd not bother so much about its outside."

"You've read it then?"

"More than once, cover to cover, after I heard them fall out in there."

"About the story?"

"Yes. She flared out at him when Dick said the murder couldn't be done like what she'd put it in the story. But that's nothing—she just wanted to hurt him. If it hadn't been one thing it would have been another."

"Well, if this is all true—"

"True?" she flamed out. "You think I'm making it up?"

He made haste to smooth her down.

"Oh, I only meant if you were right in thinking there's a connection between the crime and this story—not about the quarrel. Still, I suppose nobody but yourself would have overheard the quarrel."

"Why should you suppose that?" she asked tartly.

"Well, people don't usually do it in public, you know."

"With her temper the way it was then, she'd not have cared who heard her. But she didn't know I'd heard it. She thought I'd gone to lunch. And Mr. Kendrew, he took so long standing brooding over the book, she'd never know he was there either."

"Mr. Kendrew—who's he? A regular customer, I suppose."

"You suppose right this time. We know him here, not because like a lot more, he's not much of a buyer, but because he's an M.P."

MacNab held up *Death at the Desk*.

"And nobody so far has bought it?"

"Not yet. But they'll soon be scrambling for it."

"Well, I'll be the first with this copy." Then he added while she got his change: "Perhaps I might have a word or two about it with Mr. Carter."

She shook her head while counting the money into his palm.

"He's away till tomorrow—at a big sale in Birmingham."

His next question was the kind of casual utterance one might make off-hand at such a moment.

"And you are in charge while he's away."

"Only so far as locking-up and opening goes. He's not such a fool as to leave that to *her*," she replied, "not after the lock went out of order."

On his way to the door he stood aside to allow a customer to enter, and then turned to examine the volumes on the shelf by the door. Taking down a book at random he turned its pages with unseeing eyes while the customer haggled and debated with Miss Jenks. He had got to find out what Miss Jenks meant about the lock. Easily though he had divined that Miss Jenks was jealous of Miss Preedy for business reasons only, Miss Jenks was not in love with Carter. Her passion centred on Dick Dodsley. That only would account for the fact that while she merely despised the Preedy girl, she hated Miss Grafton. But he must find out why Preedy could not be entrusted with the keys of the shop. He was still intently absorbed in *The Keys of the Kingdom*: sermons by the Rev. John Purdy, D.D. when Miss Jenks, the customer gone, sauntered up to look over his shoulder.

"Interested in sermons?" she inquired.

"Well, professionally I'm more interested in keys," he replied with a smile.

"Yes, I noticed how you stopped when I mentioned the

lock," she said. "But there's nothing in it. The real key to your problem you'll find in the novel."

Sure that she only meant there was nothing in it that could direct suspicion towards Miss Grafton, he said invitingly as he replaced the volume.

"Still, I'd like to hear what happened to the lock."

"Oh, it simply—well—collapsed, I suppose you might call it. That happened last Wednesday when Mr. Carter was away at another sale and Miss Preedy left the key at home. I had a few things to say to her while she fumbled among her lip-sticks and salves for, being late, she'd kept me waiting at the door. Then, to show you the kind of fool she is, when I told her it was a Yale lock and she'd better go back home for the key, what does she do but cry out she knew a man in Crown Court who had a Yale lock to his flat and ran off to catch him before he went out. I let her go. If that was all she knew about Yale locks, she'd better have her lesson.

"In ten minutes she was back with a key in her hand and a smile as broad as any open door. This was going to be a lesson to Mr. Carter, I thought to myself—to trust the likes of her with a key of the shop. And then, just as I was wondering how he'd look when he heard of it, she pops in her friend's key and throws open the door."

"What!" MacNab cried incredulously.

"She pops in his key and opens the door," Miss Jenks repeated impressively, stressing each word. "Oh, of course, it was something inside the lock that had got broken and allowed the key to turn. But it was only a fool like her that would have done a thing like that and so find it out. Mr. Carter was so upset when he heard about it. He had the lock changed at once and handed over the key to me."

MacNab waved an appreciative hand. "Very sensible of

Mr. Carter. And now, of course, the shop is opened to the minute," he remarked.

Miss Jenks, however, had still her grievance.

"But fancy leaving *her* in charge behind. She knows no more about rare books than she knows about Yale locks."

Miss Jenks had given MacNab something to think about as he walked back to the Adelphi. He was deeply interested in that curious incident connected with the Yale lock, to which Miss Jenks herself attached no importance. Of course it was quite natural that Mr. Carter should be upset by the discovery of the lock's condition. Being in charge of the business for the time being it was a serious matter for him that the shop could apparently be entered by any one who had a key which could enter the lock. But how long had it been in that condition? That was another question he would put to Inspector Mallet later on. As for the suggestions the girl had made about *Death at the Desk*, MacNab dismissed them as fantastic notions, bred by her hatred and jealousy of Miss Grafton. What alone interested him about the book was the fact that Mr. Carter had laid in a stock of two hundred copies, for that at least proved that Mr. Carter, for some reason known to himself, anticipated a heavy demand for the book later on.

With his thoughts still whirling, MacNab arrived at his flat to find young Brewster already there. He seemed excited and came towards MacNab like a man who has had to suppress bad news overlong. No greeting passed; Brewster, as it were, flinging his news straight into MacNab's face.

"They're going to arrest Dick as soon as he's fit to move."

MacNab pushed him into a chair.

"Sit down and tell me how you know that."

"They've got a man watching outside the hospital. They

came back, you know, after you left, to put poor Margery through it again. It seems George has made an ass of himself—told them some lie, thinking he would save her from being troubled. And they know he wasn't telling the truth."

"You know what the lie was?"

Brewster nodded.

"He denied being with Margery outside the shop in his lunch hour on the day of Dodsley's death, and she admitted being there with him. That was nothing in itself, but it opened the flood-gates on poor Margery."

"She told you all about it?"

"As much as she could, but she came back in an almost dazed condition. She was, in fact, almost incoherent in her terror."

MacNab looked up sharply.

"Terror?" he repeated incredulously.

Brewster faced him with misery in his eyes.

"You think that an exaggeration? There's no other word to describe her condition. Margery's not easily frightened. Not the sort to wring her hands or take to hysterics. If she got her good looks from her mother, she has got her father's courage and grit." Impulsively he seized MacNab's arm. "Look here, this can't go on. Something must be done at once. We've got to get hold of something tangible—to put that damned, stupid, pig-headed inspector's nose on the right scent."

In the convulsively trembling hand gripping his biceps, MacNab detected the measure of the young man's sympathy and anxiety for Margery Grafton. Laying his free hand gently on Owen Brewster's shoulder, he pushed him back into a chair.

"Listen to me," he said. "Things aren't so black against

young Dodsley as she seems to think. Mallet is pushing her because he is certain there was a woman in it. So am I, for that matter. But Mallet is wrong both about the man and the woman. We've simply, as you said, got to put his nose on the right scent, and he'll do the rest."

Brewster, more self-controlled, sat forward.

"He seems to think Margery met Dick in the shop that night after I'd left her at the club. God knows why he does."

"Did she tell you that?"

"No; that's what I gathered from the questions he put to her. Oh, very politely. He—he had her novel—produced it from his pocket unexpectedly. And then proceeded to take her through it, point by point, comparing the story with the actual crime and begging her, as an authority in that sort of thing, to suggest to him where the murderer had made a mistake in the Dodsley case. And, of course, she couldn't do it. And so the questioning went on—the same thing over and over again. But the one thing about which she seems certain is that Mallet suspects that Dick was in London that night."

"Well," MacNab said, "Mallet could get nothing out of her to corroborate that suspicion except through you."

"No, but the persistent devil would have got it out of her if I had told her," Brewster admitted.

MacNab pondered for a minute. Then he said:

"And Dick must have denied it to Mallet, as he did to me."

The reminder pained Brewster. He jumped to his feet resentfully.

"Dick would be the last man to make the denial had he been himself," he said with heat. "He would have told the truth and damned the consequences."

MacNab, whose mind had turned to the girl distraught

with fear for her lover, allowed Brewster to work off his heat by pacing about the room. Dodsley, of course, could not have admitted to Mallet that he had been in town that night, otherwise Mallet would have had no need to question Margery Grafton so relentlessly on that point. But had Mallet found some one who, like Brewster, had chanced to see Dick somewhere in town that night? If so, his cross-questioning of the girl would mean that he suspected her to be the woman in the case. He must see Mallet. After all, even if Mallet had established the fact that Dick had been in London at the time his uncle was murdered, his denial by itself proved nothing against him, since any doctor would be ready enough to testify that a temporary loss of memory was a frequent consequence of severe cerebral concussion. But it would certainly be very awkward if when Dick Dodsley's memory returned, he admitted being in town that night. And from what Brewster said of him, there was no doubt that he would admit the visit, whatever the consequences. MacNab turned to Brewster who stood rather dejectedly gazing out of the window.

"Look here," he cried briskly, "before your friend's memory returns, we've got to put our hands on the man who murdered his uncle."

Brewster, who had faced round and brightened up at the purposeful tone, approached the table.

"Well," he said, "to do that would be the best we could do for Dick. But how can we?"

"Oh, I think we can if you and I lay our heads together," MacNab said encouragingly. "No need to be downhearted yet."

Brewster slipped more hopefully into a chair.

"Oh, if we could! It's Margery I'm thinking of. She's nearly broken, you know," he said.

MacNab seemed much moved by the young man's concern.

He stopped turning the pages of his notebook as if Brewster's hopeful exclamation had given his thoughts a new turn.

"What about her father?" he asked. "He must know the trouble she's in."

"He does. But they're not on good terms. And as it's chiefly over her association with Dick, his attitude now is— well—pretty much that of her stepmother, who says the only thing for people in their position to do with a girl who has so disgraced them is to let it be known that they had washed their hands of her."

MacNab sat up in his surprise.

"But you," he said, "you are his secretary."

Brewster smiled bitterly.

"You mean Grafton's likely to—well—resent my acting in the matter? That's quite likely. And he can damage me." Brewster, pausing, stretched his hands thoughtfully over the polished surface of the table. "Of course I have my ambitions. Who hasn't? I want to enter Parliament. And that is where Mr. Grafton could help me. Make it, indeed, a certainty. Possibly he won't now. But what was I to do? Margery is my friend and so is Dick. In fact, they'd never have met but for me."

MacNab's sympathy impelled him to stretch out his own hand and touch Brewster's gently.

"Your loyalty does you honour," he said. "And I don't doubt that in the end Mr. Grafton will come to recognise you could have done him no better service than that of freeing his daughter and young Dodsley from any connection with this brutal murder."

Brewster grasped the hand laid on his own and squeezed it with almost convulsive gratitude.

"Thank you," he cried, "thank you." Then, as if embarrassed by such a display of his emotion, dropped the hand as he added: "But how are we to fasten the crime on any one else if the only key was in Dick's possession?"

"And the shop wasn't broken into you mean? Well, the murderer might have gone there by appointment."

The suggestion startled Brewster.

"Is there anything to show he did?"

"Nothing at all. But Inspector Mallet has evidence that there were two people already in the shop waiting for Dodsley's return to complete a catalogue for which the printer was waiting."

Brewster's forehead furrowed.

"Two?" he repeated. "Is that certain?"

"A man and a woman."

"Then they must have known he was coming and they must have had a key."

MacNab smiled his appreciation.

"Good again, Watson," he said. "Your finger has gone to the salient points."

"But there was only Dick's key."

"Ah," MacNab nodded, as he glanced at the clock, "that's what I'm going to see Mallet about. And I fancy he'd be glad if I saw him before he puts in his daily report to the commissioner."

"About the key?"

"Something that widens the field indefinitely."

Brewster's eyes dilated with surprise and pleasure.

"Please Holmes, tell me all about it," he pleaded. "This is great news."

MacNab laughed.

"If you remember, Watson, I never took your views on any half-established facts. In any case I must see Mallet first."

Brewster protested:

"But surely you can tell me."

"No," MacNab cut in, getting to his feet. "Not yet. Afterwards."

"After what? My God, MacNab, you can at least be quite as irritating and aggravating as Sherlock himself ever was."

"Thank you, Brewster. It's something to me to resemble that great man, even in his defects."

Brewster's petulance gave way as he got to his feet.

"Oh, go to the devil," he said with a laugh. "I see you've got something good, anyway."

"Yes, I think so. But I mean to keep it up my sleeve till I'm sure a young woman hasn't been telling me lies, and for that I'll have to go to the House of Commons."

Brewster almost dropped his hat.

"Eh," he cried, "go to the House?" Then perceiving that MacNab did not mean to enlighten him, his youthful impatience boiled over again. "Oh, go to the devil," he repeated violently, and suddenly started for the door. But MacNab intercepted him.

"Look here, Brewster," he said quietly. "The best service you can do your friend Dick is to return to Lymington by the next train and watch over him."

Influenced by the other's new and serious tone, Brewster ceased his attempts to push his way past MacNab.

"Watch over him?"

"Yes, watch over him like a father. Then the moment he shows you he recalls what happened before his crash, let me know. That's your share in the work for the moment."

Brewster, turning his hat in his hand, considered this thoughtfully.

"It's a pretty inactive rôle," he complained.

MacNab patted his shoulder.

"But absolutely essential. Leave the rest to me. You'll have enough of the active stuff later on, I promise you."

Brewster sighed.

"All right," he said resignedly. "I see what you mean. It's this interval, before Dick remembers the past and admits being in town that you need to get on the track of the real man."

"Something like that. And you can tell Miss Grafton from me that with the help you have given me, I have every hope of getting him."

With that he pushed his over-zealous young assistant to the door and got ready for his call on Chief Inspector Mallet.

CHAPTER IV
MacNab at the Yard

MALLET WAS BUSY WITH HIS NOTES WHEN MACNAB'S name came up on the 'phone. So busy, indeed, that Detective-Sergeant Crabb, who took the message, hesitated before putting the request for an interview before his superior. Mallet himself hesitated. Then he laid down his pen grudgingly.

"All right. Tell them to send him along."

But his greeting was hearty enough.

"So you're back in town. Nice little place, Lymington."

"Yes, I thought so too, though I saw less of it than you."

Sergeant Crabb's minute grunt of disgust drew Mallet's attention.

"Nice place I'd say to recuperate. I'm thinking of sending Crabb there for his throat trouble. Patients in that little hospital seem to do very well."

"If they don't talk too much to their visitors," MacNab agreed.

Mallet laughed as he motioned to a chair.

"Sit down. As a visitor you may talk as much as you like. I

want to hear why you went there, you know, if you're not still after those missing books." Mallet held out the box of cigarettes.

MacNab was not a cigarette smoker, but he accepted the offer and delayed his reply till he applied the match.

"I went there for your protection," he said, depositing the match in the ash tray. Crabb's indrawn breath was quite audible in the momentary silence.

"My protection?" Mallet echoed with a frown.

MacNab nodded.

"I put it like that deliberately," he said.

"Will you explain, please?"

Mallet's tone was curt. All his good humour seemed to have gone. MacNab leant forward.

"As I see it," he said, "you are in grave danger of making a mistake in the matter of young Dodsley. How much you have got against him I do not of course know, but I now know enough of the case to be certain an arrest on a charge of murder would be a blunder for which you would never forgive yourself."

Mallet and Sergeant Crabb exchanged a look. But the tone of extreme gravity with which MacNab spoke had its weight with Mallet. After moving for a moment uneasily in his chair, he sat still, thinking hard, his eyes on the floor. Then he looked up.

"It's very good of you," he said, "to come here and say what you have said; but I suppose you're not here on my behalf exclusively?"

"No; I'm engaged by Miss Grafton in Dodsley's interests. And if he is charged, I think I've made enough points to—well—please any counsel engaged in his defence."

This time Mallet and Sergeant Crabb held each other's eyes for an appreciable time. Then Mallet shook his head.

"My poor chap," he said slowly, "the mistake is yours. You're altogether astray."

The tone of pity, and the condescending smile, brought MacNab out of his chair almost with a bound.

"No," he cried, "I am not wrong. I know the case against Dodsley, and, aware of its strength as well as its weakness, I say it will be met and answered. You are so sure of young Dodsley that you haven't considered the case against any one else."

"Any one else? Who else is there?"

"Well—there's Carter for one."

"Carter? There's no case against Carter."

"Isn't there? I'd have said it was stronger than any you can have against Dodsley."

The emphasis laid on the "you" made Crabb shuffle his feet impatiently. But Mallet's professional pride was piqued, and he rose to the challenge when MacNab followed up with a request for the most damaging fact he had against Dick Dodsley.

"The key," Mallet replied.

MacNab thrilled. So they did not know Dick had been in town on the night of the murder. This was all he had wanted to be sure of.

"The key?" he repeated.

"Dodsley had a key, Carter had not. The person or persons who waited for Mr. Dodsley in the shop must have used a key to enter. And it was not Dodsley's key or he could not himself have entered. Those in the shop locked the door behind them when they entered, lest the officer on his round might find the door open. So they knew both that Dodsley had a key and that he was coming there that night. Now as only two keys existed, and as those two persons entered first, the key used must have been used either by young Dodsley himself, or some one who got it from him."

"Very well," MacNab said. "Couldn't Carter have got—"

But Mallet's impressively upraised hand stopped him. This was what he had waited for.

"The second key was found in the young man's pocket at the hospital."

MacNab dropped the knee he had been so confidently nursing.

"I see," he said. "You assume the key had been placed there by some one else after it had been used."

"Got it at last," Mallet nodded, sitting up straight. Then, leaning forward, he went on: "You surely don't ask us to believe that person was Carter? To assume that would be to assume Carter had foreknowledge of the accident, and had access to young Dodsley's clothes at the hospital next morning, at the very time we were interviewing him in the shop."

Mallet was completely satisfied when he saw the stare of stupefaction his words evoked. Then, while his visitor sat dumb, the grin of satisfaction his devastating conclusion drew from Sergeant Crabb, led Mallet on to add: "The mistake is yours. You interrupted me when I said you were wrong; I was about to tell you we did *not* suspect young Dodsley. We never have, as a matter of fact. You said you came here to save us from making a blunder. That was well intentioned. The least I can do is to return the kindness, by advising you to wash your hands of the whole business."

Mallet stopped twiddling his thumbs and stood up. Crabb moved to open the door. Then MacNab jumped to his feet and gripped the back of his chair.

"Look here," he began, in a voice that made Crabb pull up short, "this, I suppose, is what the stop-press meant by 'developments of a sensational character which lift the bookshop murder out of the class of squalid crimes to which it seemed to belong.' Well, I got something this afternoon which looks like putting it back again."

"What on earth do you mean?" Mallet asked, perturbed by the other's vehemence.

"Any key could have opened the shop door."

"What?"

"At least a chance key used by an idiot assistant did it."

Mallet stepped over and pushed MacNab back into his chair, with hands that almost trembled.

"Sit down and tell us about that," he commanded.

By the time MacNab finished stating the facts about the forgotten key and the changed lock, Mallet's usual imperturbability was far to see.

"Carter ought to have reported this to us at once," he said in a flash of anger.

"Carter again, you see," MacNab could not resist saying as Mallet, hands clasped behind his back, began to pace restlessly about in an attempt to envisage the possibilities of the new situation. But the mere mention of Carter's name appeared to clarify Mallet's mind. He turned swiftly to face MacNab and swung up a clenched fist.

"No! There are too many other established facts for this to affect what we know." The memory of a long line of mechanics at a bench in Topham's garage floated back to him. "If any trick was played with that lock, we can put our hands on the man responsible."

Mallet was angry. Angry with Carter for failing to report the discovery of the lock's inefficiency, and also, less reasonably, with MacNab, for attempting to sow doubts in his mind.

As for MacNab, he left the office satisfied of one fact: Mallet knew nothing of Dick Dodsley's presence in London. More than that: Mallet did not suspect Dick at all. He would be able to tell Brewster that Dick was in no danger of arrest. But would Brewster be so relieved when he learned that Margery Grafton was the new suspect? Suddenly, as he walked along the Embankment, he saw the problem which his young assistant would have to face. He pulled up just short of the railway bridge and, turning to the river, leant his elbows on the parapet to think it out, with nothing but the grey river before his eyes.

Of course, he told himself, it was the problem of the Lady or the Tiger over again. Brewster might have to choose between Dick and Margery. While Dick was in danger he had kept silent about his friend's visit to London. But what would he do if Margery were seriously involved? It looked as if he must either sacrifice Dick to save Margery or sacrifice Margery to save Dick.

At a later period MacNab was to remember this moment when his arms rested on that parapet, and he considered the probabilities while the river was darkening and the lights on the Surrey side began to shine from the houses opposite like little stars. He did not believe the choice would be easy for Owen Brewster. To most men the choice would be simple. Not only chivalry but truth itself ought to weigh the scales. Yet, as MacNab now recalled, Brewster at their first interview had declared with a force that had impressed him, while asserting his friend's innocence, that he himself would lie sooner than tell. And recalling Brewster's passionate outburst: "Good God, Dick never did it. I know him and I'd have to *see* him do it before I could believe it," MacNab shook his head doubtfully at the dark river. Probing for the cause of his disquiet, he found it circled round Margery Grafton herself. Mallet must be in possession of facts about her and her brother George of which he was ignorant. Mallet, indeed, had almost said as much in advising him to wash his hands of the whole business.

That night MacNab did not go to bed till he had finished *Death at the Desk*. It left him more perplexed than ever. But he was fairly sure of one thing: he did not believe that Mallet was yet in possession of evidence sufficient to warrant the arrest of any one for the murder of Richard Dodsley.

CHAPTER V
The Book Dodsley
Did Not Miss

FOR THE NEXT TEN DAYS IT SEEMED THAT HIS CONCLU-
sion was justified. No arrest came. And some of the newspapers, which had whetted their readers' appetites by the
promise of developments of a sensational nature, grew res-
tive. A leader in the *Evening Record*, while admitting that the
recent advance in the modern scientific detection of crime
claimed by Scotland Yard was evidence of good intentions,
yet pessimistically observed that since the bookshop murder
seemed destined to be included in the long list of unsolved
mysteries, the advance made by the Yard in the science of
detection must be much less than the advance made by the
modern criminal in the science of evasion.

MacNab, reading this particular gibe, felt sorry for
Chief Inspector Mallet. He knew what he must be hearing
and feeling at the Yard. In any other profession there are
many degrees of success and failure. A general may even
lose a battle and yet be a glorious soldier. But for a detective, each battle is for him either a complete success or an
utter failure.

MacNab by this time felt able to view the Dodsley case detachedly. He was out of it. Employed by Miss Grafton in her fiancé's interest, his job was over now that the young man had been freed from suspicion. It was no part of his duty to fasten the guilt on any one. Yet that did not prevent him from feeling very uneasy about this strange case. In the interests of justice perhaps it was his duty to assist Mallet. But all he had learned or divined he had got through being employed by Miss Grafton herself, which made it awkward; and anyway, Mallet had shown no desire for his help. Mallet, in fact, had advised him to wash his hands of the case; and he had taken that advice. Still, somehow, MacNab was far from easy in his mind, and this gibe in the *Record* reawakened his disquiet.

He tossed the paper away and stood up to stare at the portrait of John Knox which hung above the fireplace. Visitors, sufficiently intimate, sometimes asked MacNab why he kept that portrait of the fiery old Scots reformer there. MacNab was believed to give a different reason to each inquirer; and no one knew the real reason. "Oh," he said once to a young journalist anxious for personal copy about the Scottish detective, "ye see I just keep him there because he makes me feel hot wi' hate every time I look at him, and then, ye see, there's no need for me to put any more coal on the fire."

As he stood staring unseeingly, he heard his bell ring and presently the door shut as Janet admitted a heavy-footed man to the hall.

MacNab was not altogether surprised to see Mallet, for his thoughts had been on him, but he wondered to see Chief Inspector Mallet carrying an obviously very heavy leather case.

"Ah," he greeted MacNab, "there you are. Glad to find you at home." Then, catching sight of the *Record* on the floor, the look of triumph was replaced by a frown. He made a kick at the paper. "Like to see that fellow's face tomorrow," he laughed.

"You've made an arrest?" MacNab cried.

Mallet nodded, beaming satisfaction.

"We've got our man."

"*Man*," MacNab interjected softly.

"And there's your missing books," Mallet slung the heavy case at MacNab's feet with a thud. MacNab disregarded the case.

"Who's the man?"

"Young Dodsley."

"*What?*"

"Yes, it's him, all right. You're surprised, eh? That's funny. I had a notion you really at bottom suspected him yourself, you know." He laughed. "That's why I let you talk so much. Thought you'd let something slip out."

MacNab stared at the leather case. Had Brewster then made his choice, between Margery and Dick? Had he, seeing the police after the girl, put them on to Dick?

"Look here," Mallet said, busy with his handkerchief at the back of his neck, "I've had a hot and busy day. I'm on my way home. But you might persuade me to stop and tell you about it if you had a drink in the house."

With the glass at his lips, he glanced over.

"Looks as if you could do with one yourself," he remarked, "to pull you together."

Mechanically MacNab poured himself out a whisky. Mallet threw himself back and settled down comfortably in his easy-chair. The chair was upholstered in a red leather which blended with his complexion.

"I suppose you know the kind of happy content that

comes to you at the end of a hard case," he remarked. "'Port after storm, home after heavy seas,' eh?"

MacNab nodded as he laid down his glass.

"How did you get him?"

Mallet, throwing one big leg over the other, winked and spoke one word:

"Carter."

MacNab steeled against surprised now, lifted his eyebrows.

"Carter?"

Mallet in crossing his legs leaned forward.

"Yes. This time Carter did not fail me, not after the word I had with him over his slackness in not reporting his discovery about the lock. By the way, there was nothing in that. The lock was just worn out, and old Dodsley too mean to put in a new one." Mallet waved a triumphant hand. "Anyhow, the lock doesn't come into the picture at all, useful though the incident was in putting Carter on the *qui vive*, as the French say."

Mallet reached for his glass and then lay back luxuriously, savouring his success in this his first moment of relaxation. With eyes twinkling benignantly he regarded his pale-faced host anew.

"You had rather a down on Carter, hadn't you? Well, it is to Carter you owe the recovery of the stolen books, which was your own job in this affair. So while you and I both owe him our thanks, you, I think, owe him an apology as well."

MacNab, with a face as grim as the portrait showing over his shoulder, nodded shortly.

"I will—when I know what he's done to merit your thanks."

Mallet looked mystified by this reply; then his face cleared.

"Ah!" he said. "I see. What you want is the story of how Carter put young Dodsley into my hands." His voice became more purposeful as his hand went to his breast pocket to fish out a notebook from which he extracted a letter. "Read that."

MacNab, taking the document, saw that it was the copy of a letter addressed to Dick Dodsley, Esq., Dodsley's Bookshop, Charing Cross Road.

"He used 'Dick' on his letters to distinguish himself from his uncle," Mallet explained as MacNab read:

THE UNICORN SAFE DEPOSIT,
110–115 ACORN SQUARE,
LONDON, S.W.1.
CS/ED

Sir,

We beg to remind you that the period for which you hired Cabinet Number 358 expired on the 30th ult. Should you desire to continue your tenancy we would greatly esteem a notice to that effect, and would remind you that our terms are payment in advance.

Awaiting the favour of an early reply.

We are,
Yours faithfully,
P.P. CYRIL SMITH,
MANAGER, THE UNICORN SAFE DEPOSIT.

MacNab returned the letter.

"Yes," Mallet said, "that's *the* little mistake made by the criminal without which there could be no detection and consequently no story. Miss Grafton was right there at least. What the young gentleman didn't foresee was his motor-cycle crash, nor Carter in charge at the shop to hand over such things to us."

"So that is where you got the stolen books?"

"It was. I want you to identify them formally, as part or whole of the stolen property."

While Mallet bent down to open the case a thought came to MacNab.

"So he's only arrested for theft?" he said.

"Quite. But when he's brought up, he'll be remanded in custody, in view of a more serious charge to be preferred later."

"Then—so far—you haven't enough to justify—"

Mallet stood up and flashed his words at MacNab.

"What d'ye take me for? That accident of his—it was genuine enough, but it happened not on his way up to town but after his return. Among the contents of his pockets, besides the key, we got a bus ticket—a Number 9 bus to Hammersmith. I didn't at first attach much importance to that. Any one may have an odd ticket in his pocket. But when this"—pointing down to the case—"turned up, I made inquiries and was able to establish the day and almost the hour when that particular ticket was issued. Further, that cigarette case—Miss Grafton herself admitted it as one she'd given him only a week before the murder. So," Mallet concluded in a caustic voice, "I'll ask you one question, Mister MacNab: if you had the authority to make an arrest, would you feel justified in arresting this young man?"

"Oh, certainly, Chief Inspector—on a theft charge, if these are the missing books."

Mallet was annoyed. He felt vaguely that his achievements were somehow being belittled. And by a man who had failed even to catch a book thief. He threw open the case.

"Very well," he said shortly. "Just see if you identify these books. Not that we have much doubt."

The first book he picked up satisfied MacNab.

"*Poems by Victor and Cazaire*," he murmured. "Yes, there's no doubt." But he went through all the fifteen, comparing each item with the entry on his list.

"Ah," Mallet remarked, complacently smiling, "so you'll have to appear for the prosecution after all, instead of the defence." Then seeing the bewildered look on the other's face his tone changed. "What's wrong now? Aren't they all there?"

MacNab, holding a book in his hand, nodded as he stared at it.

"Yes; not one missing. But this one isn't on my list."

Mallet took it over.

"*Edmund Burke: his Speeches and Achievements*," he read. "Well, I expect Dodsley didn't miss this one—that's all."

MacNab wouldn't have this.

"No; this book was never in his shop. I'd like to keep this—for a day or two," he said.

But Mallet rejected the request. He could not allow any of the books out of their possession. All MacNab got was another careful scrutiny of the book's condition before it was replaced in the case with the other volumes.

Mallet's opinion of MacNab had fallen as his acquaintance increased. How the devil the fellow could assert that book had never been in Dodsley's shop he couldn't imagine. But he would have a good look at it himself later on, though it did sound merely like some of the far-fetched nonsense

Crabb might read in one of his detective stories. One might be able to tell in what shop a book had been, but not one in which it had not. Pulling the strap tight, Mallet stood up, case in hand, ready to depart. But just as, remembering the whisky, he held out his hand, MacNab surprised him by a question.

"You didn't take that bus ticket found on him as evidence of his presence in London?"

Mallet, still grateful for the whisky, replied patiently.

"Not at first," he admitted, "since the doctor would not commit himself as to when the accident could have occurred, and Roberts failed to identify him."

"But that Safe Deposit letter convinced you?"

Mallet set down the case, and with forefinger extended, took a step nearer:

"Look here," he said, "if you must know, it was neither this thing nor that, but the whole of them put together. A man may carry a bus ticket for weeks in his pocket; a man may lose his cigarette case and the finder drop it near the loser's place of employment; a man may quarrel with his uncle and yet not be his murderer; a man may not be the murderer though he happens to have provided himself with an alibi; a man may not be guilty even though he is one who had special knowledge of where the murdered man would be at an unusual hour, and himself have the *only* key by which to get at him—any one of those facts might be mere coincidence; but not all, and taken together, I can tell you from my experience, I do not believe there is a jury in England who would refuse to convict."

After this burst of eloquence, which left him more red than rosy, Mallet picked up his case, leaving MacNab a little stunned. At the door, however, the Chief Inspector turned.

"But thanks for the Scotch," he said, recovering his usual geniality, "it's made me feel good."

MacNab, however, got no such beneficial "kick" out of it when he took up his own as yet untasted whisky. Even the hissing of the syphon as the soda streamed into his glass sounded like some one mocking at him.

CHAPTER VI
Mr. Carter's Opinion of MacNab

NEXT MORNING, HOWEVER, HE FELT BETTER. HIS PAPER had nothing about the arrest. But, of course, there would be nothing until Dodsley was brought up on the theft charge.

Just before nine he sent off a wire to Owen Brewster as the only man in the case upon whom he could rely for help. He had taken note of the fact last night that Brewster, after all, had not been forced to make his choice between Dick and Margery. Mallet most obviously was still without any positive evidence that young Dodsley had been seen in London. Otherwise, worked up as he had been last night, he would certainly have said so, since it would for him have clinched his case.

After waiting impatiently for over an hour MacNab received his reply: *Hope to bring her home this afternoon. See you about two-thirty.*

Yes, he had not thought of it; the girl must be prostrate. But two-thirty would do. Meanwhile he could make certain of one or two things which he and Brewster could work up together.

Shortly after ten he was walking briskly up Charing Cross Road. Outside Dodsley's, on seeing Miss Jenks engaged in dressing the window shelves with copies of *Death at the Desk*, he stopped. The jacket made an almost startling splash of fresh colour behind the soberly bound books below. Inside he found Mr. Carter, who greeted him warmly, and with a confidence born of his own increased importance in the establishment. A table stood littered with *Death at the Desk*, ready for Miss Jenks's adjusting hand. MacNab nodded at the girl's back.

"Making a special display of it?" he queried lightly. "Had a good sale already, I suppose."

Mr. Carter smiled tolerantly.

"Well, hardly that. Haven't read it myself, but I'm told it's only a blackmail story."

"But you believe in it—for the public, eh?"

"Oh well, many factors, apart from literary merit, make a book sell, you know. As a matter of fact, I'm featuring the book from a variety of motives. The authoress, you see, is engaged to young Dick. And she, being the daughter of Mr. David Grafton—" Mr. Carter finished with an airy gesture, which indicated that no more need be said. MacNab then got in his real business. Did Mr. Carter know he had been engaged by Mr. Dodsley to trace certain books which had disappeared in mysterious circumstances? Mr. Carter admitted he did, although the fact had been withheld from him.

"Well, could I see the lock you discovered to be imperfect?" MacNab finally asked as Miss Jenks crept out of the window.

Mr. Carter shook his head doubtfully.

"I don't know what happened to the old lock," he said. "Probably it went into the dust-bin."

Miss Jenks, overhearing, turned with an armful of *Death at the Desk*.

"The man from Granger's took it away when he put on the new lock," she said. Then, with a knowing nod to MacNab and at the volumes in her arms, she struggled into the window.

MacNab, having got Granger's address, went round to the locksmith in St. Martin's Lane. After some delay the discarded lock was unearthed. In the presence of the interested workmen, MacNab, verifying that any key of the right size did operate the lock, proceeded to take it to pieces. And then the locksmith, with a whistle of surprise, saw just why any Yale key could perform that miracle.

It was the first blood MacNab had tasted since coming in the case; and it whetted his appetite for more. That took him straight to Soho with a job for Jim Peters. The little shop was crowded when MacNab entered, Mrs. Peters at her counter being busy searching for a bottle of pickles for one woman, while another was clamouring for a tin of sardines. Jim at his counter was weighing out an ounce of shag, with his eye on a youngster foraging among Jim's more bloodthirsty periodicals. MacNab stood on the doorstep until the smoker's departure provided enough room at the counter. The whispered exchange between MacNab and his handy-man instantly attracted the urchin's attention, and he turned to watch. All he contrived to see, however, was a slip of paper passed across the counter, though he did also overhear MacNab say something about the possibility of its being a long job. But Jim was so deeply attentive to the whispered instructions he was receiving that the nimble-fingered urchin was able to get away with five of the Twopenny Wild West Series while paying for but one.

MacNab himself wore a look of abstraction as he walked down Dean Street and turned into Shaftesbury Avenue. Outside a milliner's shop at the corner of Coventry Street his thoughts brought him to an abrupt halt.

"Of course I simply have to find a woman," he said to himself. Unaware he had spoken aloud with such emphasis, he did not see the old lady gazing at the window display almost run away with a look of horror on her face.

He remained for a moment pondering over this part of his problem. A woman certainly was mixed up with the crime. And Scotland Yard must have some theory as to her identity. It was not the man concerned he had now much doubt about, but the woman did bother him. If he could only get a hint from the Yard it might perhaps be a help. Crossing the street he entered the 'phone box in Leicester Square and dialled 1212—the number with the quickest response in England. Almost at once he got the reply that Chief Inspector Mallet was at the Yard but his lunch hour was due in twelve minutes.

The taxi set him down at the steps in five. Mallet, alone when he entered, looked up from his desk.

"'Morning," he greeted his visitor, indicating a chair with his pen.

"It's about that lock," MacNab said. "You satisfied yourself about it, I suppose?"

"Naturally," Mallet replied tolerantly. Such a question might well have met with a stiffer rejoinder.

"You are convinced Carter was unaware of its condition?"

Mallet put down his pen and started to twiddle his thumbs.

"Neither Carter nor any one else knew. That sort of thing can happen to such locks. The trunnions get worn down and allow any key which can enter to operate. Dodsley was too much of a skinflint to have a new one fitted. But of course he was no more aware of this than any one else. No, take it from me, there's nothing in that."

"Have you read *Death at the Desk*?" MacNab plumped out.

Mallet chuckled.

"I ploughed through it—the first since I was a youngster. It was my youthful taste for detective stories that made me join the force. But that's all the good they ever did me."

"So you found no—good, let's say, in this one?"

This time the question evoked a laugh.

"Ah, that tells me you've been talking to Miss Jenks. It's her notion there's a connection between the story and Dodsley's death. Well, I don't mind telling you, since you're almost one of ourselves, my first thought was that she was trying to throw suspicion on Miss Grafton, thinking we suspected herself."

"Miss Jenks?"

Mallet nodded.

"Oh, there were one or two things—a scratch on her hand, for instance—which raised my doubts. But there was nothing in it—nor in the story either. The story had, of course, similarities to the crime, but it had also differences, which is what could be said of any detective yarn, I suppose."

MacNab thought for a moment.

"I've read it too," he said, "and I agree with you. The love interest doesn't come into the story. In fact there's no woman even remotely connected with the book."

Mallet yawned and without disconnecting his clasped hands, glanced at the clock.

"Except the authoress herself," he nodded as he got to his feet.

MacNab was startled. Too startled to mention the special display Mr. Carter was giving to the despised publication. But before he could be sure anything lay behind, Mallet, on their way to the door, laid a hand on his shoulder.

"Why didn't you join the police yourself?" he inquired. "We could have made a first-rate officer out of stuff like you."

The question was not new to MacNab. He answered it as he answered all such questions.

"Well," he said, with confidential seriousness, "ye see, my father, who was a police inspector, married a very little woman. In a just world I ought to have had his physique and her brains. Unfortunately, what I did get was her physique and his brains."

Still, if he departed leaving Mallet doubtful of what this answer implied, he himself was no less doubtful as to what Mallet meant by his reference to the authoress of the novel. Did it mean that Miss Grafton was the woman the police believed to be the woman in the case? It looked like it since they seemed to have rejected Miss Jenks. Who else was there—except Miss Preedy?

Following a hasty lunch at a tea shop, MacNab's afternoon was filled up by an interview with the Manager of the Unicorn Safe Deposit, and a journey by bus to Hammersmith, from which he reached his flat soon after three o'clock. He found Miss Grafton and Brewster already there. Indeed, just as his old housekeeper started scolding him for not coming back for lunch, Brewster in his eagerness for news came into the hall, closing the study door gently behind him.

"We were just taking him away when they arrested him," he whispered. "It was awful."

"How is she?"

"Better—more self-controlled. But it was awful. I

wouldn't sit through that night again for a seat in the House of Lords itself." He smiled wanly at the inadequacy of his own suggested recompense and then gripped MacNab's arm. "But remember if she is more self-controlled now it's because she trusts in you. So, for God's sake, say nothing to shatter her hopes."

Whatever was true in MacNab's case, it was true of Margery Grafton that, unlike her brother, she had much more of her father in her than her mother. Fine looking girl as he had thought her at Lymington, there was now that in her eyes and the contour of her face which made her very nearly beautiful. It was as if all the Grafton in her had been purified and refined by suffering, transformed, as it were, into some fibre of a nobler quality which Grafton had derived, and passed on unused, from some ancestor of his own. At least so MacNab thought as he took her trembling hand and noted her extreme pallor.

"You will help me," she breathed, holding on to his hand.

"Of course I will," he said. "I've been at it all day, you know."

The hand in his own quivered like a little bird, warm and soft, and as in eager pleading she almost drew him to her, the intensely alluring feminine quality of her whole personality mounted to his head like the perfume of a flower. It was a new experience, and he was not sure he liked it.

Disengaging his hand, he showed her to a chair. At first he scarcely heard her pleading voice, feeling a queer thrill of small resentment, suspecting her of consciously using her charm, as some women do, to bend a man to some purpose of their own. Then Brewster intervened.

"Margery," he entreated, "don't cry—please. He'll do all man can do for Dick."

As she gazed over at him with tear-dimmed eyes MacNab's discomfort deepened.

"Will you?" she asked. "Will you? You promise?"

A sudden gust of anger swept over MacNab.

"By God, I will," he cried with unexpected vehemence. "Whatever can be done, I'll do."

She jumped to her feet.

"Thank you, oh, thank you."

But he waved her away almost rudely.

"Don't thank me. If that young man is released it's Mr. Brewster you'll have to thank. He has helped me. You have him to thank for what I have done and may do." He himself took a step closer to her. "Listen, Miss Grafton, there was a time when you yourself were suspected in connection with this crime."

"Me?" she echoed faintly.

"Yes—you. And Mr. Brewster knew it. He also knew something extremely damaging against your fiancé. But, knowing that he was innocent, he kept his knowledge from all except myself."

As if confused by the speed and the harsh tone of his words, her hand went to her brow and then, speaking a little uncertainly, she turned to Brewster.

"Thank you, Owen. I—I—" she broke off.

"Yes, you do owe him thanks. In his place I certainly would not have kept such knowledge to myself."

While she stood silent he put a question to her.

"Miss Grafton, have you never thought of taking your father into your confidence about all this?"

"My father?" she repeated, as if she had not heard aright.

"Yes. He's a man who—"

"No, no, no!" she burst out uncontrollably. "Oh, please don't, don't!" Covering her face with her hands, she almost fell into the chair. As MacNab stood watching her, Brewster, stepping quickly up, gripped him by the arm.

"What did you mean by that?" he demanded in a fierce whisper. "Don't you know the terms on which they are?"

MacNab disengaged his arm.

"Sorry," he murmured. "My mistake."

Brewster, mollified, whispered into his ear:

"Tell her something to—encourage her, then, before I take her away."

With very obvious contrition MacNab went over to the sobbing girl lying with covered face, all relaxed and huddled up in her chair.

"Miss Grafton."

He had to speak twice before she removed her hands. He read either terror or horror in her eyes.

"Miss Grafton," he said with quiet deliberation and confidence, "I can promise you this much. If any one is going to be convicted for this crime it will not be Dick."

She was looking into his eyes.

"Doesn't that satisfy you?" he asked.

She bent her head.

"Yes," she said. "Thank you. I'm sorry I made a fool of myself," she added, as if to cover the banality of her thanks.

Brewster, taking her under the arm, helped her to her feet. Her muscles ceased to be flaccid, and she recovered her self-possession with the promptness of Grafton himself, as holding out her hand she said: "I can ring you up for news, can't I? I'll be at my rooms in Bloomsbury."

He told her to ring up as often as she liked. "But I think," he added, "I may have something to tell you some time tomorrow."

As she passed out Brewster hung behind for an instant.

"That all right then?" MacNab asked in the bright manner of a man satisfied with his own work.

"Ye-s," Brewster hesitated. "But, damn it all, man, was it necessary to tell her such a lie about Dick's chances?"

MacNab walked back to his hearthrug, feeling contrite. So Brewster believed Dick had no chance? He smiled up at John Knox. Young Brewster in that case would get the surprise of his life. With that he dismissed Brewster and gave his mind to Miss Grafton herself. If only he could rely on Miss Jenks! The tale she had told him about the quarrel between Dick and his fiancée she had evidently told the police also. Mallet had dismissed the story as a mere attempt to divert suspicion from herself. It might be that and something else as well—the jealousy she felt against Miss Grafton on Dick's account, the mad jealousy of the plain woman who has long nursed a secret passion for an attractive man who has succumbed at once to another woman of superior charms. Was that story of the overheard quarrel an invention, the wish for it being father to the thought? Amelia Jenks's venom had been something easy to read. But could jealousy have so blinded her that she did not perceive how in trying to throw suspicion on Miss Grafton she was also compromising her beloved Dick?

Suddenly he thought of a line of investigation which might quickly settle the question. Miss Jenks had mentioned the name of some customer who had been in the shop while the quarrel was proceeding. What was the name?—some Member of Parliament. Andrews, was it, or Hendren? Not that, but something like it. He struggled after the name, feeling near to it and yet being eluded by it. At last he ran it down. Kendrew, that was the name.

He put through a call to the House of Commons, from

which he was referred to Mr. Kendrew's club in Carlton Terrace. But Mr. Kendrew not being there, he was advised to try for him at his flat in Curzon Street. And all the time, while search was being made for Kendrew, MacNab kept thinking of the terror he had read in Margery Grafton's eyes. But the flat didn't keep him waiting. Mr. Kendrew had been away for the week-end at Buckler's Hard, and was not expected before two-thirty next day. There was nothing for it but to wait.

To pass the time he again took up *Death at the Desk*. His aim was not to consider the one mistake in the story which led to the arrest of the criminal. That was useless, for if there was any connection between the story and the actual crime that mistake would be the one most carefully avoided. Rather his object was to discover any unconscious similarities between the real and the fictitious murder. On the question of opportunity he found the similarities abundant. There was the appointment made by the bookmaker, in his own empty office and in the middle of the night—a far-fetched notion that! Yet it had actually been followed in the real crime, the one victim being a bookseller and the other a bookmaker. Still, though in each case the murderer had a talk with a police officer afterwards, the dissimilarities were more numerous.

His mind turned on what he had seen in the shop—the cigarette-ends, the hair slide, the books removed to make a peep-hole for spying—there was no parallel to these in the story. Besides, there was no woman in the story, and now, fairly certain he knew who the man was, it was the woman he must identify before he dare try to prove his case against the man.

MacNab sat up suddenly like a man struck unexpectedly

in the face. Had the woman entered the shop that night by accident? No—that was unlikely at such an hour, even if, as was equally unlikely in such circumstances, the door had been left open. No, but a woman who *suspected* something, who knew something and who, having the means to enter, came there, as the peep-hole made among the books seemed to show, to spy. On whom? On the murderer to see he did his work? Surely not; but on the person with whom Dodsley had made an appointment!

He laid down the book gently, feeling chilled as he perceived the implications. Still in the dark as to what could be the motive for the crime, he felt certain that if Miss Jenks had lied about the quarrel it would not be hard to find the woman.

Then the 'phone buzzed and, taking up the receiver, the voice of Jim Peters was in his ear:

"I got it," the voice whispered. "It's Davis and Newman's in Oxford Street."

Twenty minutes later MacNab was in consultation with the manager of the Oxford Street booksellers, Davis and Newman, after which he made for Charing Cross Road, reaching Dodsley's just before the shop closed. Mr. Carter, in fact, was in the office, entering up the sales for the day, with Miss Jenks at his elbow assisting. Mr. Carter, occupying Dodsley's seat at the desk, did not rise but nodded a greeting.

"Mind waiting a minute; Miss Jenks wants to get away," he said.

MacNab did not mind. It interested him to cast his eye about to see what changes the new management had introduced. Apart from Mr. Carter and Miss Jenks, the place did not seem much smarter. But there was less dust about and things seemed more in their proper place. Those bookcases had certainly been repolished, and the old painted Roman lettering on each section had been replaced by washable china letters. But were the volumes inside the case equally free from dust? Like a housekeeper who looks under the mats, MacNab stepped over to the section marked III and picked out a volume. Section III happened to stand behind Carter's chair, and so neither he nor Miss Jenks, with their heads together over their work, observed him. MacNab, after turning over some pages, replaced the volume just as Carter got up.

"Well, and what can I do for you now?" the manager inquired brightly.

"I'm looking for a book: *Edmund Burke: his Speeches and Achievements.*"

Mr. Carter shook his head and began to jingle the money in his pocket.

"Sorry. Haven't got it."

"Sure?"

Mr. Carter smiled indulgently.

"It's my business to be. I can be sure of more: I don't believe we've ever had it on our shelves."

Miss Jenks looked up from her accounts.

"We could advertise for it—if you wanted it particularly."

"Oh," MacNab said lightly, "I don't want it so much as all that—just a fancy I had."

When he had gone, Miss Jenks again got her addition wrong.

"That's a queer book for him to ask for," she remarked, beginning again.

Mr. Carter laughed lightly as he took up the brush for his bowler hat.

"Come," he said, "can you always fit in a customer to the book he asks for?"

"No, but all the same—"

"Very well. I suppose there never was a failure who didn't dream of great achievements. It's a form of vanity men who are failures indulge in. He sees himself making equally mighty speeches and doing mighty things. Pathetic, if you like; but quite harmless."

This time Miss Jenks got her totals correct.

CHAPTER VII
An Interview
Is Arranged

THE LAST DAY OPENED IN A WAY THAT SEEMED TO JUS-
tify Mr. Carter's opinion of MacNab. He passed the morning in what looked like idle dreaming, broken into by a
book—not *Burke* but *Death at the Desk*, which he read by
fits and starts. Once he 'phoned up the Yard; but Mallet was
too busy to see him. Mallet, in fact, was rather curt. Once
he himself was called up by Owen Brewster, who wanted
to know if he had got any good news for Margery. MacNab
tried to be cheery, but it was clear Brewster's own hopes
were at their lowest ebb.

Then at two-thirty the long hours of inaction ended for
MacNab, and he set out eagerly for Curzon Street.

Mr. Kendrew did not keep him waiting in the room into
which he had been shown. Holding his seat by a majority of
almost microscopic dimensions, the insistence with which
MacNab had stressed his request for an immediate interview
on a matter of the gravest importance led him to fear some
new trouble in his constituency. Shaking MacNab's hand
with great cordiality and enthusiasm, and then planting him

in his most comfortable chair, Kendrew stood regarding him rather apprehensively. MacNab came at once to the point.

"It's about a young man whose life is in danger," he began.

Mr. Kendrew's look changed from apprehension to sympathy.

"So sorry. If I can be of any service, please tell me."

His face, however, reflected a much greater variety of emotions while his visitor explained that he did not come up from his constituency and had not stayed the night in town because Mr. Kendrew had been called away from his duties, but did wish to verify a shop assistant's statement as to something he, Mr. Kendrew, might have overheard in a bookshop. At the word bookshop Mr. Kendrew almost jumped, the word having for so long been on every one's lips in connection with the murder.

"Yes," he said when the circumstance had been set forth. "Yes, I remember perfectly well being in the shop that day, between one and two it was. But no one else was there, except a woman assistant. At least if there was any one behind I was not aware of it, and I certainly heard no quarrel going on."

"Try to remember," MacNab begged. "It was about a book; that may stimulate your memory. About this book," he added, producing *Death at the Desk* from his pocket.

Kendrew's eyes narrowed into a perplexed stare.

"I've seen that somewhere," he said thoughtfully. "Now where on earth was it?" Then, catching sight of the author's name, "Good Lord, of course. Why, it was in the House on the night of the murder."

The surprise was MacNab's this time.

"In the house—whose house?" he said.

"Why, the House of Commons—in the reading-room, I

mean. Let me see! A moment, please! Why, yes, of course, it was Male."

"Male?" MacNab echoed.

"He had picked the book off a chair where it had been lying face down, and—" He broke off abruptly and shouting, "Male, Male, come here," threw open the door. In a moment Commander Male appeared in the doorway. Kendrew pointed to the book in MacNab's hands.

"You remember that?" Kendrew said excitedly.

The Commander, self-possessed and unflurried, came across.

"Of course," he said, "it's the book Grafton was reading before the division on clause nine that night."

The book nearly fell from MacNab's hand.

"Grafton," he cried. "Are you sure?"

Male saved the book by taking possession of it himself.

"I'll show you a place somebody marked in it, if you like." He flicked over the pages. "I remember being surprised at his nerve, reading this with a speech coming on. As soon have seen myself playing dominoes before going into action. But, after all, he hadn't stuck it long, for I saw him on the terrace when I went out after the fifth divide, and he didn't come back to it. Yes, here it is: 'The prophet who was slain by a lion had a nobler end than Bishop Hatto who was eaten by rats.'"

"Right you are, Male," Kendrew said. "And you remember the *Record* notice of the book, making fun of it?"

"Of course, Charles. Something about a bookie who was a secret blackmailer and who caught a hawk when he thought he'd only a pigeon. That's it, wasn't it?"

"Something like it. I remember there was a lot about birds in it."

"But look here," Male said purposefully. "What's all this about anyway?"

At the question MacNab struggled to his feet, a little unsteadily. He was not unused to surprise; but the flood of light thrown all unconsciously on the death of Mr. Dodsley by these two men left him dazed. He got away murmuring some almost incoherent excuses.

"Good heavens," Male said, as soon as he disappeared. "Why, the fellow's drunk—he can hardly walk."

And it looked as if Male were right, after MacNab had tumbled his way to the street, for he took the first taxi he saw as if he could not trust his own legs.

"House of Commons," he said.

He was ashamed of his loss of self-control. Yet all the way he kept softly repeating that phrase some one marked in the book Grafton had been reading. And all the time he kept on seeing Margery Grafton's face of horror—yes, it was horror—at his suggestion that she might consult her father. But by the time the taxi set him down at the office entrance, he found himself ready for what lay ahead.

He had some influence in a certain quarter at the House. But it took time before that influence could be brought to bear on the official responsible. An hour afterwards, however, he found himself in possession of the list of members who had gone into the division lobbies on the night the Government met with its reverse. What he sought in the list he soon found. Between the hours of 1 a.m. and 3.15 there had been several divisions. And David Grafton had recorded his vote on two occasions only, these being the first and the last.

But the time of the last division was decisive. If David Grafton voted in the 3.15 division, he could not have been present at a murder in Charing Cross Road, which, as the time on the watch proved, took place at 3.4. And, as a matter of fact, to which the newspapers witnessed, Mr. Grafton was actually making his great speech at the very moment the murder took place.

MacNab breathed more freely. He was not one of those who like to see a big man brought low.

Nevertheless, on reaching his flat, he got to work again on the book, that strange phrase about the prophet and Bishop Hatto running in his head. For he was, it seemed, still unsure of the woman in the case. But when, about six, he abandoned the novel and turned to the extracts which had attracted his attention in the murdered man's diary, he was able to see these entries in a new perspective.

He, in fact, found something which on the instant sent him off in search of P. C. Roberts. At the station they told him Roberts was somewhere on his beat, his night-duty shift having expired.

After scouring through half the streets in E division, he ran his man to earth at the top of St. Martin's Lane.

Roberts remembered MacNab, but when told some details were required on the report he put in with regard to his discovery of the murder, his mouth tightened.

"I can't talk about that," he said firmly, preparing to continue his round.

"That's a pity," MacNab remarked. "I wouldn't know anything about your report unless Inspector Mallet had given it to me to read."

Roberts hesitated.

"What do you want to know?"

"Whether you put everything in about the young man you met that night."

Roberts, his eye following a speeding car, smiled a trifle bitterly.

"I did," he said; "if I had to do it again I might put in less."

"Well," MacNab went on persuasively, "as you'll certainly be again questioned tomorrow by the Inspector on one or two new points, hadn't you better go over them now, with me?"

Roberts pondered for a moment.

"What are they? I don't want to be put through it again as I was over that cigarette case."

"Are you quite sure as to the exact time you found the body?"

"Dead sure: it was 3.16. Besides, that was corroborated by my call to the station."

"And the time on the watch was 3.4."

"Right again; that was something they didn't need my word for."

"But here's something I need your word for now. How long do you think the young man was in your company?"

"Is this a question I'll be asked tomorrow?"

"Most probably," MacNab replied, trying to keep cool.

Roberts's brow furrowed in thought. He was obviously reckoning the time he stood talking, then traversing the street, almost counting the steps up and then across the road, to get him out of his own division.

"Might be a matter of fifteen to twenty minutes—not more," he said at last.

"All right. Now this question. Did you, during that time, happen to see the young man glance at his wrist-watch?"

Roberts again made his effort, but this time without result.

"No," he said. "I don't remember that."

"Try," MacNab urged; "it's important."

Roberts tried again for a few breathless moments. Then

MacNab's hopes sank as he saw the constable's negative shake of the head about to come. But it did not come. Instead, Roberts's head suddenly lifted.

"Fancy me forgetting that," he said. "It must have been on account of your trying to make me think of a wrist-watch."

"He hadn't a wrist-watch?"

"No; it was a thin gold watch he took out of his waistcoat. Of course I remember now. He took it out four or five times in all, I'd say. I recollect intending to warn him against showing it off so much, in his state at that time, but he kept on babbling so I never had a chance. Fancy me forgetting that," Roberts cried in self-derision.

MacNab returned to the E Divisional station, and after a talk with the D. D. Inspector, rang up Mallet at the Yard to inquire about Dick Dodsley.

Mallet, evidently quoting, replied:

"Remanded in custody, bail being refused in view of a more serious charge likely to be preferred later."

"Meanwhile, you want evidence bearing on the more serious charge," MacNab suggested.

"I want evidence—all I can get and wherever it can be got. But it's got to be evidence, not theory."

"Well, I've got evidence as to the identity of the woman and the man. Would you like to hear it tonight, at nine, in the shop, or would you prefer not to know what it is until it is offered in Court in Dodsley's defence?"

That appeared to knock the wind out of Chief Inspector Mallet. A pause followed. Then Mallet, evidently distrusting his ears, asked MacNab if he would mind saying that again. MacNab did not mind.

"Look here, man," Mallet expostulated. "You can't be serious. You don't know the strength of the case against him."

"No; but I know the strength of the case against some one else. I only want you to hear my witnesses. It is you only who can compel their attendance." Then, as Mallet hesitated, he added urgently: "Listen, Mallet! I admit I have no proof. This is merely an attempt to get it—on the scene of the crime, and in your presence. You can't refuse. This looks like being a tremendous *coup* for you."

Mallet capitulated.

"All right. Who are the persons you want us to call up?"

"The shop assistants, Carter, Amelia Jenks, and June Preedy; P. C. Roberts, George and Margery Grafton."

In the act of taking down the names, Mallet, as if to cover the thrill he felt, said half jocularly:

"You don't want Mr. Grafton himself then?"

That was a startler for MacNab. But perceiving it to be meant for something between a jeer and a jest, he replied quietly:

"No, I can make sure of his attendance myself."

And this time it was Chief Inspector Mallet who got the shock.

BOOK IV

CHAPTER I
On the Scene
of the Crime

MACNAB ARRIVED AT THE SHOP JUST BEFORE NINE.
For half an hour he had been waiting at home for Owen
Brewster to turn up. His plan of operations could not be carried through without Brewster's assistance, and the young
man was held up by some pressing work for Mr. Grafton. As
a result, when he did appear, there was no time left in which
to acquaint him with the new turn the case had taken. But
merely to hear something had come to light which looked
like clearing Dick was enough to send Brewster's heart
racing with excitement.

"Lord!" he cried, "that's good news. Tell me all about it."

But MacNab, no less excited if more self-controlled,
refused with a laugh.

"No, no, Watson," he said. "Remember, it is my custom
to explain in detail only after the case is finished."

"But, my dear Holmes, I can't even guess what it is," the
young fellow protested.

In reaching up for his hat MacNab stopped to point a
reproving finger at him. "That's just it! You're Watson to the

life. If you made the obvious deduction from the facts you know already, you would know as much as I do."

Sergeant Barrett and Constable Copping were again in charge of the shop door, and the sergeant ushered them into the office where they found Inspector Mallet, Detective-Sergeant Crabb, and the acting manager, Mr. Carter. The inspector rather lifted his eyebrows over Brewster's presence, but MacNab explained that Mr. Grafton's secretary had been of great assistance to him and could not be left out now.

Mallet, in fact, had expected to see Grafton himself. MacNab's confident assertion over the 'phone, following his own jocular question had, almost literally, knocked him over. But now he took it that Grafton, having sent his secretary as a substitute, MacNab's influence was not quite so great as had been suggested. So while Mr. Carter, with a proprietary air, began to exhibit the literary treasures in the glass cases, he drew MacNab aside.

"Mr. Grafton isn't coming then?" he whispered.

"Oh, yes—later. Ten was the hour I gave him," MacNab replied.

Mallet would have asked for more, but just then, on the stroke of nine, Sergeant Barrett ushered in Miss Jenks and Miss Preedy. Both almost tiptoed to their chairs by the wall, Miss Jenks in the sad, subdued manner of one attending a funeral, Miss Preedy thrilling like a gate-crasher who cannot feel quite safe till she is seated. Sergeant Crabb, on the outlook to read the symptoms, was quick to note the differences. Miss Jenks, having in a rapid glance taken in the occupants of the room, sat stiff and still with downcast head, while Miss Preedy's excited eyes roamed everywhere, bright with a lively expectancy. But Miss Jenks did lift her sombre eyes for more than a moment at Brewster's exclamation when George and Margery Grafton entered. Brewster started forward.

"Why, Margery!" he cried. "I didn't know—" He turned to MacNab. "Was this necessary?"

"Absolutely," MacNab replied. "Please sit down, Miss Grafton."

He would have spared the girl, who looked so ill. He had, indeed, so arranged her father's attendance as to spare her the worst; but she had not been frank with him; she had withheld essential facts—or so he thought—and in consequence he was not disposed to let her off even if her presence had not been necessary to his case. All the same, Brewster did not find it easy to forgive MacNab for bringing the nerve-racked girl there. However good his intentions were for Dick's release, it appeared to him a stupid and unimaginative thing to do. But, now that he thought of it, this was quite on a par with his previous thick-witted suggestion to her that she should consult her father. Consult her father—on Dick's behalf. Dick, on whose account she had quarrelled with her father and left home!

For the first time Brewster experienced a little gust of resentment against MacNab.

Mallet, with a few words, explained why they had been called together.

"You will understand," he began "that this is a purely informal meeting, called at the request of my friend here to help the ends of Justice. You have each of you already made statements to me in connection with what you know. Each of these statements you will see"—he touched the pile of documents before him on the table—"I have here with me for reference. But it seems necessary, for reasons which will no doubt be given later, to go over the evidence again. So I beg you to listen carefully, and be ready to afford us all the help in your power. I am sure," he added, "you are each of you as anxious to see the innocent cleared, and the guilty convicted, as any of us at Scotland Yard."

MacNab began almost diffidently. He was, indeed, more nervous than he seemed, aware that he could not avoid, as Mallet had done, all reference to the most painful aspects of the case.

"My own connection with the case," he said, "came about through the disappearance of valuable books from this shop. I was called in by Mr. Dodsley himself, but entirely failed to discover by whom, or when, the thefts were carried out. Later on Mr. Dodsley was found here, dead. And, as you have no doubt seen in your evening paper, his nephew has been today remanded in custody for the thefts, the police objecting to bail on the ground of a more serious charge likely to be preferred later. That charge is, of course, the murder of his uncle."

Interrupted by an abrupt sob from Margery Grafton, a whispered "*Ss-h*" from George, and a murmured "Gee!" from the absorbed Miss Preedy, he went on hurriedly:

"You have each given statements, but none of you knows what the others have said. So I want to put the whole police case as it stands before you."

Mallet looked up sharply, about to interrupt. But realising that MacNab could not know the whole police case, allowed him to proceed.

"It is in evidence that the constable on the beat, finding the shop door open, entered, the time he gave being three-sixteen, and found Mr. Dodsley dead in this office. Mr. Dodsley had, according to Mr. Carter, come here to work on a catalogue which had to be ready next morning for the printer. In addition to Mr. Carter, only Mr. Dick Dodsley knew Mr. Dodsley would be so engaged that night. Now we know the shop had been entered by some one with a key before Mr. Dodsley himself arrived. And while the nephew had a key, and knew his uncle would be coming there, Mr. Carter, the only other person who shared that knowledge with him, had no key. Yet, though Mr. Carter was on the spot, and the nephew was away in the New Forest, there is strong evidence not only that young Dodsley intended to return to town that night, but also that he actually did so."

So unexpected was this that, as Mallet noted, several heads sharply lifted to stare at the speaker.

"Oh, I know there is evidence against that. He had an accident on the way up on his motor-cycle. And when I saw him in hospital down there he denied being in London. But there is still stronger evidence that the accident occurred not on his way up but on the way back from town; that, in fact, he left his cycle at Hammersmith and completed the journey in a bus. For the police found a No. 297 night service bus ticket in his pocket after the accident. Besides," MacNab said with slow deliberation, "he was seen that night in a No. 9 bus by Mr. Brewster here."

Evading the hand MacNab would have laid on his shoulder, Brewster jumped to his feet, white with anger.

"You damn fool," he cried. "You—you traitor to tell them that!"

Mallet instinctively rose.

"But you don't deny you saw him?" he said to Brewster. Brewster hesitated.

"Come now!" Mallet cried sharply.

"No, it wouldn't matter much now if I did," Brewster

replied dejectedly. He glanced along the room to where Miss Grafton sat in a state of collapse, with George's arm encircling her. The sight so moved him that he turned again on MacNab.

"She brought you in to help Dick," he cried, "and now you've done for him. You pretended to make me your assistant, and got my confidence! God—if only I had guessed why you wanted my help!"

As a man Mallet's sympathy was with Brewster, but as a detective he felt grateful to MacNab. And since at Scotland Yard duty comes before emotion, he brusquely ordered Brewster to be silent. MacNab resumed amid a tense and painful silence.

"My young assistant is afraid of the truth. I am not. He is firmly convinced his friend is innocent. So am I. The difference between us is that I am not afraid of any apparently awkward facts coming to light, though, like him, I might have wanted to conceal them if I did not feel able to establish young Dodsley's innocence."

The assurance in his voice arrested Crabb's pencil in the middle of a word. He sat back and looked up to see if he had heard aright. Glancing along the table, the first thing his eye lit on was Mallet's dropped jaw, then Brewster's head screwed round to stare up at the speaker, and, after twisting round his own head, Margery Grafton sitting forward, her eyes dilating with new hope. Some one tittered nervously as MacNab, after a forced little laugh as if struck by the absurdity of suspecting Dick, resumed:

"Why, I'd undertake to make out as strong a case against Mr. Carter himself."

Mr. Carter almost jumped at the mention of his name.

"I've seen Mr. Carter's statement. It was he who gave the

police information about the quarrels between uncle and nephew; it was he who told them of the nephew's intention to return that night; it was he alone who shared with the nephew the knowledge that Mr. Dodsley would be in the shop at that hour; and it was he who told them the nephew had the only available key. But what he *omitted* to tell them was that he and Miss Preedy spent some time at a night club not more than a stone's throw from the shop, about the time the murder took place. In other words, he told them all that compromised the nephew, and concealed what might compromise himself."

With a queer strangled cry Carter got shakily to his feet.

"There's a reason for that," he said hoarsely. "I—I don't as a rule go to such places, and didn't want it known. Mr. Dodsley would be—it would have been as much as my place is worth if he knew."

"But Mr. Dodsley was dead when you made the statement."

"Yes… Yes, he was." Carter looked bewildered. "It was just instinct—habit, I suppose. But I had no key. I had no key to the shop. You can't get over that, if I was at the *Cynara*."

"Oh," MacNab said soothingly, "I'm only dealing with the question of opportunity. If that were all I might as well suspect my assistant, Mr. Brewster here, for he also was at the *Cynara* then. You see," he added lightly, in a way that made the uncomfortable tension relax still further, "at three in the morning, though most of us are in bed, few of us are seen there, and as none of us is chained down to it, to be in bed is no real alibi. That night, in fact, few could have unshakable alibis, except, possibly, the Members of Parliament at the all-night sitting."

On this point Inspector Mallet saw fit to put in a word in season.

"Those who tell the truth and all the truth have nothing to fear from the police," he said, leaning forward. "Those who don't—" he finished with a rattle of his knuckles on the table.

Mr. Carter, whose breathing was still unsteady from the shock to his heart, spoke up.

"What about the key?" he demanded. "How does he get over that?"

MacNab knew the question was dictated by resentment against himself.

"If the man came there by appointment, he did not need a key," he replied.

Mallet and Crabb's glances met.

"That's from the novel," Crabb said under his breath. "Nothing in it."

Suddenly an interruption came from an unexpected source. Miss Jenks, who had been sitting, unlike the others, without a sign of life, got to her feet. Pointing at George Grafton who sat against the opposite wall, she cried:

"That is the young man I saw hanging about outside on the day of the murder waiting for Miss Grafton."

Then, before any one could speak, Miss Preedy, as if not to be outdone in dramatic denunciation by Miss Jenks, or perhaps responding to the feeling of tension which had been developing, as abruptly pointed at Brewster:

"And he's the swell I saw with her the same night the old man was bumped off."

Nobody felt more outraged than Sergeant Crabb. This was the sort of thing one might expect from such irregular procedure. Mallet himself seemed conscious that his willingness to take evidence when, where, and how he could get it, was being reduced to a melodramatic absurdity. Angrily, he tapped the table.

"No more of that, please. You are here, not to make speeches, but to answer in each other's presence such questions as may be put to you."

Brewster, moved by disgust, rose from his seat at the end of the table. He spoke slowly, cold with anger.

"I do not wish to make a speech, but I do wish to offer an explanation. I said nothing to you about seeing Dick in London because Dick had denied being there just before you came, and I thought it likely he would repeat that denial to you a few minutes later. His denial, of course, was due to the concussion following his accident, which temporarily destroyed his memory of past events. In those circumstances I thought it safer not to volunteer information on a matter on which I was never questioned."

Mallet accepted the explanation with his characteristic gesture.

"It's always safer to trust the police," he reiterated.

"Quite," Brewster nodded. "I see that now."

Carter, still smarting under his grievance, burst in.

"But what about that key? I made no secret of that, anyway, and I'd like to know what he has to say about it."

Mallet, about to rebuke the interrupter, stopped when MacNab's left hand pressed his right arm gently.

"Let me satisfy Mr. Carter at once," MacNab said. "The key forms the least of my difficulties, for the fact is the person who entered the shop to wait for Mr. Dodsley needed no key at all."

"Eh? What's that?" Mallet was startled. "No key? You mean he concealed himself before the shop closed?"

"No. There's another explanation." Looking round his listeners he avoided Mr. Carter by keeping his eyes on Miss Grafton. "The lock had been doctored so as to allow any key of the right size to work it."

"Not doctored—worn out, you mean."

"No. I took the lock to pieces at the locksmith's and found the drop trunnions had been removed. So there was nothing to stop the key going full circle. In fact it didn't even need a key. A hair slide would do as well."

"A hair slide!" Mallet echoed shakily.

"A hair slide or any piece of metal which would enter the keyhole," MacNab insisted. "Any locksmith will confirm what I say."

Mechanically, Mallet began to stroke his chin, lost in thought.

Owen Brewster, at MacNab's elbow, nodded his appreciation.

"That's good anyway," he whispered. "By the Lord, but you have got poor old Dick over a nasty hurdle."

"So," Mallet remarked, letting his hand fall to the table, "there needn't have been a woman in it at all."

MacNab agreed.

"We assumed there was on too slender evidence." Mallet sat still, badly shaken.

"The question is: who played that trick with the lock?"

Carter looked sullen.

"I didn't. I didn't even know it was out of order till Miss Preedy here found out."

"But even then you didn't report it to us."

Mr. Carter turned plaintive.

"How was I to know it had anything to do with the case?" he quavered.

Inspector Mallet, already far away in thought, gave no heed to such an absurd question. Every one, indeed, seemed similarly affected by what had been revealed—every one, that is, except Mr. Carter, who broke into Miss Preedy's vain attempts to remember a like situation on the movies. But if few could see all the implications Mallet perceived, not one but saw how much MacNab's discovery did for Dick Dodsley.

Margery Grafton perceived more, as was perhaps natural in an author of detective fiction. She, along with Mallet, knew that by this one single stroke, Dick, from being the one man most open to suspicion, had become the one man in London least open to it. And that for the self-same reason, since he having a key had less need than any one for a doctored lock.

Unobtrusively, she squeezed her brother's hand, and unobtrusively, but more strongly, George returned the grip as she glanced along and saw Owen Brewster's face wreathed in smiles.

Finally Mallet spoke:

"Well, it's clear now, there need only have been one man waiting for Mr. Dodsley that night. For such a purpose that hair clip is as useful to a man as to a woman." He turned his eyes on Carter in a way that made Carter want to wipe his forehead. "Tell me, Mr. Carter, do *you* own a motor-cycle too?"

"Not for years I haven't." Carter did use his handkerchief this time. After a pause he burst out suddenly: "I'll tell you the truth. Now he's gone, it don't matter who knows."

"That's right! It's always better to trust the police." Mallet nodded. "Well?"

"Well, occasionally I've hired a combination to take Miss Preedy out. She's—she likes rides in the moonlight."

Recalling Miss Preedy's tastes, Mallet's mind was instantly pierced by a sharper ray than any moon can shed.

"I see," he said innocently. "And on those night excursions, with so many road-bandits about, of course you carried a revolver for self-defence?"

Miss Preedy laughed outright.

"D'ye see him with a gun?"

"I can easily see you with one," Mallet sharply rejoined. "If I had been Dodsley, I'd sooner have sacked him than you."

June Preedy's blue eyes hardened.

"Look here. What's the idea?" she demanded. "You trying a frame-up against him and me?"

"My question has not been answered," Mallet quietly reminded her.

"Very well, I'll answer it," she retorted with eyes ablaze. "If we had carried any lead-squirt I'd have handled it; but we'd no call to, and we didn't."

It was at this point that, to MacNab's satisfaction, Brewster intervened to smooth things out. He rose as it were to a point of order. Already familiar with the procedure of the House of Commons in which one day he hoped to achieve distinction, his feelings were, even more than MacNab's, outraged by the unseemly heat which threatened to develop.

"Sir," he said to Mallet, "there's a saying to the effect that it's wiser to be off with the old love before one is on with the new. May I, with all deference, suggest that the same is true of a suspect. I came here to see my friend cleared, as I was led to believe he would be. So far, he has been only partially cleared, and perhaps you will understand my anxiety and forgive my impatience to see the process completed."

Privately, Sergeant Crabb thought this cheek, in spite of the respectful tone. But apparently Mallet did not resent it. With a smile to Brewster he nodded at MacNab.

"I've been waiting to see that done, Mr. Brewster. We are here at his request, for that purpose. So far he's only taken us to the door." He looked up at MacNab. "That point you made about the lock—a fine bit of work—but—"

"Just luck," MacNab cut in. "If you had chanced on the same hint, Inspector—"

"But not in itself conclusive, you know—not with so much still left unexplained."

"Still," Brewster argued, "surely another great point in Dick's favour is that no weapon was found on him, as it must have been after his crash."

Mallet and Crabb met each other's eyes.

"No, all we got on him was a bus ticket."

"But that's nothing; it may have been in his pocket for weeks."

"This one wasn't."

MacNab, appreciating the fight Brewster was putting up, slipped into the seat between his assistant and the inspector. He was more than content to listen and watch. The moment for which he had been angling and scheming might come of itself. But Mallet's quietly confident assertion about the ticket, obviously bothered Brewster.

"How on earth can you know that?" he asked after a moment.

"Why shouldn't we? You yourself admitted seeing him in the No. 9 which issues that ticket."

MacNab suspected, however, that Mallet had a better reason which he was not at that stage willing to disclose. Meanwhile, Brewster seemed to have missed this possibility.

"Isn't it far more probable," he suggested, "that the shop was entered by a burglar—one of those fellows who carry a few dozen keys on them—and who unexpectedly finding the old man there, shot him before he could give the alarm? Then while he ransacked the office, his confederate outside on the watch, tricked your unsuspecting constable."

Mallet demolished this far-fetched theory with great good humour.

"Burglars don't smoke cigarettes and examine books to pass the time till an owner enters; the place was not ransacked, and Mr. Dodsley was shot while sitting in his chair. Besides which, Mr. Brewster, your theory does not account for one small but conclusive fact."

"And that is?"

"The finding of a hair clip prepared for use as a key. Your supposed burglar must have been in the secret of the lock."

Pugnaciously, Brewster stuck to his great point.

"Well, anyhow, Dick had no need to use that."

"Admitted. And if that alone stood against him, he would not now be under arrest," Mallet agreed.

Brewster glanced at MacNab and then at Mallet.

"I'd much like to hear the full strength of your case then. We can hardly answer it till we do," he said.

The inspector did not mind humouring the secretary of a distinguished man who might one day become Home Secretary; but he considered indulgence had gone far enough. As to MacNab, Mallet felt rather sore, judging that his lucky discovery of the lock's condition had alone led him to predict a great *coup* for the police. And what about MacNab's confident assertion that Mr. Grafton himself would be present! Just as a little derisive smile was forming, another thought came. Perhaps Grafton would turn up after all, with the idea of putting pressure on them. Well, no! He would know better than that. But, at least, his aim might be—since he had been in the law, and might well object to having his name given publicity in such a connection—yes, he might want to see what he himself could do to weaken their case against the man to whom his daughter was engaged. Shock tactics!

But Mallet was really amused when Brewster repeated his wish to hear the full police case.

"After all, no weapon was found," the young man insisted.

"Our case will be stated only at the proper time, and place," Mallet said with finality. "We came here to collect new evidence, not to submit the evidence we already have."

"Which amounts to a bus ticket. That won't carry you far—now that the key no longer counts," Brewster commented, with a provocative laugh.

Mallet got to his feet, signalling Crabb to follow his example. He had intended to say no more; but the opening Brewster offered was too tempting to resist. With his hands at the back of his chair he bent forward:

"It's a ticket that looks like being valid for a much longer journey than Hammersmith, Mr. Brewster, thanks to your assistance."

"To me?" Brewster cried. "You—"

Mallet's upraised finger stopped him.

"Yes, and in return I'll tell you what you seemed anxious to know. The Basingstoke police were yesterday handed a revolver firing a cartridge of a calibre corresponding to the extracted bullet."

"The Basingstoke police?"

"Yes, the Basingstoke police, after it was found by a roadman in a ditch in the by-pass. So you see, what with the cigarette case outside the shop, the revolver about half-way down the road, and the bus ticket at the journey's end, well—you'll no doubt hear counsel try to explain these facts away when you appear as a witness for the prosecution."

Brewster jumped to his feet, breathless in his agitation.

"Never!" he cried. "Never that, at least. I'll say I may have been mistaken in thinking I saw him in that bus."

Mallet shook his head.

"There's no such damaging witness," he said slowly, "as an unwilling witness compelled by his oath to tell the truth."

Brewster threw up his hand in a gesture of despair. Mallet stood waiting while Crabb packed up his papers. MacNab and Miss Grafton, with George bending over her, alone remained seated.

MacNab said: "If you don't mind, Inspector, I'd like to go on with my case."

Mallet's ear was caught not so much by the request as by the tone in which it was made.

"What—after your—your young assistant, Mr. Brewster's admission?"

It was clear that Mallet considered Brewster had given the case away.

"Chiefly because of it," MacNab affirmed.

Mallet opened his eyes, thought hard for a moment, then, making nothing of it, sat down and told MacNab to go ahead. All the others followed his example expectantly.

"Suppose," MacNab began nervously, "all this is what Miss Preedy called a frame-up, not against Mr. Carter and herself, but against your prisoner, you would expect it to begin with that trick with the lock?"

"Well, perhaps," Mallet conceded, "young Dodsley, apart from his uncle, being the only person possessing a key."

"And the time would be ripe for the frame-up after that quarrel between uncle and nephew?"

"The quarrel was testified to by Miss Jenks as well as Mr. Carter and Miss Preedy; are you suggesting—"

"Not any more than I'm so far suggesting Mr. Carter doctored the lock. I'm only considering the possibilities as yet."

Mallet might have gone no further but for his certainty that something lay behind MacNab's method. He remembered the squeeze on his arm. His respect for MacNab had deepened as a consequence both of his discovery of the trick with the lock and his fearless avowal in regard to Dodsley's visit to London. Crabb, too, divined something behind, for instead of now standing with one knee on his chair and the dispatch-case in his hand, he dropped into his former seat at the end of the table.

Instinctively, Mallet and MacNab's voices had lowered, so that it is doubtful if at first the others, except Brewster facing Crabb, caught much of what passed.

"But if it was a plot, it must have been hatched by some one who knew the old man would be there that night," Mallet pointed out.

"And, secondly, some one who knew Dick meant to return that night."

When Mallet perceived the absurd implications this involved, he began to doubt MacNab. The lock discovery had been no more than a lucky fluke.

"Very well," he said, "the first involves Carter, the second Carter, Mr. Brewster, and Miss Grafton herself. We are getting on," he added in an aside to Brewster.

To Mallet, this frame-up theory seemed as far-fetched as Miss Preedy's fanciful suggestion of a similar plot against herself and Carter. Indeed, he now felt sure MacNab's fantastic theory had most likely been derived from the cinema-nourished imagination of Miss Preedy herself. To reduce it to instant absurdity, Mallet blurted out: "And the cigarette case, and the books and the bus ticket and the revolver, how many more do these implicate?"

Crabb and Brewster both smiled—with the difference that while Crabb's was triumphant, Brewster's had in it the sad acquiescence of a man who accepts inevitable defeat. But it looked as if he could appreciate the hopeless fight put up by his friend, for he turned to wait his response to the challenge.

MacNab hesitated.

"The bus ticket seems to involve Miss Grafton and Mr. Brewster," he said, "who alone had the chance so soon to place it in his pocket. The books would seem to point to Mr. Carter, who knew their value, and who might have used Dick's name; the revolver might have been planted where it was found by Carter and Miss Preedy or by Mr. Brewster; the cigarette case—"

Mallet put up a hand.

"Not Mr. Carter again! He'd have left it in the shop."

MacNab knew they were laughing at him. His face hardened suddenly.

"Would he? That would have suggested nothing. Dick might have left it there himself, at any time. But outside the shop—a gold cigarette case, at night, with his uncle dead inside and himself supposed to be about a hundred miles away, and afterwards denying he'd been in town at the time—"

Mallet's patience gave out.

"Your theory involves too many people," he said. "Even if it wasn't absolutely destroyed by a single, simple fact within our knowledge."

"And that fact?" MacNab asked.

"The fact that he actually was in London that night."

"But he denies he was."

"Oh, naturally; it was to his interest to do so. Unfortunately for him, in addition to these clues, we have the evidence of Mr. Brewster here, however unwillingly given."

"But I entirely reject Mr. Brewster's evidence."

The words, spoken with slow, emphatic deliberation, astounded Mallet. Brewster, indeed, recovered first.

"You think I was mistaken? Well—I may have been. I've already admitted as much, of course."

Mallet was indignant.

"This won't do, you know. You can't withdraw—"

MacNab interposed.

"No, Brewster, that will not do for us now." He turned to Mallet. "Listen! When young Dodsley denied he was in town on the night of the murder, it was clear to me he was either lying or telling the truth."

This time it was Brewster who cut in.

"Not at all. He was suffering from concussion which made him forget. Any doctor will tell you that," he asserted with angry impatience.

"He was either lying or telling the truth," MacNab repeated quietly. "And the one thing of which I was quite certain was that he was *not* lying through loss of memory. He was either lying consciously and deliberately or telling me the simple truth."

Brewster gasped out his disgust, and shot out a restraining hand at MacNab.

"Don't you see? You're giving him away again," he muttered.

Mallet, however, was deeply interested.

"Go ahead! How could you know there was no loss of memory?"

"Because when I put some questions to him about Carter,

he not only remembered him, but spoke of his abilities and ambitions. Now, as any doctor will tell you, loss of memory following concussion, is never partial. Mr. Carter belonged to Dick Dodsley's past as much as did the previous night. If he recalled the one, he could have recalled the other. If he forgot his own journey he should have forgotten Mr. Carter."

Brewster struck the table.

"By Jove, I never saw that!" he said with admiration.

Mallet was still more interested.

"But you didn't think he was lying," he eagerly suggested.

"No, I didn't think *he* was."

Brewster sat up abruptly with a changed face.

"You're not suggesting I was lying about seeing him in town, are you?"

"Well, at the time I couldn't be sure of that," MacNab said.

Brewster looked round at the others and then back at MacNab.

"You couldn't be sure! Well, this *is* a nice return for all the help I've given. Haven't I always asserted my belief in Dick's innocence?"

MacNab agreed.

"You could have gone further, Brewster. You could have asserted your knowledge of Dick's innocence, since you yourself are the man who shot his uncle."

So quietly was the charge made that only Mallet and Crabb heard it. Even Mr. Carter, who ever since the mention of his own name had been sitting forward with neck outstretched, did not overhear the accusation. And at the table Brewster was the first to react.

"You lunatic, you damned lunatic," he breathed. "Who put you right when you thought it was Carter?"

"You did, by professing belief in Dick and yet always heading me off Carter back on to your friend Dick."

It was the drawn-back fist that released both Mallet and Carter from the paralysing inertia which held them. Brewster's fist flashed out before Crabb was on his feet, but MacNab dodged it in time. Brewster, under the momentum of the miss, went to the floor, and before he could rise, Crabb was on his top. Some one screamed as George Grafton jumped to Brewster's assistance. But Mallet intervened and Crabb, raising Brewster, dumped him back into his chair while George with his fists still shut, looked on uncertainly.

"What's all this about?" he demanded.

Brewster, badly shaken up by his fall and Crabb's weight, smiled feebly:

"Sorry, George. But this idiot had just suggested I should be where Dick is now."

All except Brewster were on their feet.

"Well?" Mallet demanded crisply.

MacNab wiped his forehead.

"I think you'll find he alone fits in," he said. "How he had the chance to doctor the lock, I don't know," he began, "but it was a first-rate trick, anyway. The cigarette case he might have stolen. The bus ticket was more easily got and planted. The revolver was an afterthought, when the Safe Deposit letter was delayed. He'd hired it for a month and hoped by that time his friend would be in gaol with his correspondence in other hands. Yes, it was an excellent idea to put the stolen books in a Safe Deposit, giving his friend's name, knowing when the renewal notice came in it would find Scotland Yard. Very original, don't you think, Inspector? I haven't met it before."

"Very," Mallet agreed shortly. "But so far I've had proof of nothing more than an attempted assault on yourself."

Brewster, who had listened with his chin cupped in his hand, laughed scornfully.

"I plead guilty to that," he said. "As for the rest, the man is a lunatic—an egoist, who'd expect his own wild fancies to be proof enough to hang a Prime Minister."

"The crime was deliberate, of course," MacNab went on evenly, "the result of much scheming and planning. Having somehow access to the shop, he carried off the books one by one. That is why all my daytime spying failed completely. At last the opportunity he waited for came. Dick had a quarrel with his uncle. His uncle may have suspected Dick of the thefts. But that may be fancy, not fact. Yet it is hard fact that there was a dispute not only with his uncle but with Miss Grafton. Dick went away for a few days to think things out, telling Carter of the time of his return and of his intention to take over the work on the catalogue. Later, he arranged to meet Miss Grafton in the *Cynara*, about one-thirty, after his work on the catalogue had been finished. Miss Grafton told Brewster of this when they had tea together, and invited him to join them at the night club. Brewster did not go to the night club. But before doing so he had been to the shop, expecting to find Dick there.

"He found the shop empty. Supposing Dick delayed, he waited on. Then in the dark some one entered and passed on to the office. Brewster stole out from behind the row of shelves where he had first taken up his position, and, looking through the little window into the now lighted office, saw not Dick but Dick's uncle, about to begin work on the catalogue. Brewster slipped in among the next set of shelves to consider the position. It did not take him long to see that, after all, his scheme had not really miscarried. If his original purpose had been to shoot Dick, and leave the weapon beside him to suggest suicide, then the subsequent discovery of the books in his name in the Safe Deposit would provide a motive, even without the quarrels with his uncle and Miss Grafton. But his quick wits almost instantly showed him the same end could be achieved by shooting the uncle, the only small difference now being that he had to take away his revolver instead of leaving it behind. So he shot Dodsley and went off to the *Cynara*, expecting to find Dick and Miss Grafton there together."

MacNab stopped to consider, and in the silence Brewster's sniff of extreme impatience was very audible.

"It must have shaken even his nerve to find Dick had not turned up. He had acted in the belief that Dick, delayed on his journey, had gone first to the night club, and that afterwards Dick would deny he had been to the shop at all, a denial which in view of the evidence Brewster had scattered about, would go for nothing. But I doubt if for all his nerve his uneasiness ceased till the news came of Dick's accident, and his wits showed him how to make even that accident subserve his own ends."

As MacNab paused, Mallet shook his head doubtfully.

"It's possible," he said. "Yes, even plausible, as a theory, but where's the evidence in support?"

Brewster, sitting up, struck the table.

"He has none! That's just it. It might all have happened as he says—with some one else playing the part he assigns me. Why accuse me? Why suspect me any more than— say—Mr. Carter there? What did I know that he didn't know? What opportunity did I have that he didn't? Those books, for instance. How could *I* get at them to carry them off one or two at a time? As for motive, I can easily imagine one in his case, but this man hasn't been able even to fancy a motive in my case."

MacNab broke in:

"Carter himself, as his statement shows, suspected Dick. For that I haven't spared him. You invariably headed me back to Dick when I affected to suspect Carter. It's much too late for you to put us on to Carter now."

Brewster looked at Mallet.

"It's rather thrilling to be charged with murder, Inspector," he said with a smile. "But, like yourself, I'm waiting with impatient curiosity for what you would accept as sufficient proof on which to arrest a kitten."

Mallet looked at MacNab.

"The proof is quite simple," MacNab nodded. "Mr. Brewster made one mistake."

Crabb still positioned behind Brewster's chair, shot a meaning glance at his superior; and Mallet remembered.

"One mistake?" he echoed.

"One little mistake," MacNab repeated. His hand went to his pocket. "When you brought me those books you had recovered from the Safe Deposit, there was one among them not on the list Mr. Dodsley had given me."

"I remember that," Mallet said.

"*Edmund Burke: his Speeches and Achievements.*"

"That was it. Well?"

"Mr. Carter says that book was never in Dodsley's shop, and Miss Jenks agrees with him."

"You mean it was stolen somewhere else?"

"No. It belonged to Mr. Brewster and by mistake he included it with the others he placed in the Safe Deposit to incriminate his friend."

Brewster leapt to his feet.

"That's a damned lie. I never had such a book. Never even heard of it."

From his pocket MacNab drew the scrap of paper he had handed to Jim Peters and passed it to Mallet. On the scrap of paper appeared the marks CW/245, at which the inspector stared blankly, while MacNab continued:

"It is customary with some booksellers to put private marks on their more or less scarce books. You will find them pencilled on one of the fly-leaves. Every bookseller has his system of marking. And these symbols, while telling an assistant both what was paid for the book and what price is expected for it, conceals both from the prospective buyer. Now, knowing the markings used by Dodsley, I was able to say that this book on Burke had never been on his shelves. But by inquiries among the booksellers, we found that those particular markings are those used by Davis and Newman. At their shop in Oxford Street I learned more. There I learned that this particular work was sold, along with some others which are, no doubt, still in his room, to Mr. Owen Brewster, secretary to Mr. David Grafton."

Mallet lifted his eyes from the scrap of paper to see what Brewster could say to this. That young man had very clearly received an unexpected shock. The inspector's eye galvanised his inaction. Abruptly, he sprang to life.

"It's a lie," he cried. "I never had the book… I mean, if I had, I'd forgotten, and some one must have stolen it and placed it among the others as a frame-up against me."

The momentary silence was broken by George Grafton.

"By God, Brewster, it's true! You did it." He turned to the others, his face flushed, and in a rush went on: "You don't know how he managed to get into the shop. I'll tell you. *I* did the trick with the lock. Margery used to go there to meet

Dick, and wanted a key for herself. But a new lock was shortly to be put on. When they thought of having a key made I told them the trick about that kind of lock, and they let me play it off, till an extra key could be got for the new lock. Brewster knew all about it. In fact, it was a joke among ourselves."

While George, breathing heavily in his agitation, was telling his story, Brewster recovered self-possession.

"I admit all that," he said calmly. "If I said nothing about the lock it was because, unlike her brother, I was unwilling to reveal a secret which might, those meetings occurring when and where they did, seriously compromise Miss Grafton's reputation."

Allowing this to sink in while he fought for breath, Brewster's glance must have told him he had, at least, made his silence seem plausible to some. Emboldened, he went on:

"It seems a poor return for my reticence to have that care for his sister's name now taken by an over-impetuous brother as a proof of murder." He shook his head. "I might even be afraid, after all you have had to listen to, unless by good luck I happened to be able to prove that actually I was standing by the young man's father, in the House of Commons, at 3.40 a.m.—the time, I believe, at which the horrible crime was committed."

Again, and for the last time as it happened, Chief Inspector Mallet's eyes questioned MacNab. Crabb, too, stopped work on the notes he had begun to make. This was the one mighty objection to any theory involving Brewster's guilt.

"Why did you go back to the scene of the crime after leaving Miss Grafton?" MacNab asked.

Brewster lifted a defiant chin:

"I didn't go back to the scene of the crime, as you put it, at all. I returned to my duties at the House."

"You went back to the shop because you were uneasy over Dick's failure to turn up. You knew he would if he could. You were afraid. You couldn't keep away. You *must* have the doubt settled as to whether he had come to town after all. Or you went to see if the watch had really stopped at the hour to which you advanced it on after shooting him. Or, if Dick Dodsley had turned up, you might be ready to shoot him too, and leave the gun in his hand, since this also would fit into the 'frame-up' you had so carefully constructed. Whatever the motive, you did go. And when you took a look at the street before leaving, you saw, or heard, one, or both, of the two officers advancing from different directions, and though you could open the door without a sound, you didn't dare, in that silence, risk the inevitable snap in shutting it. Neither, Brewster, did you dare risk losing your alibi if the officer coming on the open door should enter and find the dead man with a watch showing he had been murdered some *half an hour later on*. So you played your little game with Roberts, holding him up, delaying him, till well *after* the time to which you had *shoved on the hands of the watch*."

"Rot," Brewster cut in. "How much more have we to listen to?"

MacNab took a step forward.

"Just this! You played the silly young fool excellently on the officer. But he remembers one thing out of key with the character you assumed. He remembers how often you looked at your watch while babbling nonsense to him. Now a young gentleman in the condition you were affecting, never does that. He is oblivious to time: he doesn't care a damn what the time is."

Brewster leaped to his feet.

"I've had enough of this," he cried. Before any one realised his intention, or could shoot out a hand to stop him, he was through the door. As Crabb started after him, Mallet yelled a warning, which was almost drowned by a woman's shriek. But there were more now in the front shop than Brewster knew. Sergeant Barrett and Constable Copping having been joined by Roberts.

When Brewster, however, was led back into the office, the fight he had made became apparent from his condition. His smooth hair was all out of position, his dinner jacket torn, his shirt front and collar crumpled, with the black tie under one ear, and his face damp with perspiration, and flushed from his exertions as by excess of wine.

MacNab's look was on Roberts who entered holding Brewster by the back of his collar while Barrett and Copping had each an arm. As soon, however, as they wheeled their captive round to face Mallet, Roberts got a shock.

"My God!" he cried, staring hard, unconscious he had spoken.

As Mallet turned to him Roberts extended a hand.

"That's him! That's the man who spoke to me that night."

Later, when the prisoner had been removed, and after Margery Grafton, in a conflict of emotions in which relief and joy triumphed, was led away by George, Mallet and Crabb stayed behind for a word with MacNab.

"The motive, of course, was Miss Grafton," Mallet said.

"Yes. I guessed that when I saw them together at Lymington," MacNab agreed.

Mallet emitted a little sigh of disgust.

"Roberts saw him there too, when I took him down to have a look at young Dodsley."

"Yes, but Roberts hadn't a fair chance. When we were speaking to you in the corridor, Brewster, I noticed, turned his back to look through the window. And when you asked him a question about Dick's condition he answered you not in words but by a shake of his head."

Mallet nodded.

"Yes, I remember that at least."

"I knew there was nothing in Dick's condition then to justify that sadly shaken head, but it was the only reply he could give you which avoided the need for the spoken words in front of Roberts."

"By George, I didn't notice that," Mallet said in self-disgust this time.

"Oh, that was different. You hadn't yet seen Dick. And my suspicions were awake by then," MacNab said. "I had just heard the man who was supposed to have lost his memory remember the past and talk about it quite normally."

"I'd like to know when you first became certain?" Mallet said.

MacNab hesitated.

"Well, not for some time after that. It struck me as odd that he should go on professing his belief in Dick's innocence and at the same time keep furnishing me with points all tending to establish his guilt."

Crabb interposed:

"He was like that with the revolver too, I thought—kept on harping about there being no weapon."

"Ah," Mallet nodded. "What he wanted was to be sure it had been found. Must have bothered him we kept dark about that—the one thing he couldn't be sure would be found, much as he wanted it to be."

"Quite," MacNab agreed. "You see the same mind at work in his story about Dick's visit to London. You heard his indignation tonight when I told you of it. But he himself had previously suggested I should tell you of it, and I refused because I was not sure there had been any visit to London."

Mallet smiled.

"And you were not sure of us, perhaps."

"Oh, you hadn't my chances, Inspector. You couldn't use Brewster as an assistant and study the man at close quarters as I did. He couldn't, for example, tell you about that supposed visit to town, since that would come out later and make him like an informer. That would not help him with Margery Grafton. But he meant you to know somehow, in a way that would not damage him in her eyes. Yes, the more I saw of him the less I liked him."

Mallet, taking up his hat, turned to Crabb.

"So you see, Crabb, there are, after all, some advantages in an unofficial position." Then as Crabb blinked his appreciation of the fact a thought occurred to Mallet. "By the way, Mr. Grafton hasn't turned up after all."

MacNab looked up in surprise.

"No more he has. That's curious. I sent him a note by hand asking him to come." His brow furrowed in perplexity.

Mallet let Crabb have a sly wink.

"Well, anyhow, he's hardly needed now, is he?"

"Not really," MacNab said. "Still, I suppose I'd better hang on a little to see."

Mallet held out his hand.

"Yes—hardly do to ask a big man like Grafton to come here and then let him find the door shut in his face."

But Mallet might have also stayed another ten minutes for the sake of meeting Mr. David Grafton had he believed the great man at all likely to come. So MacNab was left in the shop, alone.

CHAPTER II
What MacNab
Kept to Himself

HALF AN HOUR LATER, STANDING IN THE DARK FRONT shop, he heard the three taps on the door for which he had asked. As he opened, a figure stepped nimbly inside. No word of greeting passed. MacNab shut the door. The man stood waiting, uncertainly.

"Straight ahead," MacNab said. "You know the way."

Without a word the other went forward between the rows of book shelves towards the office, his broad shoulders silhouetted against the light from the office window. Once inside the two men faced each other.

"Please take a seat, Mr. Grafton," MacNab said, indicating a chair.

Grafton, at a disadvantage, obviously perplexed, but with set jaw and suspicious eyes, let the invitation pass unheeded.

"What do you want with me?" he demanded. "Come out with it. Time presses."

"Not so much, surely, as the last time you were here."

Grafton's eyes widened.

"The last time I was here?"

"Yes, in response to a call up by Mr. Dodsley on the twenty-first of May. You came here two days later, on the night Mr. Dodsley was shot, if you remember."

For all his self-possession and invulnerability to attack, the quiet reply went home. He started as if he himself had been shot, and then placed a hand on the table to steady himself as MacNab sat down, facing him.

"You—you don't suppose I had any hand in that?" he said. The dominating note had gone from his voice.

"No, but till half an hour ago I wasn't sure you were not involved in it," MacNab said.

Grafton waited a moment, and then, having moistened his lips, got his question out.

"Then... what do you want me for?"

"Why, Mr. Grafton, merely to give you what you came for that night, and didn't get. Let me see. There were twelve letters, were there not?"

Grafton edged along the table and then sat down heavily to stare at MacNab turning over the leaves of his notebook.

"You are a strange man," he said. "You seem to know more of my affairs than my own secretary."

"Oh, you're wrong there," MacNab said. "But never mind, the letters alone are important to you?"

"Ah, so you've read them, and want your price, like Dodsley himself."

MacNab laid down his notebook.

"Mr. Grafton, I have not read one of them; but I have my price, though it is nothing like Dodsley's."

"How much?"

"I'll tell you that when the letters are in your hands." Then, as Grafton stared, he added: "As a matter of fact it was your daughter who put me on to them."

"Margery?"

"Yes; it's her you have to thank."

"Thank!" Grafton cried.

"Yes. I got the essential hint from her book. Oh, but I was very stupid, you understand. I oughtn't to have needed it. Never saw what stared me in the face. Didn't see the forest for the trees, as it were."

"What, in God's name, are you talking about?" Grafton burst out.

"Oh, it's quite simple. While we had one or two people under suspicion for the murder—"

"You are a detective, then?"

MacNab smiled.

"I used to think I was. Now I'm not so sure. But, as I was saying while we were considering the possibilities in the crime, among other things we went into there was Mr. Dodsley's diary. Several entries took our attention. Among them this:

"*May 15th, acquired the A. L. Collection by D. G.*

"The same initials reappeared on the 21st.

"*Note by hand, D. G.*

"At first I thought this worth looking into. But it was pointed out by a smart young officer who knew Latin that D. G. stood for *Dei Gratia*, and merely indicated that the late Mr. Dodsley, being a man of pious disposition, was ready to acknowledge that but for the divine assistance he would never have made so good a bargain."

Grafton nodded.

"I see," he said.

"Quite. And as the entry *Note by hand, D. G.*, closely followed a sale for which he had expressed a doubt of ever seeing his money, I fell into the same error. Very stupid, that was. For you see I had heard Mr. Dodsley's charwoman and two of his assistants tell us things about him which might have saved even a lunatic from supposing him the kind of person likely to interlard his diary with pious expressions."

Grafton, who was looking more or less calmly at the entries from the diary copied by MacNab into his note-book, nodded.

"Of course," he said, "you should have seen that if D. G. was a Latin abbreviation the 'by' in the first entry was redundant."

"Quite," MacNab agreed, "but I didn't know, you see, how much Dodsley himself knew about the ablative case; and anyway, I missed seeing things equally obvious later on."

"Such as?" Grafton prompted when he heard MacNab's sigh.

"Well, the significance of terror your daughter showed at the mention of your name."

Grafton was visibly shocked.

"No, no," he said. "We're not on good terms. She's left home on account of this young fellow, but terror on that account—no! That is ridiculous."

"So I should have seen," MacNab agreed. "But, besides that, I missed taking the hint given me in her new book."

"*Death at the Desk*, you mean?"

"Yes. You've read it, I understand. We've all been reading it. I spent hours over it, seeking for clues, like the others. And I clean overlooked the one clue that suggested the motive for Dodsley's murder."

Grafton seemed to be running over the story in his mind.

"Blackmail," MacNab nodded.

After a moment Grafton sat up:

"Surely to God you don't suspect me?" he cried.

"No, but your daughter did."

As Grafton stared incredulously, MacNab put out his hand:

"Your daughter has been going through hell, Mr. Grafton. You were quite right in saying it was ridiculous to suppose her disagreement with you could account for her terrified and broken condition."

"Oh, but—"

"Listen! She knew you had read her book, and she thought you had imitated and improved on its plot. If that were all she had to go through it would be enough."

"What else?" Grafton was insistent. But the other man could be as firm, though seeming less so.

"No," MacNab said. "I have a notion it's your turn now, and I'm curious to hear your story."

After some thought Grafton looked up.

"Very well," he said. "I'll tell you everything. What you still withhold I don't know; but if it's something by which you can test the truth of what is said, I'm not afraid.

"I did come here that night in response to a note sent by Dodsley. The tone of the note, like the one you yourself sent, made me suspect what the business was about. Those letters have been in existence many years. They belong to my past, and bear witness to an indiscretion which if published would mean for me the end of everything. But on the other hand, they were letters which if destroyed would end that danger for ever. So I came here ready to pay a big price. Dodsley, as arranged, met me at the door. We sat down here in this office. Having made sure what the letters were, I asked him his price. Then came the shock. He coolly informed me they were not on sale as a collection. My autograph, he said, was bound to increase in value the higher I rose in the political sphere. So he proposed to sell me the letters singly, at intervals of perhaps a year, the price, of course, naturally rising, as he put it, in proportion to my own rise in fame.

"We argued for some time. I found him as hard and unyielding as a flint. No, he asserted, he felt sure of big money, for at the last resort my political enemies, at least, would not underestimate the value of my signature. So the debate went on, he assuring me he would not have made me the offer he then made but for the badness of the book trade at the moment. Just at that point my ear caught a slight sound from the back shop. He saw me listening and laughed. 'It's only the cat,' he said. 'Like his master tonight he's caught a mouse.' That satisfied me for the moment, and the haggling continued till I heard another noise. It was different. First like books falling to the floor, followed by a scurry of light footsteps, like some one running.

"That was enough for me! Sure Dodsley meant some trickery, I thought it prudent to give him no more time to bring it off. So I got up without a word and walked quickly out of his shop. Next morning I learned from the papers he'd been shot about an hour afterwards."

MacNab shook his head.

"A minute or two afterwards would be nearer," he said. Then in reply to Grafton's stare he added: "You see, he was shot by your secretary."

"By—by Brewster?" Wide-eyed with amazement, Grafton cried: "Why, man, you're mad. The thing's incredible. Why should Brewster shoot him? What motive could he have? And how could he be there at such an hour?"

"Mr. Grafton, that note by hand from Dodsley, what happened to it?"

Grafton thought for a moment.

"Well, after it was brought to me and I'd considered it, I

tore it up. Of course it wasn't the sort of thing to leave lying about."

"And you sat some time considering it?"

"Naturally; it was a new experience for me."

"Brewster being present?"

"Oh, yes, but he couldn't possibly know. He didn't see the letter. I took care of that."

"Not enough, Mr. Grafton. Coming by hand, and seeing you troubled, possibly, by the letter and, probably, tearing it into very small pieces—a job you perhaps usually left to him?"

"Yes, I did—but—"

"All that so aroused his curiosity that he picked the small pieces out of your waste-paper basket and put them together."

"Oh, that you can't know," Grafton interrupted uneasily.

"Why not? How else did he know when and where to follow you that night?"

Grafton, still incredulous, said:

"You suggest he followed me out of curiosity and shot Dodsley when Dodsley found him in his shop?"

"Not quite that. Brewster followed you to learn what hold Dodsley had which could make you come at such an hour to his whistle, so to speak. He wanted to have a hold on you himself, so that you might second his ambitions. But it was for quite another reason he shot Dodsley after your daughter ran from the shop."

Staggered, but impressed by MacNab's tone of certainty, Grafton's hand went out.

"You say Margery was there too?"

"She was there before you, waiting for Dick's arrival, impatient to see him after their quarrel. It was she you overheard running away. Brewster, who was among the books behind her, of course heard her too, and knew who she must be. So after you left, he came out and shot Dodsley."

"But—in God's name, *why*?"

"Because, to put it briefly, he saw how easily suspicion would fall on young Dodsley. Because he wanted to have a hold on you, and above all, because he wanted your daughter. Mr. Grafton," MacNab went on in a new tone, "do you realise what your daughter has had to go through since that night? She knew you were there. And next morning when, like yourself, she read of the murder—well, there was one sentence marked in the copy of her book you read."

"How can you know that?"

"That's no matter! You remember it? *The prophet who was slain by a lion had a nobler death than Bishop Hatto who was eaten by rats.* Well, she probably heard enough that night to know Dodsley was blackmailing you. What wonder if, knowing you so well, she thought you had turned and slain this particular rat? And not this: all these days, though certain Dick was guiltless, she kept silent, even to me, whom she had employed on his behalf, about your own presence here that night."

Grafton's face, as MacNab finished, twitched and changed and, as if ashamed of his emotion, he lowered his head.

"Now about those letters," MacNab said, shifting his attention to his notebook.

"Now in the hands of the police, I suppose," Grafton said resignedly.

"No, neither with them or Brewster, though he came back to look for them. Look at this." MacNab passed his open notebook across the table. "That also is an entry from Dodsley's diary."

Grafton scanned the figures indicated:

VIII 45, IX 23, X 16
I 54, II 32, III 16

He looked up in perplexity to see MacNab pointing at the glass-fronted bookcases. But he did not comprehend till MacNab said:

"Try the case marked VIII. You should get two of your twelve letters in the fourth and fifth volumes from the top left-hand corner."

When Grafton had all the twelve letters in his pocket he crossed towards his chair like a man rescued from a sinking ship. He found the chair but could not find his voice.

"Yes," MacNab said, "a good place to hide them. No one had access to those cases except himself. But we ought to have found them sooner. An artificial arrangement of figures like that—and the Roman numerals on the bookcases staring us in the face!"

"But the police!" Grafton said, touching the letters in his pocket. "They must—"

"They know nothing of that side of the affair, hard put to it though I was tonight to keep you out of it."

"Thank you indeed. I—I—don't know how—"

"Oh, don't thank me. After all, it was your daughter who employed me," MacNab interrupted, almost roughly. "If Dodsley was a rat, I am no lion; and anyway, in these days prophets are scarce."

THE END

If you've enjoyed *Death of Mr. Dodsley*,
you won't want to miss

the most recent BRITISH LIBRARY CRIME CLASSIC

published by Poisoned Pen Press, an imprint of Sourcebooks.

Praise for the
British Library Crime Classics

"Carr is at the top of his game in this taut whodunit... The British Library Crime Classics series has unearthed another worthy golden age puzzle."

—*Publishers Weekly*, STARRED Review,
for *The Lost Gallows*

"A wonderful rediscovery."
—*Booklist*, STARRED Review, for *The Sussex Downs Murder*

"First-rate mystery and an engrossing view into a vanished world."
—*Booklist*, STARRED Review, for *Death of an Airman*

"A cunningly concocted locked-room mystery, a staple of Golden Age detective fiction."
—*Booklist*, STARRED Review, for *Murder of a Lady*

"The book is both utterly of its time and utterly ahead of it."
—*New York Times Book Review* for *The Notting Hill Mystery*

"As with the best of such compilations, readers of classic mysteries will relish discovering unfamiliar authors, along with old favorites such as Arthur Conan Doyle and G.K. Chesterton."
—*Publishers Weekly*, STARRED Review, for *Continental Crimes*

"In this imaginative anthology, Edwards—president of Britain's Detection Club—has gathered together overlooked criminous gems."

—*Washington Post* for *Crimson Snow*

"The degree of suspense Crofts achieves by showing the growing obsession and planning is worthy of Hitchcock. Another first-rate reissue from the British Library Crime Classics series."

—*Booklist*, STARRED Review, for *The 12.30 from Croydon*

"Not only is this a first-rate puzzler, but Crofts's outrage over the financial firm's betrayal of the public trust should resonate with today's readers."

—*Booklist*, STARRED Review, for *Mystery in the Channel*

"This reissue exemplifies the mission of the British Library Crime Classics series in making an outstanding and original mystery accessible to a modern audience."

—*Publishers Weekly*, STARRED Review, for *Excellent Intentions*

"A book to delight every puzzle-suspense enthusiast"

—*New York Times* for *The Colour of Murder*

"Edwards's outstanding third winter-themed anthology show-cases 11 uniformly clever and entertaining stories, mostly from lesser known authors, providing further evidence of the editor's expertise… This entry in the British Library Crime Classics series will be a welcome holiday gift for fans of the golden age of detection."

—*Publishers Weekly*, STARRED Review, for
The Christmas Card Crime and Other Stories

Poisoned Pen
PRESS

poisonedpenpress.com